THE KEY TO EVERYTHING

THE KEY TO EVERYTHING

VALERIE FRASER LUESSE

THORNDIKE PRESS
A part of Gale, a Cengage Company

**LIBRARY OF CONGRESS CIP DATA ON FILE.
CATALOGUING IN PUBLICATION FOR THIS BOOK
IS AVAILABLE FROM THE LIBRARY OF CONGRESS**

ISBN-13: 978-1-4328-8171-9 (hardcover alk. paper)

Published in 2020 by arrangement with Revell Books, a division of Baker Publishing Group

Printed in Mexico
Print Number: 01   Print Year: 2020

For my friend Holly and two special dads — hers, who inspired this story, and mine, who taught me the alphabet on a little slate and has encouraged my writing ever since.

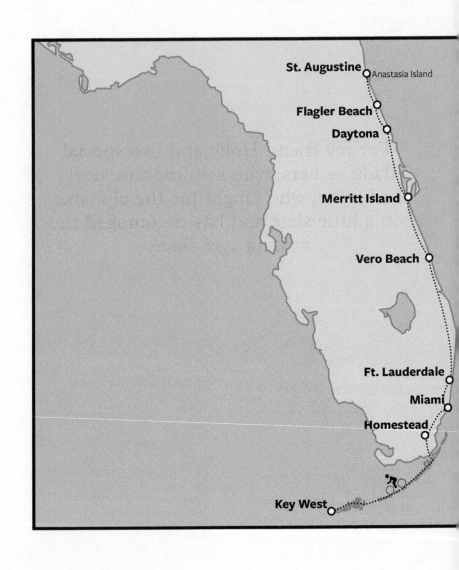

ONE

Though he couldn't have known, nor ever guessed, Peyton Cabot had just witnessed a bittersweet kiss goodbye. There they stood, a man and a woman, in the center of his grandfather's library, a mahogany-paneled sanctuary that always smelled of polished wood and old leather, parchment and pipe tobacco. It was empty now, with all the family outside for their annual picnic — empty but for these two.

As Peyton looked on, the couple shared an embrace so passionate that he knew he should turn away, for he realized in that moment that he had become the worst kind of intruder, spying on his own parents. Right now they didn't look like parents — she a blonde all-American beauty, he a larger-than-life movie idol. They looked like two strangers whose past he didn't share, whose present he couldn't comprehend. More than

7

the embrace itself, that's what he found so arresting — the realization that his parents were more than a mother and father, that they did, in fact, have a life before him, apart from him entirely, one they would've shared even if he had never been born.

The revelation took him by surprise, and he fled to the cover of his grandparents' front porch, sinking into their boisterous Georgia clan as he longed to sink into a pool of water that could wash away his transgression, for he knew good and well that he was guilty of theft. He had stolen a private moment that his mother and father never meant to share.

Peyton would spend this afternoon like so many others — swapping jokes with his boy cousins and listening to the uncles tell their stories (the same ones they told at every family picnic, but everybody laughed just the same). Still, the image of that kiss would be etched on his memory, not just for the rest of this sunny afternoon but for the rest of his life.

For years, the Cabots had been gathering for a spring picnic at the family estate on the Isle of Hope. It was a show of togetherness mandated by Peyton's grandmother and held religiously, regardless of weather, on the Saturday before Easter. Attending the picnic was like performing a role in a play or a movie, the men costumed in their linen and seersucker, the ladies in tea-party dresses and wide-brimmed hats. All the children wore croquet whites, swinging their mallets in an orderly fashion until they got bored and started chasing each other all over the place, like a band of well-dressed jackrabbits.

Picnic tables were covered in starched white linens and dotted with crystal pitchers filled with fresh flowers. Even the ice cream would be served on china with sterling silver spoons. Servants ferried food out of the kitchen and dirty dishes back in. Over the course of an afternoon, the Cabots would consume platters mounded with fried chicken, country ham, and homemade biscuits slathered with fresh-churned butter; sweet potato casserole, corn on the cob, green beans, and black-eyed peas; ambrosia, Grandmother Cabot's coconut cake, Doxie's chocolate cake (she had to make three to satisfy all the family), homemade ice cream with Georgia peaches; and enough sweet tea and lemonade to float a barge — this in addition to the steady flow of cocktails mixed by the uncles.

For all appearances, the annual picnic was

a grand gathering of one of the richest clans in Georgia. But the truth, Peyton knew, was that none of his aunts and uncles particularly liked each other. Moreover, they were all jealous of his father, the eldest — and reluctant favorite — son. Peyton's grandmother — instigator of the whole thing — never appeared to enjoy the picnic. In fact, it would eventually give her "a case of nerves," and she would retire well before sunset.

The center of activity was the lower front porch of his grandparents' Greek Revival house, which crowned a gently sloping, half-acre front lawn, parted down the center by a hundred-year-old live oak allée and bordered with deep pink azaleas almost as tall as Peyton. Lacy white spirea and more azaleas framed the house with its eight soaring columns. The white wicker porch furniture had been in the family for years, and while his grandmother frequently complained that it was old and needed replacing, his grandfather had it painstakingly repaired and restored every year. For whatever reason, he could not let it go.

Right now the porch was full to overflowing with relatives. Peyton leaned against one of the columns, watching a flock of his little cousins chase each other across the pristine carpet of zoysia grass that was his grand-father's pride and joy. Though he had two gardeners, George Cabot still surveyed the zoysia daily, bending down to pull an offending weed here or dig up a wild violet there. The aunts fretted over his weeding. He was not as spry as he used to be and was starting to repeat himself more than usual. *Now, Daddy, if you fall and break a hip you're gonna be in a mess.* Still, he weeded.

With his back to the family, Peyton could listen to all of their conversations, tuning in and out as if he were turning the dial on a radio.

His father's two sisters, Aunt Camille and Aunt Charlotte, were sharing the porch swing closest to Peyton:

"Could you believe that dress Arlie Seton wore to her own daughter's wedding?"

"Ridiculous. It was cut clear to here and twice too short for a woman half her age."

Uncle Julian, the middle son, was doing what he always did — trying to sell Grand-daddy Cabot on one of his big ideas: "We could parcel off a thousand acres over by Reidsville and turn it into a residential development. We'd make a fortune. Can't you see that?"

"Julian, Reidsville's not close enough to anything — not Atlanta, not Savannah. All

11

those vets settin' up housekeepin' want to be close to a city where they can find work."

Nothing about Peyton's Uncle Julian was genuine — not his smile, not his concern, and certainly not his devotion to the family. Whenever there was any heavy lifting to be done, you could count on Uncle Julian to be needed elsewhere. Peyton's mother had once said that he was "doomed to go through life feeling cheated" because he believed any good fortune that fell on someone else rightly belonged to him. He fancied himself a statesman but so far couldn't even win a seat on the Savannah city council.

Peyton spotted two of his cousins on a quilt underneath the Ghost Oak and decided to join them. Their grandfather had named the tree long ago, and the moniker was apt. Sit beneath it on a breezy night — better yet, a stormy one — and the rustle of leaves did indeed sound like a swirl of specters communing overhead. When they were children, Peyton and his cousins would dare each other to sit under the tree on windy evenings while the others hid in the azaleas, calling out into the darkness, "Ooooooooo, I am the ghost of Ernestine Cabot, dead from the fever of 1824 . . . Ooooooooo, I am Ol' Rawhead, swamp monster of the Okefenokee . . ."

Peyton had never been afraid of the family ghosts or the tree they supposedly haunted. There was something to be discovered way up in those branches, and he had always been more curious than fearful.

Stepping off the porch, he dipped himself some homemade ice cream from a wooden freezer that was probably older than he was and sat down on the quilt with his cousins Prentiss and Winston.

"Somebody's goin' home mighty early." Prentiss nodded toward Peyton's mother, who was walking slowly up a dirt road that led from the main house to a pretty lakeside cottage about a quarter mile away.

Peyton watched his mother's back as she moved farther and farther away from the family, now and again raising a hand to her face. Just then his father appeared, following a path that led from the back of the house, through a pecan grove, and out to the stables. In one hand was a highball glass, already filled. The other held his ever-present companion since he had come home from the Pacific, a bottle of bourbon.

Peyton's aunts said it was "the worst kind of stupid" for the Army to draft men in their thirties, but once everybody younger was already over there, they had no choice.

Peyton's father was gone for just over a year before the Japanese surrendered, but by then the war had done its damage. The war was still doing its damage.

"Don't look good, does it?" Winston asked him.

"No," Peyton said, watching his father disappear into the pecan trees.

Winston swatted at a bee circling his head. "Hey, Peyton, how come you didn't bring Lisa?"

"To face the whole clan? Way too early for that. Might scare her off." Peyton finished his ice cream and stretched out on the quilt. Closing his eyes against the sun filtering through the branches overhead, he pictured the girl who was never far from his thoughts.

Lisa Wallace had transferred to his school in January, when her family moved to Savannah from Augusta. She was the prettiest girl in the whole town, the prettiest girl Peyton had ever seen. But there was more to her than that. For one thing, she didn't flirt, a rarity in a Georgia beauty. Then again, she didn't have to. Every boy in school wanted to go out with her. Her hair was deep auburn and fell in long glossy waves down her back. Her eyes were blue, with just a hint of green, and she had a complexion like ice cream.

The minute she walked into his home-room class, he knew. He felt it in his gut or his heart or whatever you want to call it. While all the other guys were working up their nerve, Peyton made a beeline for Lisa in the lunchroom that first day and offered to carry her tray to her table. She had smiled up at him and said, "You don't waste any time, do you?"

As beautiful as she was, Lisa wasn't interested in sitting on anybody's pedestal and looking pretty. Once, Peyton had invited her to a skeet shoot Winston put together. After watching all the guys complete their first round, Lisa had tapped him on the shoulder and said, "Don't I get a turn?" He handed her his gun and watched her take down every clay.

Peyton often found her sitting next to unpopular kids in the cafeteria so they wouldn't feel lonesome. One girl in their class was a little slow and didn't have the nerve to ask the teachers questions, so she came to Lisa, who would spend her whole study hall tutoring instead of doing her own homework. When Lisa was excited about something, she talked with her hands, and Peyton found himself staring at them as they lithely fluttered in the air, waving her timid pupil toward the correct answer.

15

Winston interrupted his reverie. "Lisa and Peyton sittin' in a tree, k-i-s-s-i-n-g. First comes love, then comes marriage —"

"Oh, shut up, Winston." Peyton threw an acorn at him.

The truth was, he was already thinking about marrying Lisa — daydreaming about it anyway. He had asked her out right after she moved to Savannah and just about every weekend since. Only a month ago, he had taken her to the spring formal, when his whole life seemed as close to perfect as it would ever get . . .

Again his cousins pulled him away from Lisa and back into the fray of a Cabot family picnic. "Listen — here it comes," Prentiss was saying, pointing toward the porch.

The boys listened as their Uncle Gil retold his favorite story, the same one he told at every spring picnic. "Marshall says to me, he says, 'I believe I've seen all this ol' camp has to offer.' And I says, 'What you plan on doin' about it?' That's when he pointed at the bicycles Papa had left for us. He says, 'I'm gonna ride my bicycle to Key West and see what those islands look like.' "

The cousins finished the story with their uncle, repeating his favorite line in unison: "And *that,* ladies and gentlemen, was the last time Marshall Cabot ever let anybody

16

tell him what to do."

Winston leaned back to rest against the oak tree. "How many times you reckon he's told that story?"

"How many spring picnics we had?" Prentiss answered. "Every time he tells it, Uncle Marshall makes the trip in less time."

Looking up at the sprawling branches above, Peyton watched one squirrel chase another, spiraling up the trunk for several feet and then racing back down again. They repeated their circular journey over and over, as if they were following a racetrack around the tree.

"Reckon they know there's a whole big world outside that oak?" he said.

"Who you talkin' about?" Winston asked.

Peyton pointed to the squirrels above. "Those little guys. Reckon they think this tree is all there is — the whole wide world up in those branches?"

"Seriously?" Winston threw a twig at him and missed. "I think a squirrel's a squirrel."

The boys were quiet for a while before Prentiss said, "How long *did* it take your daddy to get to that dang island?"

Peyton listened to the oak tree sighing in the spring breeze. "I got his old map out and figured it up. Looks like it's somewhere in the neighborhood o' six hundred miles from that old boys' camp on the Okefeno-kee to Key West, so twelve hundred there and back. And he wrote dates on different spots on the map — not everywhere he stopped because the dates are too far apart. No way he pedaled two hundred miles without resting somewhere — doubt any-body could make it more than fifty in a day. And it looked like he stayed awhile in St. Augustine. But judging by the dates after he left there, I'd say that leg of it, at least, took him about a month."

"And nobody came after him?" Prentiss wanted to know.

"He said he promised Granddaddy Cabot that if they'd let him be, he'd call collect every Sunday to let 'em know he was al-right, which he did."

"Ain't no way he saddled a bicycle for a month," Winston said. "He musta thumbed some rides."

"Well, hold on now," Peyton said, sitting up. " 'Course you'd have to stop and rest along the way. You'd have to figure all that out before you left. And you'd prob'ly wear out your tires over and over, so that'd have to be worked out. Then there's your clothes and food . . ."

"You sure have given this a lotta thought." Now Prentiss was interested. "Why don't you just ask Uncle Marshall how he did it?"

"I have — lotsa times," Peyton answered. "He just smiles and says that's something I'll have to figure out for myself."

"Uncle Gil always tells the story like it was a spur-o'-the-minute thing," Prentiss said.

Peyton ran a finger along a seam on the quilt where they sat, absently tracing its north-south path. "I don't think so. The map has a price tag on it from the Savannah Shop 'n Go, so he bought it here. And it's dated 1921 — that year Daddy woulda been 13, but he didn't make the trip till he was 15, same as us. Maybe he didn't mark all his stops ahead o' time. Can't really tell. But I believe he was thinking about it before he left for camp."

"You believe it's possible — that he rode the whole way on his bike, I mean?" Prentiss asked him.

Peyton nodded. "Yeah, I do. It wouldn'a been easy, but it's possible. I know his first stop in Florida was Aunt Rosalie's in Jacksonville. That's seventy-five miles from the camp. Aunt Lily's family lives in St. Augustine — maybe he stayed there awhile to visit with them because he didn't get to Flagler Beach till nearly two weeks later, and it's only thirty miles away. The trick would be figuring out where to stay and where to get supplies — food and water and someplace to wash your clothes. 'Specially if you went in the summertime, it'd be hot as blue blazes, so you'd be sweatin' like a pig."

"I got fifty bucks that says you'll never do it," Winston said.

"Me too," Prentiss said. "I'll put down fifty bucks."

"I never said I was gonna *do* it. I just said I think it's possible."

"Sounds like he's bailin'," Winston said.

"Yep," Prentiss agreed.

" 'Course I'm bailin'," Peyton said. "Why would I want to spend my summer pedaling a bicycle and let some other guy move in on Lisa?"

"You got a point," Prentiss said.

Peyton picked a dandelion and held it up in the breeze to watch its feathers fly. "Y'all would seriously pay me a hundred bucks if I did it?"

"Yeah, but if you start the ride and quit, you gotta pay us fifty bucks apiece," Winston said. "Wanna bet?"

"Not yet," Peyton said. "But I'll think about it."

They looked up as a horse appeared from the pecan grove. Actually, they heard it before they saw it — a thunder of hooves

20

hitting the ground as a powerful Thorough-bred named Bootlegger raced around the border of the front lawn and made his way to the rear garden before following the same dirt road Peyton's mother had taken. The rider, at once familiar and foreign, looked reckless even at this distance, holding the reins in one hand and a bottle of bourbon in the other, his boots tight against the horse's sides, his sandy hair blown by the spring breeze.

Peyton was at once sickened and mesmerized by the sight of it. He heard the familiar murmurs rippling across the porch. "I'm tellin' you, he's gonna kill hisself with that bottle . . ."

Horse and rider reached the crest of a hill that blocked the view of Peyton's house — the cottage his mother had fled to. Peyton heard the horse snort and saw it pawing at the ground, impatient to release the energy rippling through its sinewy legs. The rider kept turning to look over the hill and then back at the main house until at last he appeared resigned to his fate. Turning toward the house, he gave the horse its head and sped back down the dirt road toward the front lawn. As Bootlegger came streaking around the grand old house, Peyton saw clumps of grass fly up each time the Thoroughbred's hooves landed. It was hypnotic, the sight of his father racing into the picnic, carrying his bourbon bottle like a knight bearing a standard, ready for the joust. Without speaking, the three boys stood but remained under the tree, only halfway trusting Peyton's father not to run them through.

Years later, when Peyton was a grown man with a family, what unfolded on this spring afternoon would replay in his mind again and again, always in slow motion. Just as his father raised the bottle to his lips, leaned his head back, and took a long draw, the two squirrels in the tree suddenly raced down the trunk and scampered into the yard. Jubal, his grandfather's Irish setter, spotted them from the porch and tore down the steps after them. Barking as he laid chase, the dog startled the horse. It balked, sending Peyton's father sailing out of the saddle, over the head of his mount, and straight into the Ghost Oak, where he hit his head with such force that it sounded like a billiard ball dropped onto an oak floor. And then nothing — lifeless silence for a split second before all the women screamed and the whole family swarmed the fallen rider.

In an instant, the slow-motion scene accelerated to lightning speed, and Peyton couldn't keep up. The three boys were unceremoniously pushed aside as an ambulance was called and a cousin visiting from Birmingham — the only doctor in the family — ran to his car to get his medical bag.

Suddenly, it hit Peyton. His mother knew nothing about this. As the ambulance sped away with his father — and before anyone else thought to do it — he ran into the library and called home.

TWO

Peyton and his mother ran all the way from the parking lot, up the front steps of the hospital, and straight to the front desk, where a receptionist waved them on. "Sixth floor, Katie!" Peyton was too preoccupied with his father to ask why a hospital receptionist would be so familiar with his mother.

They arrived at the waiting room just in time to see a tall, forbidding nurse bring order to the chaotic Cabots. "That's enough!" they heard her shout as they stood just outside the room full of family. The Cabots, who generally obeyed no one but their patriarch, fell silent. "You will *not* disturb my patients. Everyone, take a seat and keep your voices *down,* or security will escort every last one of you to the lobby. You'll be updated shortly."

The nurse spun around and marched into the corridor where Peyton and his mother stood. She stopped when she saw them.

Peyton expected her to bark them out of the hospital, but instead she took his mother's hand and said, "Oh, Katydid." Peyton's mother fell sobbing into the nurse's sympathetic embrace, leaving him to wonder whether he really knew his own parents at all.

When his mother finally collected herself, she opened her purse and handed the nurse a white envelope. "He gave me his power of attorney before he shipped out," she said.

The nurse nodded. "Well and good. Come with me."

Peyton could only follow behind, as his mother and the nurse seemed to forget he was there. Only when the two women entered a conference room and the nurse turned to close the door did she notice that a teenage boy was trailing them.

"Who are you?" she demanded.

Peyton's mother looked surprised to see him standing there. "Oh, honey, I'm so sorry!" she said, taking him by the hand and pulling him into the conference room. "Ida, this is our son, Peyton. Sweetheart, this is my dear friend, Nurse Ida Buck."

"Pleased to meet you," Peyton said.

"I'm pleased to meet you too. Now look after your mama or you'll have me to deal with — understand?"

"Yes, ma'am."

Nurse Buck left them alone in the windowless conference room, closing the door behind her. Peyton's mother took a seat and patted the chair next to her. "Come and sit down, honey."

He sat beside her and wondered what he should be doing as she blotted her eyes with a tissue and took one deep breath after another. He had never seen his mother like this. Peyton's father used to tell her she was like a Roman candle — small but full of fire. Right now his mother seemed small, alright. But there was no fire, at least none Peyton could see. She looked like someone in dire need of protection, but her protector had ridden a bourbon bottle into a tree and was now himself helpless, lying unconscious on a gurney somewhere down one of these aimless corridors.

She jumped slightly when the door opened and Nurse Buck ushered a doctor in. "Mrs. Cabot, I'm Doctor Crenshaw. I'm head of neurology here at the hospital."

"Thank you so much for taking care of Marshall," his mother said as Nurse Buck made her exit. "This is our son, Peyton."

"I understand you have your husband's power of attorney, so you needn't worry about interference from anyone else. I don't have to tell you it's serious . . ."

Peyton was aware of sound coming from the doctor's mouth, but he couldn't distinguish the words swirling out. He had the sense of being unplugged, still taking up space and filling a chair, but unable to think or speak or feel.

He found himself staring at the doctor's wristwatch, which looked very old and expensive. Had it belonged to his father? Maybe the dad was also a doctor. Was the watch a gift from father to son — a passing of the torch, a reward for footsteps followed?

As sound kept flowing from the doctor's mouth, Peyton's mother reached over and took his hand as if she knew he was adrift and instinctively offered an anchor. What was happening in this room, now a matter-of-fact occurrence, would've seemed unthinkable just yesterday — just this morning. It was unthinkable still.

Peyton hovered outside the waiting room, where the Cabots couldn't see him, and listened. Once concern for his mother broke through the fog in his brain, he had asked her to explain everything the doctor said and then volunteered to update the family himself. Just the thought of dealing with them, he knew, was too much for her right now. As he had done earlier that day on his grandparents' porch, Peyton stood still in the hospital corridor and tuned in to one voice after another.

Aunt Camille: "Did you see that bunch o' rednecks that looked in here like they wanted a seat?"

Aunt Charlotte: "Lucky we fill up the waiting room. Can you even *imagine* being cooped up in here with white trash?"

Uncle Julian: "Do you *finally* see, Daddy, why you cannot afford to have Marshall in charge of the family holdings?"

Granddaddy Cabot: "There's no such thing as the family holdings, Julian. They're all *my* holdings. I earned them, I own them, and I'll direct them as I see fit."

Grandmother Cabot: "Do you think, George, we should perhaps resume our lovely picnic and await word at the house? There doesn't seem to be anything we can do here, and we'd all be so much more comfortable on the porch."

Peyton felt a tingly wave that started at the base of his spine and quickly moved up, all the way to his temples. He had felt it only once before in his life — right before lightning struck a tree by the stadium during a Georgia game. As the lightning cracked and a tall pine split apart with a deafening pop, his father, in one swift motion, had dropped the Coke and hot dog he was holding and wrapped his arms protectively around Peyton. It was a memory he hadn't revisited in ages, but the tingling brought it back. He stepped inside the waiting room just in time to see his grandfather wince, reach for his head, and slump over.

Peyton's grandmother looked down in horror. Without touching her husband, who had fallen into her lap, she repeated over and over, in an eerily calm voice, "George? George, dear, get up. George, do get up . . ."

THREE

They buried Peyton's grandfather on a rainy afternoon, the Monday after Easter. Tuesday morning, his father's law office called to say that Uncle Julian had just been there, urging the partners to "expedite the will." Peyton still couldn't believe it. They had gone from a family picnic to a hospital to a funeral, but the death they half expected hadn't happened, while one they never saw coming delivered a blow.

For the next few days, Peyton spent most of his time at the hospital with his mother, sitting on a stiff, uncomfortable sofa in the sixth-floor waiting room until visiting hours finally rolled around. School would be out soon anyway, so his mother had arranged for him to finish his studies at home — "home," for now, being the hospital. His father was occasionally responsive but never spoke and didn't rest easy with anybody except Peyton's mother, who hadn't left for a second since the accident.

When Winston and Prentiss called to see if Peyton wanted to go fishing, she insisted that he take the opportunity to escape the oppressive confines of sickness and get some fresh air. The three boys rode their bikes to a put-in on the Skidaway River. It was the great indignity of being fifteen that all three of them could drive — and freely motored around the family farmland in work trucks — but out here, on the open road, they were not allowed behind the wheel without an adult. They remained one birthday away from a driver's license and its promise of manhood.

Propping their bikes against some scrub pines, they headed for a johnboat that was resting upside down by the water. It wasn't secured and never had been. All the locals used it and recognized it, so any thief would be summarily caught and throttled. Everybody knew to return it to this exact spot when they were done. Out of habit, the trio jumped back as they flipped the boat over, a precaution against any water moccasins that might've nested there since the last time it was in the river.

"Grab the cooler," Winston said to Peyton as he laid their fishing rods in the boat. In any given situation, Winston assumed au-

31

thority, even when he had no idea what he was doing. It had been so since they were kids. Peyton would go along unless Winston headed in a particularly stupid direction, and then he would find a way to change their course while making his cousin believe he was still in charge. It kept the peace and kept them out of harm's way.

He unstrapped the small cooler from the rack on the back of his bike and loaded it in before they shoved off and jumped into the boat. Peyton winked at Prentiss as the two of them took up oars and let Winston have the front seat they knew he wanted — the captain's position, of course. Prentiss grinned back at him as they dipped their oars into the water and the boat glided downriver.

They were quiet for a while before Prentiss said, "You been stayin' at the hospital an awful lot."

"Don't want to leave Mama by herself," Peyton said with a shrug.

"What do the doctors say?" Prentiss asked.

"Some of 'em say Daddy'll get better, some of 'em say he won't. This one says he's gotta have brain surgery, that one says it'll kill him. I don't know how Mama stands it — 'specially with Uncle Julian over there every day telling her she's too emotional to make decisions and needs to let him do her thinking for her. She won't, though, and I'm glad."

"You better be," Winston chimed in. "Whole family knows he's always wanted to take over everything. Hey, head for that fork over there."

Peyton and Prentiss rowed toward a favorite spot on the Skidaway, one where the fish were generally biting this time of the morning. Peyton was thinking about the day his grandfather announced that he was retiring and would be handing the reins of his estate to his eldest son. Granddaddy Cabot had made a big production of it, gathering the whole clan and having a shrimp boil for the occasion. All the adults had circled around the big mahogany desk in the library to witness his grandfather signing the papers, rolling them into a scroll, and handing them to Peyton's father like a runner passing the baton. Then they all had a champagne toast.

He tried to remember his dad that day, during the gathering his aunts sarcastically called The Coronation. How had his father looked? What had he said? Was he happy to be taking over the estate? Somehow Peyton didn't think so, but the details wouldn't come to him.

As for Granddaddy Cabot, he and Peyton

had always had a strange relationship. On the one hand, the elder Cabot had made it clear that Marshall was his favorite child and Peyton, by extension, his favorite grandchild. Whenever there was a prized shotgun to be passed down or extra spending money slipped into a palm, these tokens of love, or at least favored status, always went to Peyton. And yet he had never had a real conversation with his grandfather.

"Let's try casting right here." Winston pulled him out of a swirl of memory and back into the johnboat he had been absently rowing.

The three boys took up their fishing rods and cast their lines. They drifted along, none of them feeling the need to talk as they watched for signs of movement on the surface of the river. As usual, Winston was the first to grow impatient, reeling in his line to try another spot.

"Peyton," he said, "I need to tell you something. Uncle Julian was over at the house last night. Heard him tell Mama, like he was all concerned, 'Baby sister, we need to get Marshall moved to Milledgeville where they can do something about his situation. I think we're the only ones who can see the truth.' Can you believe that? 'Baby sister,' my hind leg. I can't believe he called her that, like they were all close and everything."

"Wait — back up," Peyton said. "Are you sure he said Milledgeville? Nothing there but the asylum."

"I know."

"But why would Uncle Julian want to put Daddy there?"

Winston stood up in the boat and cast his line near some stumps protruding from the water. "I'll give you two guesses and the first one don't count. He told Mama he'd already started the paperwork to have Uncle Marshall declared mentally unfit to run the estate."

Peyton gave his reel a few turns, adjusting his line as he thought it over. "He can't send Daddy to Milledgeville unless Mama agrees to it, and she never will."

"Maybe not, but Uncle Julian knows a lot o' powerful people in Savannah. Sooner or later, he'll find a way. Just giving you fair warning so you can head him off."

Peyton knew what his cousin said was true. Despite his mother's best efforts, Uncle Julian might find a way to do this horrific thing. Not only that, but he'd enjoy every minute of it. Without stopping to weigh his options, Peyton threw down his fishing rod and jumped in the river.

"Where in the Sam Hill are you going?" Winston shouted as he and Prentiss, both looking stunned, sat together in the boat, now oblivious to the fishing rods dangling from their hands.

"Back to the hospital!" Peyton shouted as he swam toward the bank. He scrambled up and ran the distance to his bicycle, then pedaled furiously up the county road.

Before he could get very far, Police Chief Herschel Bramlett pulled up beside him in his pickup truck. "Son, you look like you need to get somewhere."

"Yes, sir, I sure do. I need to get to the hospital to see about Daddy."

The chief's eyes narrowed. "Marshall take a turn?"

"No, sir," Peyton panted. "I just all of a sudden feel like I need to get back."

"Well, throw your bike in the truck bed and climb in."

"I can just sit in the back. I'm all wet from jumping in the river."

"I ain't worried about that," the chief said as Peyton lifted his bicycle into the truck. "I keep some old towels under the seat for emergencies. Looks like you got one. Climb in and you can dry off on the way."

Peyton took the passenger's seat and began drying off with the towels as the chief headed for the hospital. Leaning his head out the window, he let the warm wind whip through his hair and hoped it would dry his clothes at least enough so he didn't drip. Dripping would most definitely get him thrown out of the hospital, especially if Nurse Buck was on duty.

"How's your mama holdin' up?" the chief asked.

"Pretty good, I reckon," Peyton said as he blotted his face with a towel. "She looks real tired, though — 'specially after a visit from Uncle Julian."

The chief frowned and scratched the back of his head. "I don't mean to speak ill o' your kin, son, but that one ain't changed one iota since he was a kid. He was useless then, and he's useless now."

"You won't get any arguments from me."

"He givin' your mama trouble?"

"Yes, sir. I just found out he's trying to get Daddy sent to Milledgeville. That's why I need to get to the hospital."

"*Milledgeville?* That's low even for Julian. Listen, son, if it looks like he's about to have his way, you get on the phone and call me, okay?"

"What could you do, Chief?"

"I could slow things down. Your uncle's got connections, but I got a lot o' people around here that I've helped out, and they owe me a favor or two. I wouldn't hesitate to call 'em in for your daddy."

"How come, if you don't mind my asking?" Peyton covered his head with one of the towels, rubbed it back and forth over his hair, and then ran his fingers through the mess he'd made to try to comb it out.

"Son, I want you to remember something," the chief said as he turned on his blinker and slowed the truck down. "Your daddy ain't a bad man. He ain't a weak one neither. He's a good man that went through some real bad stuff. I'm still hoping he can find his way back — for your sake as much as anybody's. And as for your mama, well . . . people don't come no finer."

"Thank you."

The chief pulled into the hospital parking lot and stopped his truck at the front entrance.

"Want me to carry these towels home and get 'em washed?" Peyton asked.

The chief took them from him and crammed them under the truck seat. "No, that's alright. Ada's used to me bringin' home something or other for her to throw in with her washin'. How 'bout I drop your bike off at your house so you don't have to fool with it?"

"I sure would 'preciate that. And everything else too."

"You're more'n welcome. Go on inside, and give your folks my best. And you remember what I said. Julian takes it too far, you gimme a call."

"I will. I promise. Say hey to Miss Ada for us."

"I'll do that."

FOUR

Inside the hospital, Peyton walked as fast as he could in hopes of escaping the required stop at the front desk. Luckily, the receptionist was away from her post.

Knocking softly on his dad's door, he could hear a man's voice on the other side and didn't have to think twice to know who was in there. As he slowly opened the door, his mother gave him a tired smile from her chair beside his father's bed.

Uncle Julian crossed the room and laid a hand on his shoulder. "It's good that you came, Peyton, but you'll need to leave now."

Peyton saw his mother rub her forehead as if she had a bad headache. "Marshall's his father, Julian."

"It's for his own good, Kate. You'll need to listen to me from now on."

Just as Peyton was about to protest, Nurse Buck came into the room. With her crisp uniform and stern demeanor, Peyton imag-

40

ined she could put General MacArthur in his place.

"Only two visitors at a time and *only* during visiting hours, which will be ending in thirty minutes," she said firmly.

Uncle Julian turned to Peyton's mother. "There now. We all agree."

Peyton doubted that his uncle was aware enough of other people to see the subtle change in his mother's expression — the tightening of her jaw, the way she balled one hand into a fist as she slowly stood from her chair.

"You've been here for an hour, Julian," she said. "And now it's Peyton's turn. Goodbye."

Uncle Julian gave her a patronizing smile, part sneer, part smirk. "Kate, I'm trying to be patient with you, but you're tired and you aren't thinking straight. Just do as I say."

"I'm very tired, but I'm thinking very straight," she said. "Peyton needs some time with his father, and he's *going* to have it."

Faced with defiance, Peyton's uncle was unable to fake civility. He glared at them as the corner of his mouth twitched.

"If you're thinking of raising your voice, think again," Nurse Buck said as she opened the door and held it open for him. "Remember to sign out as you leave."

Uncle Julian tried to give the nurse a condescending smile, but he had to look up to do it, which rendered the effect more comical than threatening.

Nurse Buck rolled her eyes as he left. "You all keep it quiet, and I'll see if I can give you an extra hour," she said, winking at Peyton's mother. She looked Peyton up and down. "You're wet."

"She's right — you *are* wet," his mother said, finally able to focus on something besides battling his uncle.

"Yes, ma'am. I was on a fishing trip when I just felt like I needed to get back here. I kinda jumped in the river."

The nurse raised an eyebrow. "You *kinda* jumped in the river?"

"I definitely jumped in the river."

Nurse Buck reached into a drawer and pulled out a hospital gown. "Put this on and leave your clothes outside the door. I'll get them dried."

"Bless you, Ida," his mother said. "You're an angel in uniform."

"Wish I could talk you back into one."

"Maybe one day."

The nurse checked his father's temperature and pulse. "About the same."

"We'll be grateful for that much," Peyton's mother said.

Nurse Buck was about to leave the room when she stopped in the doorway, turned, and said, "You stay strong now, Katydid, and let me know if you need anything."

As the nurse closed the door, Peyton stepped into the bathroom and changed, then stacked his wet clothes outside in the hallway and pulled up a chair. "Why does she call you Katydid?"

"Didn't you know your mama's a spy? That's my secret code name when I parachute behind enemy lines."

"I'm trying to picture you in combat boots, jumping out of a plane," he said with a frown.

"You don't think I could pull it off?"

Peyton reached over and gently tugged at the string of pearls around his mother's neck. "You're way too girly to be a spy. And way too honest."

She brushed at his hair with her fingertips. "You need a haircut."

"You always think I need a haircut."

"Do I? I'm sorry. I never wanted to be one o' those naggin' mamas."

"Don't worry. You're not. I just like to give you a hard time so you'll have to earn that Mother's Day corsage every year."

She held his chin in her hand and sighed. "I see so much of him in you — your daddy,

43

I mean. You're tall like him. Same broad shoulders. Same high cheekbones and strong jawline. Same silky hair."

"Different color though."

"True. I guess you reached way back yonder to some ancestor with dark hair and eyes. My whole family's fair. Marshall's hair used to turn nearly blond in the summertime, back when we lived on Tybee and spent so much time at the beach. You can still see little flecks of gold in it."

"Lisa thinks he looks like Gary Cooper."

Peyton's mother winked at him. "Gary Cooper should be so lucky." She looked at his father with such a lonely expression that Peyton tried to distract her.

"Tell me about Katydid."

She attempted a smile but appeared too exhausted to manage it. "That was my nickname when I worked here. Ida called me Katydid one day in the cafeteria and it stuck."

Peyton couldn't believe what he was hearing. "You worked with Nurse Drill Sergeant?"

"Sure did."

"How long were you a nurse?"

"Four or five years, I guess, counting my student nursing."

"How come I never knew that before?"

She squeezed his hand. "Because that part of my life was over by the time you came along, and a boy has more important things to do than pry into his mama's sordid past."

As an image of the library kiss drifted back into his mind, Peyton suddenly had all sorts of questions that had never occurred to him before. "Where'd you meet Daddy?"

She didn't take her eyes off his father, lying unconscious and still.

"Mama?" He reached over and touched her arm, knowing that he really should tell her what Uncle Julian was up to. But she looked so forlorn right now that he couldn't bring himself to do it. "Why don't you tell me the happy part?"

She turned to face him, absently running a finger over the pearls around her neck. "Okay, honey. I'll tell you the happy part." They settled back into their chairs as she began. "I met your father when we were teenagers — on the beach in St. Augustine, when he was just beginning his famous bike ride to Key West."

"You gotta be kidding me!"

She laughed and held up her right hand. "The truth, the whole truth, and nothing but the truth."

"Wait a minute — what were you doing in St. Augustine?"

"You've always heard me talk about Aunt Gert, right?"

"Yes, ma'am."

"Well, honey, Aunt Gert raised me from the time I was about nine years old. Daddy died from a heart attack when I was eight. And remember, I was the baby of ten children."

"I can't even imagine a house with that many kids."

She opened her purse, pulled out a couple of lemon drops, and gave one to Peyton. "People in the country had big families back then so all the kids could help work the farm. Still do, I guess. You were just never around mine because my brothers and sisters all scattered. Most of us didn't grow up together."

Peyton bit down on the tart candy and squinted at its sour punch. "Was that because your daddy died?"

She crunched on the candy, apparently unfazed by the sharp burst of lemon. "Back then, if the man of the house passed, it could break up a family. Five of my brothers and sisters had already married and left home, but that still left five more for my mother to try and feed — with no education and no assistance from anybody but her older children, who had their own financial struggles. She knew I loved Aunt Gert and asked her to take me in. My two sisters who were still at home went to live with another aunt and uncle who didn't have any children, and the boys stayed with Mama to help on the farm. By the time you were born, she had died of the flu. The boys sold the farm and moved as far away from it as they could get. I guess they'd had their fill of the mules and the plows."

"How did you even know Aunt Gert," he asked, "with y'all in Mississippi and her down in Florida?"

"My folks never had enough money for vacations, but Aunt Gert would always invite us down there to spend a couple of weeks with her every summer. If Daddy could scrape together gas money once the cotton was planted, we'd go — all of us kids riding in the back of his old farm truck. He would pitch us a big tent by the river in Aunt Gert's backyard, where the breezes were cool. Can you even imagine doing that now? People think they can't go anywhere without a hotel room, but we sure did."

His mother ran her fingers through her hair, as if she were remembering the river-front winds of St. Augustine. "Anyway, Aunt Gert and I took a quick shine to each other. We were always close."

"So you were actually living in St. Augustine when Daddy came through on his bike?"

She brushed a piece of lint from her skirt. "His Aunt Lily — she's your granddaddy's sister — lives down there, so he stopped to rest and wash his clothes before he set off again."

"Where were you when the two of you met?"

"On Anastasia Island, near the lighthouse. You could bike there from Aunt Gert's — it was just over the old wooden bridge that was there before they built the one with the lion statues. She'd let me go by myself as long as I promised not to wade out too far." She closed her eyes and leaned her head back for just a moment. "Oh, it was wonderful — that first taste of freedom for a teenage girl."

"That's where you met Daddy?"

She laughed as she held her hands over her heart and made a fluttering motion like a dove flapping its wings. "Yes, that's where I met my sweetheart."

"How?"

"I had walked out onto a sandbar to gather seashells, and I wasn't paying attention when high tide started coming in. The next thing I knew, my sandbar was going under, and the surf between me and the shore was probably four feet deep. I was starting to panic when I looked up and saw this tall, tan boy waving at me from the beach. He called out to see if I needed help and then ran into the waves like he was born in the ocean. By the time he climbed onto the sliver of sand that was left, I was so scared that I was crying." She stopped and stared out the window, as if she were hoping to see the image of that boy and girl, alone on their tiny island in the Atlantic Ocean.

"What did Daddy do?"

"He looked down at me and smiled," she said, turning back to Peyton. "Then he took me by the hand and said, 'It's just a little water.' Right away I trusted him, even as young as he was. He picked me up and carried me to the shore. We sat together on my beach quilt — it was an old one Aunt Gert had given me — and we just talked and talked for the longest time . . ."

"And?"

"And . . . we both had it bad. Don't ever let anybody tell you there's no such thing as love at first sight — or that puppy love can't be the real thing. Aunt Gert could see it right away."

"You took Daddy to meet her?"

49

"Yes, stupid me!" His mother rolled her eyes and laughed. "I could've spent a lot more time alone with him if I'd had sense enough to keep my mouth shut, but I never could keep a secret from Aunt Gert, so I invited him to supper that night. I can still see it to this day: Aunt Gert, a force of nature — lots of drama — and your pensive father together at the supper table, along with smitten little me who couldn't eat a bite, I was so in love with Marshall."

Peyton frowned. "But how could you be sure? You were just kids."

"About like you and Lisa?" she answered, eyebrows raised.

"No fair changing the subject. What did you and Daddy do about it?"

"Got married."

Peyton's jaw dropped. *"Then?"*

"Not *right* then, but pretty soon. Marshall wanted to cancel his bike ride and stay in St. Augustine with me, but Aunt Gert put her foot down. She told him a boy who couldn't finish what he started would grow up to be a man who never finished anything. He biked down to Key West and pedaled back as far as Miami, but then he got impatient and caught the train to St. Augustine. He tried to get Aunt Gert to take us to the courthouse when we picked him up at the train station. You can imagine how that went over. She told him if he was too young to drive to the courthouse, he was too young to get married there. But she promised us both that Marshall could visit as often as he wanted, and as long as we both finished high school and behaved ourselves, we would have her blessing."

"So that's what you did?"

"That's what we did. We both turned sixteen that fall. Marshall got his driver's license and came down literally every single weekend our junior and senior years of high school. He graduated first, then came to St. Augustine for my ceremony — Aunt Gert said she wouldn't hear of a wedding till we both had diplomas. But once we did, she signed her permission for the judge."

"Who signed Daddy's?"

"That's a whole other story. But the short answer is a fisherman named Finn, who pretended to be your daddy's guardian. And then Aunt Gert took us to her church and had her preacher marry us again, 'just to make sure it took,' as she put it. Once Marshall carried me home to meet his family, your granddaddy was worried I might not be legally protected, so *he* took us to the courthouse and signed your daddy's permission, and we got married *again*. Bet you never suspected your daddy was my third husband — and my first and my second."

Peyton tried to picture his parents as a teenage bride and groom. "Where did the rest o' the Cabots figure into all of this?"

"For a long time, they didn't," his mother said with a sigh. "Your granddaddy always supported us, and I don't have to tell you that what he said was the law of the land, as far as the Cabots were concerned. The rest of the clan didn't really care where your daddy was or what he did as long as he was right there with the money when they needed it." She paused and looked at Peyton. "I'm sorry, son. They're your family, and I shouldn't talk about them like that."

"It's weird. Except for Winston and Prentiss, they don't feel like family right now."

"I know how confusing all of this is," his mother said as she reached over and squeezed his hand lightly, "and I'm so sorry to put you through it."

"It's not your fault." Still, he had more questions. "So you and Daddy married right outta high school and then you went to UGA with him?"

"I did. At first, I got a job as a receptionist at the local hospital, but once I made friends with some of the nurses there, I started to think about becoming one. Your daddy always encouraged me to do whatever I wanted to. Thanks to the Cabot money, neither of us really had to work, but we both wanted to do something with our lives — something meaningful. I got accepted into the hospital's nursing school, and by the time Marshall was in law school in Athens, I was a travel nurse, going out into all these little rural communities to help families that didn't have a doctor. He talked about becoming a public defender for a while. But in the end . . . well . . ."

"In the end?" Peyton prompted.

"In the end . . . his family overwhelmed him," she said in a voice filled with sadness and regret. "Once Marshall finished his law degree, we moved to Tybee. Over time, though, his work for the estate pulled us off our little island and into the Cabot fray. I got a job at this hospital, working with Ida — Nurse Drill Sergeant, as you so affectionately call her — and stayed till I found out I was expecting you."

They sat watching Peyton's father breathe in and out, praying he didn't stop.

His mother put her arm around his shoulders. "I know his drinking has been hard on you, Peyton. But you have to believe me — he loves you very much. I know it doesn't make sense, but in his way, your daddy's trying to protect you by keeping his distance."

"Protect me from what?"

"From himself. From whatever followed him home from the war."

They were quiet again before Peyton said, "He used to come to all o' my games."

"He still does."

"Ma'am?"

"It's true — he comes to every single one."

"I never see him there."

"I know. I've done all I can to talk him into showing himself. But he says a boy ought to be able to play ball for the sheer fun of it and not spend his time on the field wondering when his father might show up drunk. So he always comes — completely sober. He makes sure he gets there after the game starts, and he watches from someplace where nobody will notice him. Your daddy's always cheering for you, honey. Just not out loud."

Peyton leaned back and rested his head against the wall. "I feel like such a dope."

"What on earth for?"

"Because I couldn't see what I couldn't see, if that makes any sense."

His mother leaned over and kissed him on the cheek, giving Peyton the courage to broach the difficult subject he dreaded most of all.

"Mama, there's something I need to —"

Interrupted by a knock on the door, he looked up to see a doctor with curly salt-and-pepper hair and wire-rimmed glasses step into the room.

His mother gasped and stood up. "Eli? I can't believe it's you!" They hugged like old friends.

"It's mighty good to see you, Katie," he said with a smile. "Sure wish the circumstances were different."

"What are you doing here?" his mother asked.

The doctor closed the door and motioned for her to sit down. Then he said, "Ida called me."

FIVE

Peyton was sitting beside the hospital bed while his mother went to the lobby to meet a courier delivering money from his father's law office. He heard footsteps in the corridor outside and looked up to see her come through the door with the girl who occupied most of his waking thoughts and all of his best dreams.

Lisa wore a white dress with a full skirt and a wide belt with little clusters of strawberries all around it. He remembered it from their last date. Her dark red hair fell onto her shoulders in a cascade of waves and soft curls.

"Son, there's someone here to see you," his mother was saying.

"Hi, Lisa." He finally managed to speak as he stood up.

She gave him an encouraging smile. "Hi."

He couldn't seem to find his voice, not with both of his parents in the room, and was grateful when his mother gave him an out. "Peyton, why don't you take Lisa to the waiting room where you can visit?"

He held the door open, then escorted her to the empty waiting room just down the hall, where they sat next to each other on the rock-hard sofa Peyton had napped on the night before.

"Sure is good to see you," he said. "Sorry I haven't been around much."

"You don't need to apologize for taking care of your family. How's your daddy?"

"Not so good. He needs surgery, and that's what we're trying to work out. Say, how'd you get out o' school to come here?"

Lisa gave him a playful nudge with her elbow. "It's Saturday, silly."

"Man," he said. "I don't even know what day it is. We've only been here a week, but it seems like forever."

The clock on the wall ticked off seconds that felt like minutes as they sat together, with Peyton searching for something — anything — to say. Alone with Lisa on a moonlit night in Savannah, he would've had so much to tell her — and so much he wanted to hear her say. But not in this place. Here, the words wouldn't come. Hospitals held such suffering that it seemed any flashes of joy inside their walls might somehow be tainted.

Finally, Lisa broke the silence. "My sister and I could run some sandwiches over for y'all. Can't imagine eating hospital food as long as you have."

"That's mighty sweet of you, but we won't be here after today. There's a doctor in from California — an old friend of Mama's. He says Daddy needs surgery and we have to get him to Atlanta right away. That's what we're doing this afternoon, before my Uncle Julian finds out. He wants to get Daddy sent to Milledgeville."

Lisa frowned. "But isn't that . . ."

"Yeah. It's where the asylum is. My uncle's not a very nice man. We don't have much time to get Daddy out o' here."

"Listen, I'm sorry I barged in like this. I shouldn't have come." Lisa stood up to leave, but he followed her to the door and took her by the hand.

"Please don't go," he said. "I'm just — I'm just so glad to see you. I really miss you, Lisa." They stood close together in the empty waiting room. Kissing a beautiful girl in such a sterile place, with his father lying unconscious down the hall and his mother hanging by a thread, would be all kinds of wrong. Even so, that's exactly what he wanted to do. But nurses kept walking by, some glancing, some glaring.

"Hey, what's goin' on out there?" he asked Lisa, nodding toward a window and taking a few steps back to get them out of the doorway.

"The usual, I guess," she said with a shrug. "Everybody goes from the lake or the beach to the movie theater and back again. Typical spring around here, from what everybody says. I imagine summer will bring more of the same."

"You been going to the movies a lot?"

"A few times."

"With your girlfriends?" Afraid of the answer, he stared at the floor as he waited for it.

"If there's something on your mind, you should tell me."

He looked up at her. Man, those eyes. "I was wondering . . . I mean . . . not that I'd blame you with me cooped up in here for so long . . . wouldn't expect you to just sit at home . . ."

"Are you trying to ask me if I've been going out with other boys?"

He took a deep breath for courage. "Yes."

"A couple of times," she said. "But only because Mama insisted. Why?"

"*Why?* Well . . . because . . ."

Now she was smiling at him. "Because why?"

Because I'm crazy about you. Because I think about you day and night. Because the sight of you makes me go weak at the knees.

Peyton could've said all of that — or any of it — and it would've been true. But instead he blurted out the one thing that wasn't. "Because, well . . . I mean, I can't ask you to sit at home and wait for me . . . It's fine with me if you want to . . . you know, go to the movies with somebody else."

"Oh, it's *fine*? With *you*?"

Immediately, he saw his mistake. Lisa's smile vanished, she pulled her hand away, and her voice trembled.

"Lisa, I didn't mean —"

"I'm yours to give away? And you're all too happy to do it?"

"No! That's not what I said."

She started for the door.

"Lisa, wait!"

"Shhhh!" Nurse Buck was passing by, holding her finger over her lips.

"Sorry," Peyton said to her before he turned back to Lisa and put his hands on her shoulders. "You've gotta believe me, Lisa — I didn't mean for it to come out like that," he pleaded as quietly as he could. "I'm just in over my head here. I don't know what's about to happen, and I don't know when we'll be back. I have no idea if Daddy'll live through this. And my crazy uncle is driving Mama up the wall. The summer I see coming isn't exactly the one I was hoping for. I was hoping to spend it with you. Picnics on the river and afternoons at the beach and movie nights and dancing and — just — just *you,* Lisa. That's what I was hoping for. That's what I want more than anything. Instead . . . Please come back inside?"

She let him hold her hand and lead her back into the waiting room. "I know this is really hard for you," she said, looking up at him as he laid his free hand against her face. "Mama says . . . she says a break might be good for us."

He let his hand glide down to her neck. "What do you say?"

She looked straight at him, shaking her head and biting her lip. "I don't know. I really don't. I wish I did because then everything wouldn't be such a muddle."

Lisa always told the truth. Her honesty was one of many things that had drawn Peyton to her from the beginning. And honesty took courage. But Lisa didn't seem so brave just now. Her eyes were welling and she looked cornered.

Peyton, who suddenly felt very selfish, bent down and softly kissed her. "I'm sorry," he said, putting his arms around her. "Last thing I'd ever want to do is make you cry."

She tightened her arms around his waist and rested her head on his shoulder. "I know that."

An image of his parents' library kiss flashed into Peyton's memory. He laid it next to another, of a boy and a girl just finding their way to each other — at least, that's what he fervently hoped he and Lisa were doing. It was a picture of loving and longing, of almost touching, soul to soul, but not quite. And sometimes it hurt like all get-out.

"Can you — can you call me whenever you get settled in Atlanta?" Lisa asked, looking up at him. "Let me know how you are — how your daddy's doing?"

He brushed a tear from her cheek and nodded.

Lisa slowly pulled away from him. "I guess I'd better go. Judy's waiting."

"Your sister drove you over?"

"Yes. Are you sure you'll be alright?"

"Yeah. I'll be okay." He walked her into the hospital corridor, where he had to stand and watch the girl of his dreams disappear into a tunnel of white tile, gray walls, and cold fluorescent light.

into a tunnel of white tile gray walls, and cold fluorescent light.

Six

Peyton was a bundle of energy, tapping his foot against the loading dock as if his own rapid motion might make everybody around him move faster. By the time Lisa left the hospital, his mother had made all the arrangements for Atlanta. Now, they were about to move his father, and so much had to go right.

Chief Bramlett pulled his mother's car around back to the service entrance, where the hospital parked ambulances that weren't in use. A rapidly emptied laundry truck had been backed up to one of the rear exits. Doctor Eli Roth and Peyton's mother helped Nurse Buck lower Marshall's hospital gurney into the back of the truck and lock the wheels. Peyton's mother and Doctor Roth climbed in, each taking a seat on metal laundry bins turned upside down on either side of the gurney. Nurse Buck handed the doctor his medical bag and gave each of them a thermos of coffee and a paper sack filled with whatever food she could quickly muster. The chief's wife had also sent along a sack of sandwiches.

"I wish I were going with you," Nurse Buck said.

Peyton's mother reached out and squeezed her hand. "So do we, precious Ida. So do we. Thank you for everything."

"We ready back here?" the chief asked as Nurse Buck stepped away from the truck.

"Ready as we'll ever be," Doctor Roth said.

The chief closed the truck's rear doors, their small square windows cracked for ventilation. "Peyton, I reckon it's time for you and me to saddle up," he said. They climbed into the cab of the truck, making ready for the trip to Atlanta. An orderly would drive an ambulance in the opposite direction, followed by a blonde student nurse in Peyton's mother's car, all in an effort to hide his father's destination from Uncle Julian's prying eyes.

As the chief pulled away from the loading dock, Peyton ducked down out of sight. A couple of days ago, the deputies had spotted a man who looked out of place in Savannah. He turned out to be a private investigator from New York, hired by Uncle Julian.

65

"Any sign o' that guy?" Peyton asked as the chief gave him the all clear.

"Drove right past him. I don't know how he expects to slip around, dressed in a black suit in the springtime. Sticks out like a preacher on Bourbon Street."

It was late afternoon when they turned onto the main highway. The sun was softening, the sky still clear and blue. For days, Peyton had longed to escape the numbing neutrality of the hospital. But now, getting doused in color just reminded him of all he was missing — a lost summer with Lisa. That was selfish, he knew, given what his parents were going through. Still, the thought of endless days in an Atlanta hospital made him feel desolate.

Peyton didn't know how on earth his mother could hold up through all of this. His father would know exactly what to do to make everything easy for her. That's what he always did — before the bourbon, anyway. He made her troubles go away. Once, when she was anxious about hosting a luncheon for Grandmother Cabot's garden club, his father brought in an extra maid and two gardeners to handle the house and yard, hired a chef and his staff to cook and serve, and booked the governor's florist to do all the decorating. Then he took Peyton's mother shopping for a new dress while her luncheon came together.

Ever since he came home from the war, it seemed as if he didn't know how to love anyone but her. That sounded petty and jealous, Peyton realized, which wasn't at all how he felt. He could never be jealous of his mother, who, in all honesty, had become his hero. Preachers were always talking about unconditional love, but he had watched his mother live it every day since the war. And if the tables were turned — if she were the one lying in that hospital bed — he knew his father would move heaven and earth to make her whole again.

"Son, if you don't quit thinkin' so hard, your head's gonna fly off," Chief Bramlett said.

"I'm not sure that'd be such a bad thing, the way my brain's twisting all around," Peyton said, rubbing his temples.

"We got five hours o' drivin' ahead," the chief said. "Want to tell me what's on your mind?"

"Just thinking about Daddy, I guess . . . . Did you know him when you were kids?"

"Sure. Everybody knew everybody around Savannah."

Peyton looked out his window at nothing in particular. They were approaching a billboard with a huge picture of Rita Hayworth holding up a bottle of RC Cola. Her auburn hair reminded him of Lisa's. Another sign promised "a burger worth fighting for" at Pop's Diner. Maybe Pop's should change their slogan now that the war was over and nobody wanted to think about it ever again.

Peyton didn't know what to expect from his next question for the chief but decided to ask it anyway. "You remember anything about him — Daddy, I mean? Do you remember what he was like back then?"

"I remember he saved baseball for us."

"Sir?"

"Saved it from your Uncle Julian. We'd start a pickup game, and sure enough, here would come Julian with his fancy glove, made special in Charleston. He couldn't play worth a flip, and he was a bad sport, so we hated to see him comin'."

"Why'd you let him in the game?"

"Because most of our parents worked in one o' your granddaddy's cotton mills. Julian would slither in an' say something like, 'First base is my spot.' If anybody protested, he'd smile and say, 'Where do your parents work again?' Whenever he dropped the ball — which was pretty much every time he touched it — he'd blame whoever threw it."

"What a fat head."

"Couldn'a said it better myself."

"So what did Daddy have to do with it?"

The chief rubbed his chin and narrowed his eyes. "If I'm rememberin' right, one o' the boys finally got a belly full o' Julian and told your daddy. Marshall kicked his brother outta the game and told us nobody had to worry about their parents' jobs. We asked him if he wanted to play, and as it turns out, he was a fine ballplayer — mighty good sport too."

"I'm not sure that story makes me feel any better, Chief. Knowing Uncle Julian, he's prob'ly still mad about it. Just gives him one more reason to hate Daddy."

"True. But here's the thing I learned about Marshall back then. Some people are just selfish and think the rules don't apply to them. That'd be your Uncle Julian. Others are law-abidin' because they don't want to get into trouble or have their neighbors think ill of 'em. That's most everybody else. And then there's a handful like your daddy — people with a strong sense o' justice. They'll do what they think is right and fair even when the law says they don't have to — even when the law says they're not s'posed to. And even when it means a sacrifice on their part. Ain't many like that,

69

Peyton."

"No, sir. I guess not." Peyton ran his finger back and forth across the dusty dashboard of the laundry truck, carefully considering his next question. "Chief . . . do you . . . do you know anything about Daddy's time in the service — what happened, I mean?"

"If you're askin' do I know what drove him into that bottle, no I don't, Peyton. If I did, I'd tell you. What I do know is this: Marshall saw some o' the worst fightin' in the Pacific. And from what the newspapers say, once the Army and the Marines finally took that bloody island, it turned out we didn't even need it."

"You mean they did all that for nothing?"

"Pretty much. You think about that for a second — months o' killin' and tryin' to stay alive and witnessin' horrors you can't even imagine, only to find out your life — all them lives — were gambled for no more than an x'd-off spot on some general's map. Knowin' how your daddy's turned, that'd be a mighty bitter pill to swallow."

The pavement sliced through cotton fields and onion fields and one sleepy rural town after another until the sun started its descent, painting the sky with shades of reddish-orange that mirrored the Georgia

70

clay down below.

"You ever hear about Daddy riding his bike from that camp on the Okefenokee down to Key West?" Peyton asked.

"I did," the chief said. "Made him a kinda hero among the teenagers in town — 'specially the girls. At first, I wondered why he never paid 'em no mind, but then word got around that he had a girl down in Florida. Now and again, I'd see him starin' at a picture o' Kate he kept taped inside his locker."

"He ever tell you how he did it — bike to Key West, I mean?"

"No, can't say that he did. Matter o' fact, he never talked about it at all, except for one time when he first got back. Bunch of us boys was takin' a water break from a pickup game, and your Uncle Gil went to tellin' us all about the bike ride to Key West: 'Marshall did this and Marshall did that.' Your daddy stayed pretty quiet until Gil started tellin' us he rode that bike all the way down there and back. That's when Marshall spoke up and said no, he only rode the bike down there — like that wasn't impressive enough. He told me he started back but didn't make it far — hopped a train in Miami so he could get back to St. Augustine and your mama. Then he took a

71

bus to Savannah."

"Is there still a train to Key West?"

"No, not anymore. Hurricane blew it away. But it was there when your daddy made his trip. Come to think of it, the railroad was *all* that was there. Marshall woulda had to ride his bike down the railroad track — and part of it ran over a seven-mile bridge out in the middle o' the ocean. He woulda had to make that crossin' between trains. It's a highway now, o' course. Trains don't run to Key West no more. Can you even imagine — ridin' a bike for seven miles right out in the middle o' the ocean? And I hear the water down there's a color like you ain't never seen. I'm gonna have to make that trip one o' these days."

Peyton grinned at the chief. "Me too."

"I got a feelin' you're gonna be thinkin' about makin' that trip more and more as your daddy gets better. You ever decide to up and ride down there, I want you to take this with you." The chief reached into his pocket, took out a piece of yellow notebook paper folded into a square, and handed it to Peyton. "You ever strike out for Key West, I want you to carry that along, okay?"

"Sure." Peyton put the note in his shirt pocket. "Mind tellin' me what it is?"

"Let's call it a letter of introduction to the police and fire chiefs in all those little towns you'll be passin' through. I'm just askin' 'em to look out for you and put you up if they can."

"Seriously? Wow, Chief, thanks. You think they'll do it?"

"I would if a fellow law enforcement officer asked me to. Gotta believe there's folks down there that'll do the right thing when the opportunity presents itself."

"You really think I can do it?"

"I really think you're *gonna* do it. You've just got sense enough to wait for the right time. And don't you worry, Peyton. It's comin'. Things are gonna turn around here in a little bit."

SEVEN

It was late on the day after surgery when Peyton and his mother were called to his father's bedside. They were standing just outside the entrance to a special ward for neurology patients. "You sure you want to go in, son?" his mother asked.

"I want to stay with you," he answered.

It was only as a courtesy to her, a fellow nurse, that the staff was allowing a teenager inside. He had sworn to be as quiet and unobtrusive as humanly possible.

As his mother led the way through big double doors, a nurse came over and squeezed her hand in a silent show of support. They followed the nurse down a corridor to a picture window that looked into a dimly lit hospital room where his father lay.

The nurse pointed to a small table and chair. "That's where I sit when I'm not in the room with him," she whispered. "He's never alone."

Peyton's mother tried and failed to smile, tears raining down her face. She reached out and took Peyton by the hand as the nurse put an arm around her shoulders and led her closer to the window.

His father lay very still. His head was bandaged, and he had a spaghetti bowl of tubes hooked up to him. Doctor Roth was standing over him, making notes on a chart. When the doctor looked up and saw them through the window, he finished his notes and came outside.

"Marshall's doing extremely well, Kate," he said. "To be honest, he came through surgery even better than I'd hoped. Let's step outside so we won't disturb the other patients, and I'll tell you everything."

Peyton's mother reached out and gently touched the picture window as if she were touching his father's face. Then she put her arm around Peyton and said, "Come on, honey. We'll let Daddy rest."

They followed Doctor Roth into a small conference room and sat down. "As we suspected," the doctor began, "Marshall has a skull fracture, and a great deal of fluid had built up against his brain. We also saw evidence of a small bleed."

"A stroke?" Peyton's mother said.

"Yes, but only a small one. We drained all

the fluid away and checked for any other damage. There's still a little swelling, but that will go down on its own. The skull fracture will heal itself over time, but he'll need to be extremely careful for a while. Definitely no horseback riding — or anything else that's strenuous — for at least six months. As for the stroke, we'll have to wait until he's conscious to see where we are. But the good news is, I believe he can make a full recovery. It won't be quick, but he can get there, with your help."

Peyton could tell his mother was still fighting for composure. "How can we ever thank you, Eli?"

Doctor Roth took off his glasses and wiped the lenses with a tissue from a box on the table. "Tell Ida I followed her orders to the letter."

EIGHT

Peyton hung up the phone and sat silently for a couple of minutes in one of many wood-and-glass phone booths lining a wall of the hospital lobby. His call hadn't gone as he had hoped. Lisa wasn't home. Even worse, her mother said she would be spending the summer with family in Miami. And here he sat on a Friday afternoon, wondering what she was doing and who she was with instead of getting ready for a date.

His mother didn't need the burden of his own disappointment, and he wasn't sure he could hide it just yet, so he headed for the hospital cafeteria to collect himself. With a Coke and a piece of pecan pie from the cafeteria line, he took a seat at a table next to a plate-glass window overlooking a hallway filled with portraits of men Peyton didn't recognize — all wearing suits or white coats. Probably the board of directors or something.

"Hey, mister, could Jasper here have a bite o' your pie?"

Peyton turned to see two children standing beside his table. The little girl looked maybe six or seven years old. She was a pretty child, with big blue eyes and long blonde hair in need of a comb. Her cotton dress was frayed around the hem, and there was a button missing from the front. She wore dingy white sneakers with a small hole in the right toe. Clutching her hand was a boy who looked younger — maybe three or four — but had the same blue eyes and blond hair as the girl. He wore jeans, patched and threadbare, and a T-shirt that looked a couple of sizes too big for him.

"Hey there," Peyton said with a smile. The children didn't smile back.

"Jasper ain't had nothin' to eat since yesterd'y, and he's real hungry," the girl said. "Can he please have a bite o' your pie?"

Peyton slid his plate toward the boy. "He can have all of it. How 'bout you? You hungry too?" The girl nodded as the little boy devoured the pie, eating it with his hands. "Y'all wait right here. I'll be back in a second."

Hurrying through the cafeteria line for fear the children would leave, Peyton filled a tray with fried chicken, mashed potatoes

78

and gravy, rolls, chocolate cake, and two Cokes. They were still there, patiently waiting at his table, when he returned. Their eyes opened wide when they saw the food.

"There you go," Peyton said.

"This here's all for us?" the little girl asked.

"All yours."

The children dug in to the food, and Peyton watched in silence until they finally began to slow down.

"What's that there?" The girl pointed to a bottle of Coke. Until then, Peyton hadn't noticed that neither of the children had taken a drink.

"It's a Coke — something good to drink," he explained.

The girl only blinked at him as the boy licked chocolate icing off his fingers.

"Just take a sip," Peyton said. "I think you'll like it."

She cautiously lifted the bottle and took a sip. A smile broke across her face. "It's bubbly and sweet," she said. "I like it."

"Thought you might."

The girl turned to her companion. "Try it."

The little boy stopped licking chocolate off his hands and took a sip of Coke. Immediately, he started giggling, which made

Peyton laugh.

"Wipe your mouth, Jasper," the girl said. The little boy cleaned his face with a napkin.

"Are you two brother and sister?" Peyton asked.

"My name's Bonnie, and this here's my brother Jasper," the girl said. "I'm seven and he's four, but Mama calls us her twins on accounta we look so much alike."

"Pleased to meet y'all. My name's Peyton."

"That's a funny name. You named after somebody?"

"Never thought to ask," Peyton said with a shrug. "What are y'all doin' at the hospital?"

"Weren't no other place for us to go. Daddy took a tumble down at the mill where he works, and they brung him here on accounta this place has a ward for people like us that ain't got no money to pay. Our other brothers and sisters is old enough to look after theyselfs, but Mama says me and Jasper's too little and we gotta stay here with her."

"Your daddy doing okay?"

"Yeah, but the doctor says he's always gonna walk with a limp. And he done lost his job. The mill fires people like Daddy that gets hurt and misses a bunch o' work."

"How'd y'all end up roaming around this place all by yourselves?"

"Just did," Bonnie said, shaking her head. "Mama's busy lookin' after Daddy up in that ward, and Jasper was hungry, so somebody needed to do somethin'. We slipped out when nobody was lookin' and asked directions from ever'body till we found the eatin' place."

"Y'all live around Atlanta?" Peyton asked as Jasper reached for the cake Bonnie hadn't finished and began peeling off the icing with his fingers.

"No, we live up on Pine Mountain. The ambulance brung Daddy here. My Uncle Willis brung the rest of us in his pickup truck. 'Course he had to get back to the farm, so we ain't sure how we gettin' home. Hitchin', I reckon."

"Wouldn't that be mighty hard on your daddy with his bad leg?"

"You got it backwards," Bonnie said with a sigh. "Daddy's the one's hard on us. If hitchin's the only way to get home, I reckon that's what we gonna do. How come you in here?"

"My daddy had an accident too."

"I bet he don't work in no mill."

"No. He took a bad fall at home."

Bonnie had another sip of her Coke and

81

crinkled her nose. "I can't get over them bubbles. I bet rich people like you knows about all kinda stuff that I ain't never heard of."

"I don't really think o' myself as rich."

"That don't mean you ain't."

"Fair enough. Say, Bonnie, is your daddy gonna be looking for work in Georgia when he gets well? Because I can help — I mean, I know grown folks who can."

"You ain't grown?"

"Fifteen."

Bonnie rolled her eyes. "That's grown, silly. Two o' my sisters got married when they was fifteen."

"Okay, then, I guess I'm grown. Y'all going back to Pine Mountain?"

"No. Daddy's got a cousin in Florida what told him there's work down there in this place called Fort Lauderdale. I wonder if there's any cowboys and Indians at the fort."

"Probably not anymore," Peyton said, smiling at her.

"Daddy says there's always sunshine down in Florida and fruit on all the trees — you can just pull off the road and pick you some whenever you get hungry. He says Florida's a land o' plenty and he's fixin' to take his share."

"When are y'all leaving?"

82

"You sure do ask a lotta questions. I don't think I ever had nobody ask me so many questions."

"I'm sorry — am I being nosy?"

"It's okay," Bonnie said, smiling at him. "I think you got a good heart."

"How can you tell?"

"Because when people's got black hearts, it shows in their eyes. There ain't no light in 'em cause there ain't no light inside. You got lots o' light."

"Thanks." Peyton took a paper napkin and wiped a stray crumb from Bonnie's chin. "I reckon I'd have to say the same about you. Tell you what — wait right here just a second."

Peyton went back through the cafeteria line and got a box of fried chicken and rolls. As he paid the cashier, he asked to borrow a pen. Then he grabbed a few paper napkins and returned to Bonnie and Jasper.

"What you writin' on that there napkin?" Bonnie asked, leaning across the table. Jasper was staring out the plate-glass window, pointing his finger at one after another of the portraits on the wall.

"I'm writing my name and my Uncle Jimmy's phone number in Savannah. Well, he's not really my uncle — he's Daddy's law partner — but I call him that, and he'll

83

know I sent you if you call him that too. If Florida doesn't work out and y'all come back to Georgia, Uncle Jimmy can get your daddy a job. What's his name?"

"Fountain Jarvis."

"Alright then. I'll let Uncle Jimmy know to be on the lookout for a call from Fountain Jarvis." Peyton slid the napkin to Bonnie, who carefully folded it and tucked it into her pocket. Then he took another napkin and wrote a note to Bonnie's mother, folded it, and tucked in some money from his wallet. "Put this in your pocket too."

"We ain't s'posed to take no handouts," Bonnie said, frowning and crossing her arms across her chest. "Handouts makes Daddy look bad."

"It's not a handout," Peyton said. "It's a thank-you for keeping me comp'ny. I woulda had to eat all by myself if you and Jasper hadn't come along. Sure is lonesome to eat by yourself."

"It sure is." She stared solemnly at Peyton. "How come you done all this for us?"

He thought about it for a second. "Because everybody oughta help everybody else when they can. You'd help me if I needed it, wouldn't you?"

Bonnie slowly nodded. "I sure would. Things just ain't never been where I could

84

help nobody."

"You're helping your mama right now by takin' care o' Jasper. And you helped Jasper when you asked me to share my pie."

"I guess I did," Bonnie said with a big grin.

"How 'bout I walk y'all back to your mama and you take her this box o' chicken?"

Bonnie and Jasper slid out of their seats as Peyton returned the pen to the cashier.

"Hey, Peyton," Bonnie said as the three of them climbed onto the elevator, "who's gonna show you the way back?"

"Reckon I'll have to find it myself."

"Well, well, well, you're not easy to find — *I* found you."

Kate looked up to see her brother-in-law standing in the doorway of the waiting room. "Congratulations," she said.

"I don't care for your tone."

"I think I can live with that."

A satisfied smile slowly spread across his face, and Kate thought, *If a snake could smile, it would smile exactly like that.*

"Now, now, let's be civil," he said, pulling up a chair and reaching into his jacket pocket to pull out a white envelope. "I've brought you something."

85

She opened the envelope and read its contents, careful to control her reaction.

"It's a subpoena," he said.

"I can see that."

"You're to turn over all of Marshall's medical records at once. The family has a right to prevent you from carrying out any risky surgeries or other procedures."

"The family?"

"I speak for the family."

"Assuming you listen for them too, you can report back that Marshall already had surgery, and it was a success."

Julian's eyes narrowed and his mouth twitched. "When?"

"A few days ago. His doctor expects him to make a full recovery."

"That's a lie. You know as well as I do he'll never be mentally competent again."

"Marshall's competence is irrelevant now. He gave executorship of the estate to his firm, with Jimmy as the trustee. If you want to fight for control, you'll have to take that fight to Jimmy. Marshall's not in it anymore."

Julian smirked at her. "He'd never give up control of all that money."

"Actually, he did — right before he shipped out. He gave me his power of attorney and Jimmy control of the estate."

Julian wasn't smirking anymore. "There's no way he would hand over everything we've built to someone outside the family."

"All the building was done by Marshall and his father, and he cared enough about it to make sure it stayed in capable hands when he returned home from the service and needed a little time to adjust. Fortunately for you, he cares more about family than power."

Julian stood up with such force that he knocked over his chair, which prompted an immediate response from the head nurse.

"What's this!" she said as she pointed at the chair.

"Nurse Parsons, this is Marshall's brother Julian," Kate said.

The nurse gave her a nod as Julian picked up the chair. "I have business with my brother," he said. "Take me to him."

"Absolutely not," the nurse answered.

"What do you mean? I'm his brother, and I have business with him."

"Then you'd better get a hotel room, because he can't have any visitors other than his wife and son for at least three more weeks."

"That's absurd. Get me his surgeon."

"No."

"I've had about enough —"

Julian was mid-sentence when Nurse Parsons stepped just outside the waiting room door and motioned for someone to join them. "Please escort this gentleman out of the hospital," she said as two security guards came into the room.

"You can't force me to leave!" Julian argued, angrily pointing his finger at the nurse.

"Hide behind a bush and watch me," she said.

Before Julian could protest, the guards took him by each arm and all but carried him out of the waiting room. Kate could hear him sputtering all the way to the elevator.

She poured herself a cup of coffee from an urn in the waiting room and returned to the sofa, where she covered her legs with a blanket. Hospitals were always cold. Getting Marshall to this one — and getting him away from his family — was the best thing she could do for him right now. Maybe she should've tried a long time ago.

"How long was Uncle Julian here?" Peyton had returned to the waiting room.

"You saw him?"

"Two guards were hauling him off the elevator as I was getting on downstairs."

Peyton sat next to her on the sofa.

"He was here just long enough to remind me how much I despise him."

"Ooh, feisty!" Peyton said with a grin. "Never heard you say that before."

"I probably shouldn't say it now, but it's true. It's a good thing he's not as smart as he thinks he is, or he might really be dangerous." She reached over and took Peyton by the hand. "How was Lisa?"

He didn't answer.

"Son — did you call her?"

Peyton leaned his head against the wall behind them. "Yes, ma'am. I called her. But she wasn't home. Her mama says she's going away for the summer."

"To where?"

"Miami."

"Does she have family down there?"

"Apparently. Her mama said she'd be spending the summer with her cousins. But Lisa never said anything about that to me. Why didn't she tell me at the hospital in Savannah when she came to visit?"

"Maybe she didn't know. Could've been a last-minute invitation."

"I doubt it. She told me her mama thinks we're getting too serious."

"Well . . . if the trip wasn't Lisa's idea, she's probably missing you as much as you're missing her."

"Think I'm that lucky?"

She put her arms around him and hugged him. "I think you're that special."

"Sure hope you're right." He stretched out on the sofa, resting his head on her lap. "I'm so tired, Mama," he said. "Aren't you?"

She stroked his hair and looked down at him. "I feel like I'm a hundred and ten. But I reckon love gives you strength — either that or it kills you dead as a hammer."

Suddenly, they were laughing together. Peyton was still giggling like a little kid as his mother tried to stop laughing and collect herself. Once she did, she hit him with a question that took him by surprise, something she seemed to do often these days. "Son, before Herschel left, he mentioned to me . . . that you might be planning a trip?"

Peyton stared up at the white ceiling, thinking about his answer. "Yes, ma'am. But he shouldn't have told you just yet. I don't want to worry you."

She ran her fingers through his hair. "Don't be upset with the chief. He just wants to make sure you know what you're getting into — and that you're prepared."

Peyton was looking up at her, trying to read her face. "You don't want me to go, do you?"

"Of course not," she said, "for all kinds of reasons that would be hard to explain. Everybody in the family — everybody in Savannah, for that matter — they talk about your dad's ride like it was some great adventure with no hardship whatsoever. But he went through a lot on that trip, Peyton. Most of it, he never shared with anybody but me. There's more to that bike ride than pedaling, son. You'll likely stir up some things about your daddy — and things about yourself — that could be painful out there all alone. Promise me you'll think about it long and hard before you decide?"

"Yes, ma'am."

Nurse Parsons came in. "He's awake," she said, motioning for them to follow her.

Peyton quickly sat up. He and his mother looked at each other in disbelief. He put his arm around her as they left the safety of the waiting room and followed the nurse through the double doors and back to his father's room, where they stopped at the picture window. A nurse was beside the hospital bed, holding up three fingers. Peyton watched, reading his father's lips as his mouth moved: *three.* The nurse gave him a big smile and a nod, then checked his IV before leaving the room.

"He's doing just beautifully," she said on

her way to the nurses' station.

"I don't have to tell you that this part can be harder than the waiting," Nurse Parsons said.

"Feel like I might dissolve into a puddle," his mother answered.

Nurse Parsons laid a hand on his mother's shoulder. "A nurse can always do what needs to be done. And you're still a nurse." She held the door open as they slowly walked into the room.

At first, Peyton's father didn't turn toward them. No doubt he thought they were just hospital staff, and he kept his gaze on the only window to the outside.

Peyton took a step back, just in case his parents needed a moment. His mother lightly touched his cheek with her hand, then stepped closer to the bed, reached down, and took his father's hand.

"Marshall?" she said.

He turned to look at her, blankly at first, but then he squinted slightly until a smile — ever so slight — curled on his lips, and he said simply, "Hoppy." It was his pet name for her, bestowed when he'd watched her decorate for their first Christmas together on Tybee and said she was hopping all over the house like a rabbit. Peyton hadn't heard him use it since he came home from the war.

Now she was crying, kissing his hand over and over, as if she were trying with all her might to get control of herself.

"Is . . . is Peyton . . . alright?" he asked her.

She reached out for Peyton and he came to his father's bedside.

"Hey, Daddy," he said.

His father looked confused, staring at Peyton as if he were a stranger. "I . . . don't . . . understand. Our Peyton's . . . four years old."

"Don't worry — he's doing a little time traveling as he comes around," said Doctor Roth, who had just come into the room. Standing on the opposite side of the bed from Kate and Peyton, he leaned over Marshall and asked, "So you say Peyton is only four?"

Marshall nodded.

"And where do you live?" Doctor Roth asked.

"Chatham Avenue . . . on . . . Tybee."

Kate's mouth flew open. "He's right. When Peyton was four, that's where we lived. We were so happy there. But then he got pulled into all the Cabot . . ."

"What year is it, Marshall?" Doctor Roth asked.

"It's 19 . . . 1936?"

"You're getting there," Doctor Roth said, giving Peyton's father an encouraging pat on the shoulder. "You're getting there."

NINE

Outside, rain was drizzling down from a dreary gray sky, and everything Peyton could see through the window looked just as bleak as the hospital room where he sat next to his father's bed, absently turning the pages of a magazine he wasn't actually reading. Over two weeks had gone by since the surgery. His father was out of the neurology ward and into a regular room now, doing physical therapy twice a day. But he still didn't recognize Peyton, and that blank stare was unnerving. It made him feel like he didn't exist anymore — that he wouldn't exist ever again, until his father said he did.

He stood up to stretch his legs and walked over to the window. This room was only three floors up, so he could see the people moving down below. Right away, he spotted them — Bonnie and Jasper standing on the sidewalk next to a man in a wheelchair be-

95

ing pushed by a nurse. A tall, thin woman stood next to the wheelchair. Soon a rattle-trap of a pickup pulled up to the curb. Bonnie and Jasper climbed into the back. The tall woman handed them a quilt from inside the truck, and the children held it over their heads — their only shelter from the rain. Then the woman climbed into the cab, followed by the man in the wheelchair, who stood up with the aid of a walking cane and limped to the passenger door. Uncle Willis must've come for them after all.

Peyton wondered how often the Jarvis children went hungry and how well they were cared for. He hoped their mother would use the money he had given them to buy food for Bonnie and Jasper.

"Peyton?"

He was startled to hear his own name and turned to see his father looking around the room. "Yes, sir?"

"Son . . . where are we?" His father looked confused about everything except one. For the first time since the accident, Peyton saw recognition in his eyes. He went to his father's bedside.

"We're at Emory University Hospital in Atlanta," Peyton explained.

"But . . . why? And . . . where's your . . . your mother?"

96

"She's here, Daddy. She's been right here the whole time. Goes to physical therapy with you twice a day. You don't remember?"

His father frowned and shook his head slowly.

"She just went down to the cafeteria while you were sleeping," Peyton went on. "You had an accident. On Bootlegger. You hit your head, and Doctor Roth did surgery a couple of weeks ago."

"Doctor Roth . . . Eli?"

"Yes, sir."

His father slowly raised his hand to touch the bandages on his head. Peyton gently pulled it back. "Prob'ly shouldn't touch that, Daddy. Not just yet."

"Shouldn't . . . shouldn't you be . . . in school?"

"No, sir, Mama got 'em to let me finish up at home since the school year's almost up. Don't go sending me back to Loony Luetrell till fall."

That brought a weak smile to his father's face. Lucy Luetrell had been terrorizing Savannah students since the 1920s and didn't show any signs of slowing down. "Wouldn't . . . wish . . . ole Loony on you."

"Daddy, the doctor always asks you what year it is when he talks to you. Do you know?"

"It's 19 . . . 47 . . . 1947 — is that right?"

"Yes, sir. It's May the second, 1947." Peyton ventured another question. "Do you know how old I am, Daddy?"

His father frowned again. "Not old enough . . . to drive . . . yet. You turned fifteen . . . last June."

Peyton felt it immediately, like one of the chemical reactions he had watched in the lab at school, first a slow bubbling — a minor disturbance — and then a roiling and churning —

He ran to his father's bathroom just in time for the heaving. Never in his life had he felt so violently ill. When at last it stopped, he flushed the toilet, washed his hands, gargled with cold water, and then splashed some on his face. He took a few deep breaths before returning to his dad, who was looking at him the way he used to before he explained whatever it was that needed explaining.

"Don't know what that was about," Peyton said with a shrug. "Must be the hospital food."

He knew his dad was watching his every move, the way he used to study players on the ballfield. "It's not really . . . the food . . . is it, Peyton?"

He looked into his father's eyes, which

saw clearly now, the way they used to. He had never lied to his dad, not just out of respect but because it would've been pointless. His father could always see through any falsehood — probably what made him such a good attorney.

"This has all been . . . just a little . . . too much . . . hasn't it, son?"

Peyton only nodded at his father, who had been functioning for some time now — carrying on conversations with the hospital staff and answering all their questions — without even being fully conscious of where he was or what he was doing. And now he had come to, fully and completely.

Just then his mother returned from the cafeteria. She took one look at them and knew. "Marshall?" she said, hurrying to his bedside.

His eyes were misty as he asked her, "How could I . . . forget . . . my own son?"

Taking his hand in hers and wrapping her other arm around Peyton, she said, "You never forgot him, Marshall. You just forgot that he grew up. We can forgive that, can't we?"

She looked at Peyton, who said, "Nothing to forgive."

"Peyton, honey, you need something to eat," his mother said, pulling money out of her wallet. "And I want you to get out of this hospital and get some fresh air now that the rain is finally letting up. Why don't you walk down to that little diner we tried by the university? Take a stroll around campus and get away from all this hospital gray."

"Okay." He grinned down at his dad, who looked so sad right now. "Want me to bring you something you're not supposed to have?"

That brought a smile. "Slip me a hot dog," his father said, "like the ones . . . we used to get . . . at the ballpark."

"You bet."

"You better *not,*" his mother said with a grin. "Take your time, honey. Spend this afternoon on yourself. We'll be here when you get back."

After Peyton left, Kate volunteered to help her husband with his afternoon exercise. She kept one hand at his back and pushed an IV cart with the other as Marshall held on to a walker and slowly inched down the corridor. He had always moved with such athletic grace. It was heartbreaking to see him struggle to put one foot in front of the other.

"Not much farther, honey," she said, "and you're doing great."

100

He sighed and looked down at her. "Liar."

"I'm giving you my professional opinion as a registered nurse, board certified by the great state of Georgia," she countered.

They made their way back to his room, where she got him settled into bed. He wanted his head raised so they could talk for a little while.

"I'm not supposed to sit on your bed, but I'm feeling a little reckless," she said as she lowered the railing and sat down facing him.

He took her hand and kissed it. "You're worn out, aren't you, Hop?"

"As a matter of fact, yes. But like Aunt Gert used to say, it's a good tired." She gently ran her fingertips across his brow, just below the white bandage that covered most of his head. "Can you tell me what you remember, Marshall?"

"It's so strange," he said. "It's like . . . all of my memories were written down in a book . . . and somebody tore out a bunch of the pages here and there."

"So it hops and skips?"

"Yes. I remember everything . . . up until Peyton was about four years old. Then I remember that awful ceremony . . . when Daddy signed over the estate. I could . . . feel the knives at my back."

"Julian was holding most of them."

101

He winked at her. "I always knew you were keeping an eye on him."

"What do you remember next?"

He stared at the ceiling, his brow slightly furrowed. "I remember shipping out. Standing on the train platform."

"Then what?"

He took his time answering. "The library. Telling you we had to split up . . . for Peyton . . . all my drinking after I came home from the war . . ." A cloud fell over his face. "Are we divorced, Hoppy?"

"No. I can't believe we even talked about it."

"It was bad, though . . . my drinking, I mean . . . I remember it was bad."

"Nothing's bad enough to separate us. We were crazy to even think about it."

He was smiling again, but she could tell he was getting tired. "I don't remember anything about the accident. Nothing after I saddled Bootlegger . . . until today when I woke up . . . and Peyton was sitting next to me."

She laid her hand against his face. "You've remembered enough for one day. Probably too much. You need to rest."

"Wait — how is Peyton? How is he handling this?"

"Oh, Marshall, you'd be so proud of him.

He has not left my side — and never complains. He's gotten real sweet on that pretty Lisa Wallace at school. But he's spending all his time in hospitals with us, and then he found out Lisa's gone to Miami to be with family. His summer's a real bust, I'm afraid."

"We could . . . maybe fix that."

"How?"

He smiled up at her. "Aunt Gert."

"What?"

He closed his eyes and nodded, still smiling. "Let's send him to her."

She bent down and kissed him. "I'll take care of it."

TEN

The sun was barely piercing the early morning darkness when Peyton said goodbye to his parents and made his way to the Atlanta Greyhound terminal. Now he was looking out the window at the Georgia countryside as the bus rolled through fields of red clay and small towns with little more than a water tower to claim their place on the map. He hadn't realized how much he needed some time away from fluorescent lights and waiting rooms and the colorless monotony of a hospital. His parents were sending him to visit a great-aunt he couldn't remember. Peyton hadn't seen Aunt Gert since he was a toddler and could only hope she wasn't a holy terror.

"Next stop, Milledgeville!" the driver called.

His heart beat faster at the name of this place. The sprawling grounds of the Milledgeville asylum were rumored to hold many graves — final resting places of all the unfortunate souls who were sent there never to return. Milledgeville was made all the more horrifying by its mystery. Most people had no idea what actually happened within its walls, and what they imagined was a collage of every bad dream they'd ever had and every horror movie they'd ever seen.

The driver turned off the main highway and headed into town. "Baldwin County Courthouse!" he called out. A giggling young couple, both dressed in their Sunday best, got off the bus. She was wearing a corsage. Likely a courthouse wedding. Peyton wondered — was that how his parents had looked on their way to the courthouse all those years ago?

"Georgia Military College!" the driver announced. Three boys in uniform, who all looked just a little older than Peyton, stepped off.

As the driver took the bus down a long street and then turned onto Broad, he called out, "Central State Hospital!"

Peyton's blood ran cold at the sight of it — an imposing brick building with white columns out front. There wasn't a living soul in sight. Were they all confined behind those high walls, with bars on their windows and locks on their doors? Or was it just like an ordinary hospital? You'd have to go in there to find out, and nobody wanted to do that.

He watched as a man about his father's age stepped aboard, taking a seat across the aisle. The man was tall, pale, and gaunt. For a fleeting moment, Peyton wondered whether he might be a Milledgeville escapee, but then, he doubted anyone fleeing this place would calmly step onto a public bus.

As the driver slowly pulled away, the man across the aisle sat perfectly still and straight, his hands folded on his lap. Peyton relaxed into his seat, leaned his head against the window, and fell asleep to the hum of the bus.

He slept through stops in little towns like Lumber City, Satilla, and Hazelhurst as the bus rambled through Georgia on its way to the coast. Somewhere along the way, he dreamed. Peyton saw himself kneeling on the grass at his grandparents' house, petting a beautiful Irish setter. The dog licked his cheek and then took a spirited run around the lawn. When it returned to Peyton, it playfully jumped on him with its front paws. Peyton was laughing, scratching the dog behind its ears, when suddenly it turned into a stallion and reared up, pawing at him.

It knocked him flat on his back. He covered his face with his arms but couldn't get up — couldn't run or scream. Finally, he heard the stallion gallop away. With great relief, he slowly lowered his trembling arms, only to see that he was strapped to a hospital gurney encircled by nurses who had no faces.

When he woke up, the man from Milledgeville was standing over him, shaking his shoulders.

"Y-you . . . o-k-kay?" The man looked concerned.

"Yes, sir. I'm sorry I bothered you. Just — had a crazy dream." Immediately, he regretted his choice of words — saying "crazy" to a man who had just gotten out of the asylum. "I didn't mean —"

"No b-bother," the man said. "I j-just . . . didn't . . . want to leave you . . . in there." He returned to his seat, stretching out his legs and looking out the window.

Peyton took a look himself and could see that they were still in Georgia. No palm trees in sight. "Excuse me, sir," he said. "Could you tell me where we are?"

"J-just north of . . . of . . . Waycross. You get off . . . in . . . Waycross?"

"No, sir, St. Augustine."

"I g-get . . . off in . . . J-Jacksonville."

107

"Thank you for your help," Peyton said with a smile.

The man tried to smile back but looked as if he hadn't done it in so long that he had forgotten how. "I have . . . a . . . b-boy your . . . age," he volunteered.

"I'll bet he's excited to see you."

The man looked confused, as if he couldn't fathom anyone being excited to see him, then turned to stare out the window again. Maybe he was just tired of talking.

Peyton opened the lunch sack his mother had packed for him and pulled out a piece of fried chicken from the hospital cafeteria. She was doing her best, he knew, to make things at least a little bit normal for him. "Sir, would you care for a piece o' chicken?" he offered. The man shook his head and turned back toward the window.

Peyton hadn't been down to Florida since he was little. His mother spent occasional long weekends with her Aunt Gert in St. Augustine, mostly in the fall and winter. She would give Peyton the option of coming with her or staying with his father, and he always took option two. During football season, his dad would take off work on Friday and they would drive to Athens, check into the best hotel in town, and go to the Georgia game on Saturday. Then they'd sleep late on Sunday and leisurely make their way home — sometimes stopping in Augusta to play a round of golf. Right now that seemed like somebody else's life.

After putting his lunch away, Peyton leaned back in his seat, closed his eyes, and thought of Lisa. Soon he was dozing again, dreaming of her. She was dressed in the emerald-green ball gown she had worn to the spring formal. It was sleeveless with a V-neck, which showed off a double strand of pearls close to her neck — nothing flashy. He had given her a single pink rose. In his dream, they were back at the dance, and he proudly escorted her onto the ballroom floor. But then a crowd of dancers swirled between them. He kept getting glimpses of Lisa in a sea of satin and silk, but he could never touch her. Every time he got close, the crowd of dancers pushed her away.

The bus driver jolted him out of his misery. "Next stop, Jacksonville station!"

As the Milledgeville man stepped into the aisle, Peyton stood up and offered his hand. "Nice traveling with you, sir," he said. Looking more apprehensive than excited to be home, the man shook hands with Peyton before making his way up the aisle and out the door.

Just before the bus pulled away, Peyton saw him step onto the platform, where a woman threw her arms around his neck. The man just stood there with his hands at his sides. The couple got smaller and smaller as the bus moved on, leaving Jacksonville and everybody in it behind. Peyton could only wonder about the boy his age waiting at home for his father to return from Milledgeville, oblivious to what was happening on the bus platform as his parents, now strangers, struggled for reunion.

ELEVEN

Peyton knew his father had biked down A1A, the coast road that hugged the Atlantic. Unfortunately, the bus route followed US 1, a faster interior highway with less enticing views — mostly Florida scrub pine, a wilderness area or two, and a gas station here and there. He had boarded in Atlanta before daylight. Since then the bus had made stop after stop at a strand of little towns until the driver at last called out, "St. Augustine station!"

Peyton and several other passengers stepped off the bus and waited at the luggage bay while the driver located their suitcases. Before Peyton could decide whether to wait on the platform or follow the others inside, he felt a hand on his shoulder and turned to see a man who looked like he had just stepped off a boat. His overalls were neatly tucked into tall black rubber boots, and the sleeves of his blue cotton shirt were rolled up to his elbows, revealing tattoos up both arms — an anchor on one and the lower half of a short-skirted woman in cowboy boots on the other. Her torso disappeared under that rolled-up sleeve. The man's skin was deeply tanned and craggy, but he was clean-shaven. Silver hair peeked out from beneath his fishing cap, which shaded eyes the color of aquamarines.

"You the boy come to see Gert?"

"Yes, sir," Peyton answered.

"Ha!" the man exclaimed with a big smile. "Ain't nobody called me 'sir' in a long time. Name's Leeward Finnegan, but ever'body just calls me Finn."

"*The* Finn?" Peyton couldn't believe he was shaking hands with the fisherman who had helped his parents get married.

"Well, I don't know about that. Are you tellin' me I'm famous in some quarters?"

"You could say that," Peyton answered. "Nice to meet you, Finn. My name's Peyton Cabot."

Finn looked him up and down as they shook hands. "Now there's a puzzle."

"Sir?"

"What I mean is, when I look past your big-house manners and really eye you good, I'd swear you got a little bit o' Gert in you

— way down in there somewheres."

"From the way Mama talks about her, I'll take that as a compliment."

"Oh, it's intended as one. Speakin' o' Gert, I reckon we'd best shove off. She'll be lookin' for us."

Finn loaded Peyton's suitcase into a battered Ford pickup truck that smelled of fish, and they both climbed in. All Peyton got to ask was, "How do you know Aunt Gert?" That set off a monologue that lasted from the bus depot, through downtown St. Augustine and all along the harbor, past the bridge with the lion statues, and onto a side street where an oyster-shell driveway led to a Florida bungalow surrounded by palm trees and banana plants. The house backed up to a river.

By the time they arrived, Peyton had learned that Finn was born and raised in Alabama, was a breech baby who nearly killed his mother, married three times and divorced three times, served in the Navy during World War I, liked rum, drank too much of it (the cause of an unfortunate tattoo on his right shoulder), once landed a two-hundred-pound blue marlin without dropping his cigarette, wondered how magicians make people disappear in those trick boxes, had never voted, was a Pisces ("ain't that a coincidence"), and hated coconut.

Also, he had met Aunt Gert at a VFW dance. She was serving the punch that he was attempting to spike. She told him rum was made for dive bars and fishing boats, and if he knew what was good for him, he'd take his flask and hightail it to one or the other. They had been friends ever since. Early on, he said, he tried to kiss her — but only once. She whacked him with her sun hat and told him there would be none of that nonsense, so he'd just as well get it out of his head.

"Yessiree, Gert says the loss of her late husband, rest his soul, is still so fresh, she'd feel like she was cheatin' on him if she took a shine to another man," Finn said, shaking his head.

"When did he die?" Peyton asked.

"Summer of '21." Finn shifted the truck into neutral and let it idle. "We'll leave your suitcase on her porch. She ain't here at the moment. The two o' you'll likely walk home from the dock, and I doubt you'd want to be a-totin' your grip all the way."

Finn unloaded the suitcase and then drove them to a marina just across the harbor. He led Peyton down a long dock, past fishing boats and trawlers, to a stunner of a wooden runabout named *Madame Queen.*

114

"Well, here we are," Finn said. "Peyton, my friend, meet the *Madame*. She usually stays at Gert's dock on the San Sebastian, but we figured it'd be easier for you here, it bein' your first acquaintance and all. Been a pleasure meetin' you. I reckon I'll see you around Gert's." He shook Peyton's hand and started to walk away.

"Hey, Finn, wait a minute!" Peyton called after him. "Where is she?"

"See that bend in the river down yonder?"

"Yes, sir."

"Go just past it, and you'll see Cap'n Davy's Seafood on your right. There's a dock there where you can tie up, and Gert'll come down to meet you. Likely waitin' there for you right now."

"You mean she wants me to drive this boat down there?"

"It's a mighty long way to swim."

"But I've never driven a boat like this."

"Ever drive a car?"

"Yes, sir."

"Same thing — or just about. Untie 'er, push the starter, and ease back on the throttle — see it right yonder? *Madame Queen*'ll get you where you're goin'. Been a pleasure!"

With that, Finn was gone, leaving Peyton to scan the dock. All the boats were bob-

115

bing in their slips, but there wasn't a person in sight. Already he was wondering if Aunt Gert had lost her marbles.

He turned his attention to the *Madame Queen.* This old boat, with its fine mahogany decking and deep-green leather seats, had to be worth a fortune. If he wrecked it, Aunt Gert might send him home in a body bag, but she hadn't left him with many options.

Peyton climbed in and untied the boat. Sliding into the captain's seat, he ran his hand along the dashboard, which was beautiful with all the silver gauges and detailing set against rich wood. He started the boat. The rumble of her engine was deep and smooth, like distant thunder. Easing back on the throttle as gently as he could, he felt the boat stop drifting and take command of the water. Soon they were gliding across the harbor, slowly at first but then faster as Peyton found his confidence. Driving the boat felt as natural as breathing.

Stealing glances at downtown St. Augustine from his watery vantage point, he was mindful to keep an eye out for any approaching boats. The scene was unbelievable. A late-afternoon Florida sun was hanging low in the sky, casting its golden glow on the Matanzas River. To his left he could see the historic district with its ancient Spanish architecture just a street crossing from the harbor. To his right were barrier islands that kept the Atlantic at bay. And what a way to see it — the wind in his face, a beautiful boat in his hands, and the water sparkling below, parting for them as they sped up the river. What was it his mother had said about her time alone on the beach here? *That first taste of freedom.*

The bend was just ahead. Peyton throttled down in case Aunt Gert should catch him speeding and judge him too reckless to ever captain the *Madame Queen* again. As Finn had promised, Cap'n Davy's was just ahead on the right. A woman was standing on the dock outside the restaurant. She waved her arms to flag him down.

"You must be Peyton!" she said as he climbed out of the boat.

"Yes, ma'am," he answered. "Are you Aunt Gert?"

"The legend in the flesh," she said as she hugged him. Aunt Gert was tall, with warm brown eyes and thick silver-white hair, which was cropped short. From what his mother had said about her, she had to be in her seventies, but her tanned face wasn't wrinkled at all. She was wearing red-and-white-checked pedal pushers, a short-sleeved white cotton blouse, a wide-brimmed straw hat with a red scarf tied around it, and leather sandals. Beside her was a picnic basket and a small cooler.

"I hear you've been havin' a rough time of it," she said to Peyton. "No sense hem-hawin' around it."

"Yes, ma'am. Mama and Daddy too."

Aunt Gert nodded. "Well, we can't do anything about them right now — they'll have to fend for themselves — but we might be able to salvage your summer. I thought we might start by havin' an early supper alfresco. Do your Aunt Gert a favor and grab that cooler. I'll get the picnic basket and we'll shove off."

Peyton and his aunt climbed into the boat with their gear. He was heading toward the passenger seat when Aunt Gert corrected him. "None o' that lazybones passenger business for you," she said. "I intend to relax and enjoy the view."

"You mean you want me to drive the boat?"

"Somebody's got to."

"Aunt Gert, I think I love you."

She threw her head back and laughed as she took off her straw hat and tucked it under her seat. Then she put on a pair of white-rimmed cat-eye sunglasses with rhinestones at the corners. "Now," she said, "let me show you how to back the boat out of the slip. And remember — from now on, you need to back it *in*. Otherwise the locals will think you're a landlubber, and we can't have that, now can we?"

"Wouldn't want to bring shame on my family," Peyton said with a solemn bow of his head.

"Ha! You're a mess, Peyton. I can tell already. We're gonna get along fine!"

Following her instructions, Peyton backed the boat out of the slip and they were off. He kept to a slow speed until Aunt Gert commanded, "For heaven's sake, son, open 'er up!"

Peyton pulled back on the throttle, and soon the *Madame Queen* was slicing through sun-kissed water, her bow rocking up and down as they streaked toward a pass up ahead, their hair blown back, their shirts flapping against them in the wind.

"That's more like it!" Aunt Gert said loudly enough to be heard over the boat. "Go through that pass and bear to your right. I'm gonna show you somethin' special."

To Peyton's amazement, the pass opened not into a bigger harbor but into the open sea — the Atlantic Ocean, whose powerful waves appeared to be napping at the moment. Aunt Gert pointed the way as they bypassed a beach that was speckled with sunbathers, motoring on to what looked like coastal wilderness. It was a beautiful beach, with pristine sand and wild dunes covered with sea oats. Aunt Gert guided him to an inlet and an old dock, applauding when he successfully backed the *Madame Queen* against it and tied up.

"What is this place, Aunt Gert?" Peyton helped her out of the boat and handed her the straw hat, then set her picnic basket and cooler on the dock.

"I'll tell you when we get there." Aunt Gert put her hat on and took up the picnic basket.

"Get where?"

"The special spot. Now grab that cooler and come on."

She led him over a high dune to the prettiest stretch of sand he had ever seen. Still she didn't stop. Only when they were just a few yards from the water and she had set the picnic basket on the sand did she dramatically spread her arms wide and proclaim, "*This* is Anastasia Island!"

"And we're here because . . . ?"

"Oh, Peyton, keep up!" she said, putting her hands on her hips. "Anastasia Island, near the lighthouse . . . ?"

He gasped as he figured it out. "This is where Mama and Daddy met!"

"Well, hallelujah, the boy's got some brain cells!" She opened her picnic basket and took out a small blanket. "Here, help me spread this."

They spread the blanket on the beach and sat down together. Aunt Gert had brought fried grouper sandwiches, hush puppies, French fries, and fudge brownies from the restaurant, along with a cooler full of Cokes. Peyton hadn't realized how hungry he was till they started eating.

"This is the best sandwich I ever had," he said, reminding himself to use a napkin now and then.

Aunt Gert took a sip of her Coke. "You're just hungry. But Davy does fry a mean grouper. It's the homemade mayonnaise that really sets off the fish. Look out there. See that?"

Peyton followed her finger to a spit of sand out in the ocean. He remembered his mother's story about collecting shells on a sandbar in St. Augustine. "That can't be the same sandbar — is it?" he asked Aunt Gert.

"No, but that's about where it was. At high tide, it'll disappear."

The two of them ate their supper and sipped their Cokes as the sky slowly washed out to a pale robin's-egg blue with faint streaks of pink and coral. After all his time in hospitals, Peyton couldn't believe how great it felt to be on the ocean. What had it been like for his parents?

"Could you tell me what they were like — back then, I mean?" he asked, turning to his aunt.

"Well, let's see. Your mother was always kind and sweet. But make no mistake, Katie's got plenty o' moxie — and a sharp, curious mind. Marshall wasn't much different back then than he is now. Your daddy was the strong, silent type even as a boy. Over the years, he became a much more lovin' person. Katie did that for him. If it wasn't for her, he mighta ended up a cold fish like the rest o' the Cabots."

"You don't care much for Daddy's people?"

"Can't stand 'em. Never could. George was pretty decent, as rich old planters go — may he rest in peace — but his lovely wife Celia's got a cold streak a mile long. Marshall's sisters never had to turn their hand, so they pretty much treat anybody outside the family like the hired help. And as for the brothers, the youngest one's kinda giddy-headed, and that Julian thinks he could ride a mule around the moon backwards, but the truth is, he ain't even got sense enough to saddle it up."

"How do you know 'em all, Aunt Gert?"

She sighed as she took off her sandals and slid her feet into the sand. "When Katie first married, she used to call down here and beg me to come up and give her a little moral support durin' that dreadful spring picnic, which I did, till you came along. I figured a baby'd give her an excuse to get away from 'em, and I just really couldn't take it anymore. It's like those people were all born with somethin' missin'. All of 'em 'cept your daddy."

"Why do you think he's different?" Peyton had unearthed a couple of seashells next to their blanket and was absently turning them over and over with his fingers.

"I 'magine he takes after his mama."

"But I thought you didn't like Grandmother Cabot."

Aunt Gert stared out at the ocean now turning soft shades of blue and gray in the early sunset. "She's not your daddy's mama."

Peyton dropped the seashells and wheeled around to face his aunt. *"Ma'am?"*

Aunt Gert took off her sunglasses and

looked straight at him. "It's not my place to tell you, but I've never been too concerned about stayin' in my place, and I believe in bein' truthful. Plus I think you'd be a lot less confused about everything if you knew what's what. So here we go. Your granddaddy didn't start off in Savannah. He started off in Louisiana. That's where he was born and raised and where he met his first wife, Julia Guidry. They were both very young when they married, and he was farmin' cotton. Julia was a dark-haired beauty and a very lovin' girl who was crazy about your granddaddy. The two of 'em didn't have much, but they were happy together."

Aunt Gert dug her feet deeper into the sand. "Poor Julia had two miscarriages before she gave birth to your daddy, and then she died in a car accident when Marshall was two. A happy life just wasn't meant to be for that girl, bless her heart. Didn't you ever wonder why there's five years between your daddy and your Uncle Julian, but all the other Cabots are just a year or so apart? Or do you not know about the birds and the bees?"

"Aunt Gert!" Peyton covered his face with his hands, embarrassed to death to be discussing the facts of life with his aunt.

Aunt Gert, in turn, laughed till she couldn't catch her breath. "I'm sorry, honey! I didn't mean to shock you. But you *do* know, don't you?"

"Yes, ma'am! But I swear if we don't get offa this subject, I'm gonna go drown myself in the ocean."

"Oh, don't kill yourself, honey. You'll miss the sunset. Anyway —"

"Now, wait a minute before you move on. You said Granddaddy Cabot was married before, but nobody's ever talked about another wife. There's no pictures of her. Daddy calls Grandmother Cabot 'Mama.' I don't get it."

"Alright. I'll tell it to you the way Doxie explained it to me."

"What's Granddaddy's cook got to do with all this?"

"Doxie's worked for him since he was a young man. And she knows plenty. Those uppity Cabots just don't have sense enough to ask her. I used to slip off to the servants' quarters to escape the family during those heinous picnics, and Doxie and me would have us a glass o' bourbon and a talk."

"You said Granddaddy Cabot started out in Louisiana — was he farming, just like in Georgia?"

"Not quite. Back then, he was on a little-bitty family farm. But rumors got to goin' around about oil bein' buried under that prairie land, so he decided to drill. And he struck oil."

"*Oil?* But he's never been in the oil business."

"That's not true. After strugglin' in the beginnin' and losin' two children, your granddaddy and Julia finally had a child — Marshall — and they had struck oil and knew they'd never want for anything ever again. They were so happy, Doxie told me, and started buildin' a fine new house. Julia went to New Orleans to pick out furniture for it. But all she settled on that day was a set o' fine white wicker porch furniture. I reckon you've been sittin' on it all your life."

"On Granddaddy's porch?" Peyton was stunned.

"That's right. Julia placed the order on Magazine Street not an hour before her driver went speedin' around a corner, goin' the wrong way on a one-way, and had a head-on collision with a bread truck. Threw 'em both outta the car and killed 'em, right there in the French Quarter. Left your granddaddy with a two-year-old child and an unfinished mansion and a whole bunch o' money that didn't mean a thing in the world to him without his wife."

Peyton ran a finger over the sand, absently drawing the outline of a palm tree. "How did Granddaddy end up in Savannah?"

"About a year after Julia died, Celia came down from Virginia to visit some cousins in New Orleans. They also knew your granddaddy and invited him to a house dance. He was lonely. She was pretty. And she can be charmin' when she wants to — when she wants something. That was that. The two of 'em agreed on a fresh start, and he had just read about a ton o' good farm land comin' available around Savannah. So they moved to Georgia, bought the land and a fine house, opened some cotton mills, and there you go. Everybody thinks cotton made him rich, but the truth is, he built those mills just to help all the poor communities around Savannah. His money came — and still comes — from those oil wells in Louisiana."

"Does everybody know about his first wife and about Daddy — everybody in the family, I mean?"

"For a long time, nobody knew except Celia and Doxie. That's how your granddaddy wanted it."

"But why?"

"Because he didn't want your daddy to be treated any differently than his other children — by the family or the community.

127

'Course, the irony o' that was that George himself always treated Marshall a whole lot *better* than his other kids."

Something moved in Peyton's peripheral vision. He looked out over the water and saw two dolphins smoothly arch above the surface, then dip back under, the pair of them in perfect sync. Peyton watched them rise and fall together twice more before they disappeared in the ocean.

"Why didn't Grandmother Cabot tell?" he wanted to know.

Aunt Gert swatted at a dragonfly strafing their blanket like a dive-bomber. "Celia didn't really want anybody to know she was wife number two, so she was happy to raise Marshall as her own child. Accordin' to Doxie, Celia's so distant with her own kids, nobody'd ever suspect Marshall was any different. And as time went on, George figured out that fillin' Celia's purse was easier than meltin' her heart, so he promised her that as long as she never told a livin' soul about Marshall, he'd make sure she had everything she wanted — but if she *did* tell, he'd cut her off. That settled it for Celia. Doxie, on the other hand, decides for herself who needs to know what, and she up and decided one day that I needed to know."

"What about Daddy? Does he know?"

Aunt Gert nodded. "They managed to keep it from him for a long time, but then when he was about fifteen years old, he was rummagin' through his daddy's closet, lookin' for a fishin' hat to carry with him to summer camp, and he uncovered a shoebox full o' pictures, includin' one o' George and Julia with a baby in her arms — a baby with eyes just like hers. Later on, Marshall told me he just had a feelin' about that picture — like it was answerin' a question he'd always had but never asked."

"If he was fifteen — that's the year he rode his bike to Key West."

Aunt Gert slapped her knee, pretending surprise. "You know, you're right!" She laughed. "Came right through St. Augustine and met a pretty girl on a sandbar."

They gazed out at the sea together, listening to the water sigh as it rolled onto the shore. Peyton finally broke the silence.

"Does Mama know?" he asked.

"She does. And no, I do not agree that keepin' it from you was wise. And yes, you've got a right to be aggravated as all get-out with both of 'em. Years after they married, your mama told me that they talked about it that very first time they met on the beach. He told her he had just found out his mama wasn't his mama, and he was

129

takin' this bike ride to try and sort things out. By the time you came along, Marshall was so tangled up in the family business that Katie knew y'all would likely be livin' amongst the Cabots. She just didn't want you to know anything that might make you feel like an outsider — which is how they always made her feel. I told her she oughta shout 'glory hallelujah' that you and your daddy are cut from a different cloth than the rest of 'em. If you ask me, that's somethin' to celebrate, not somethin' to hide."

"Why do you think Daddy let 'em do it — tangle him up in the family business, I mean?"

"Because he respected his father, and he knew the rest of 'em didn't have sense enough to preserve what your granddaddy worked hard to build. He also knew the rest o' the Cabots didn't give a flyin' rip about all the poor families who depended on your granddaddy's cotton mills for work."

They listened to the water lap against the sand before Peyton said, "I'm glad you told me. I really am. It feels weird to know I'm not one o' the Cabots, but —"

"Now hold it right there. That's not what I said. You are one hundred percent one o' the Cabots. You just don't have any o' that crazy Kelly blood from Celia's side o' the family, which is all to the good, if you want my opinion. And somewhere in Louisiana, you've got some family you never even met. Prob'ly Cajun. You feel particularly musical all of a sudden?"

Peyton laughed and kicked off his sneakers so he could shove his feet into the cool sand like Aunt Gert. "No, ma'am."

"Well, that's too bad. Maybe we'll find out you can cook. Louisiana people can cook like nobody's business."

"I'm not much use in the kitchen, but I'm pretty good with a grill or a pit. Does that count?"

"I'm not sure. We'll have to make that determination somehow. I expect you'll need skill with crustaceans to be considered legit." Aunt Gert pointed out to sea. "Well, would you look at that!"

What an amazing sight it was. As they'd talked past sunset and let the sky darken, the moon had risen over the water and was casting its glow over the placid sea. After daybreak the Atlantic would awaken with a thunderous roil of salty spray, but for now, it was like dark glass reflecting moonbeams back into the sky.

"You just missed the full. You know what the Indians called the full moon in May?" she asked.

"No, ma'am."

"The Flower Moon — because it appeared the same time all the flowers were in bloom."

In the shimmering silver light, Peyton could picture a single pink rose next to an emerald-green ball gown. And he could only imagine what it would feel like to sit here on the cool sand some balmy evening and hold a beautiful girl with auburn hair and skin like ice cream.

TWELVE

Sometime during the night, it had begun to rain, a steady downpour pelting the tin roof of Aunt Gert's bungalow and lightly misting Peyton's face. The temperature dropped a few more degrees, sending a brisk, cool breeze across the screened porch. Peyton could hear distant thunder and the sigh of palm trees rustling in the wind. Frogs were singing on the river. He could listen to those sounds forever.

When he and Aunt Gert had come home from the marina, she told him to put his things in her spare bedroom but offered him the option of her sleeping porch if he preferred it. The deep screened porch ran all the way across the back of the bungalow, which was painted purple with white trim. In the center of the porch were two twin beds made of cypress, just like the floors throughout the house. They were positioned end to end, running parallel to the back wall of the house to allow as much shelter from the elements as possible, but the thunderstorm that was rolling in now blew the rain farther into the porch than usual.

Peyton didn't care. Pulling the covers higher to keep the mist off his face, he listened to the sounds of rain and thunder as the wind rustled the palms and thought of another rainy night back in March. He had invited Lisa to a St. Patrick's Day concert in Forsyth Park. They caught the bus downtown and danced in front of the bandstand. Peyton knew he should insist that they leave when the early evening breeze gusted and he could see lightning off in the distance. But he couldn't bring himself to end a night out with Lisa. By the time thunder rumbled and they felt the first drops of rain, it was far too late to make it to the bus stop. Peyton wrapped his arm around her as they sprinted to the front porch of a grand old mansion fronting the park. It was mostly dark inside, and Peyton could only hope the owners didn't come home before the rain stopped.

He and Lisa were both drenched. As he frantically apologized and brushed her dripping red hair out of her eyes, she looked up at him, somber at first, but then her lips curled into a smile and she laughed.

Still fussing with her hair but now laughing with her, Peyton said, "I'm sorry, Lisa. I wanted to show you such a good time —"

"Who says you didn't?" she said. She was beginning to shiver in the cool March air, so he took off his jacket and wrapped it around her. As he did, she slipped her arms around his waist . . .

Peyton drifted off to sleep, listening to a Florida rain splash against the river and the palms, dreaming of a girl with long auburn hair dripping wet and a beautiful face that felt so soft in his hands.

Hours later, when his dreams of Lisa were fading, he awoke to a strange tapping sound. Or was it whapping? He wasn't awake enough to tell, but this much was sure — it was unrelenting. *Whap . . . whap . . . whap-whap-whap-whap. Whap . . . whap . . . whap-whap-whap-whap.* When he couldn't stand it anymore, he sat up in bed to find the biggest, most gorgeous cat he had ever seen pawing at the screen door. For a couple of seconds, it would sit and bang the door with one paw. Then it would stand on its back paws and whap with its front ones, like a boxer going after a punching bag. Standing on its hind legs, the cat had to be three feet tall, with a thick coat of silver, charcoal, and white all blended together. Its long tail was as fluffy as a feather duster, and it had pointed ears like a bobcat.

Peyton got out of bed and opened the door. The cat paid him no mind, calmly proceeding across the porch, through a cat door, and into the house. Peyton went inside, stopping by his room to get dressed before he followed the smell of bacon into Aunt Gert's kitchen.

"Mornin', sleepyhead," she said as she used her spatula to splash bacon grease on the eggs she was frying.

"Mornin'," Peyton said.

"I guess I don't need to ask if you slept good." Aunt Gert cracked the oven door and took a quick peek inside.

"No, ma'am. That thunderstorm put me out like a light."

"Well, good. You needed some sleep. I expect you've met Pirate?" She nodded toward the cat having his breakfast from a bowl underneath the table.

"Yes, ma'am." Peyton eyed the cat's bowl. "You fry your cat bacon?"

Aunt Gert pulled a small pan of biscuits out of the oven and set it on a pot holder on the kitchen table. "Not every meal," she said as she brought a butter dish and a pitcher of orange juice out of the icebox.

"He only likes it for breakfast. By the way, I don't b'lieve in dirtyin' up a bunch o' dishes if I don't have to, so help yourself to biscuits and butter and pour you some juice while I finish up the rest of it."

"Thank you," Peyton said, buttering a hot, fluffy biscuit from the pan and filling the glass next to his plate. "Man, Aunt Gert," he said after he drained his glass. "I never had orange juice like that."

She slid two eggs out of her skillet and onto his plate. "Squeezed it myself. Got an orange tree right out back. There's plenty more where that came from, so drink up."

He refilled his glass as she loaded him up with bacon. Right before she sat down, she put a steaming cup of coffee next to each of their plates.

"Uh . . . I don't usually drink coffee, Aunt Gert," he said.

"That's because you've never had mine." She offered thanks and told him to dig in. "Well, go on," she said, pointing to the coffee. "Give it a try. You don't have to drink it if you don't like it."

Peyton had to admit, Aunt Gert's coffee didn't look like any he had ever seen. She served it in a glass cup. It was dark brown — almost black — with a frothy cream on top. He took a cautious sip.

She raised an eyebrow as she watched him. "Well?"

He broke into a smile. "That's good stuff."

"I know! Drink up. It'll put hair on your chest."

Peyton set down his fork and slapped his forehead with his hand. "Oh, man! I forgot to call her last night."

"Your mama?"

"Yes, ma'am."

"I called her."

Peyton sighed with relief. "Thank you."

"You're welcome. But if you ever forget to call *me* when you're supposed to, I'll tan your hide."

"Yes, ma'am," he said as he dove back into his breakfast. "Did she say how Daddy's doin'?"

" 'Bout the same, but he's not goin' backwards, which is the important thing."

Peyton buttered another biscuit and asked, "Is there anything you need me to help you with today?"

"Your mama told you to say that, didn't she?"

"Yes, ma'am."

"Ha! I appreciate your honesty, son. There's plenty I'll need help with, but not now. Today, I want you to ramble. Go walk around town and get your bearin's. Take the *Madame* out and explore the harbor and the beach. Introduce yourself to St. Augustine."

"Don't you want to come?"

"I do not. You're on your own. Here, take this money and stick it in your pocket for lunch in town so you don't have to eat here and be tied to a clock."

"Mama gave me money."

"I know. But you're my guest, so you eat on me. And that's that."

"Thank you." Peyton stuffed the bills into his hip pocket. "I still can't believe you let me drive the *Madame*."

"Everything worth knowin' has to be learned by doin'. And if there's anything worth knowin' in Florida, it's how to swim, how to fish, and how to handle a boat. You can swim, can't you?"

"Yes, ma'am. I'm a pretty decent swimmer."

"And fish? You know how to cast a line?"

"Yes, ma'am."

"Alright then. Master the *Madame* and you're good to go. There's fishin' gear in the toolshed if you want to take a rod and reel out with you. Just stay on the shoreline for now. I'll get Finn to show you the ropes in the deep sea, but you're not ready yet, so stay where you can see the beaches."

"Yes, ma'am. What are you gonna do while I'm gone?"

"None o' your business."

St. Augustine was a marvel. Peyton had grown up around historic architecture in Savannah, but this place was seriously old. Everywhere, you could see remnants of Spanish buildings — and others still intact and in use. Tourists swarmed the centuries-old fort on the waterfront. He picked up a map in a candy shop, where he couldn't resist the aroma of chocolate, and wandered cobblestone streets while he nibbled on fudge.

Eventually, he made his way to the Ponce de Leon, a grand hotel built by the man who had dreamed up the railroad to Key West. It looked like something out of *The Arabian Nights.*

Following the map to the corner of Valencia and Sevilla, Peyton took a short walk to Memorial Presbyterian Church, which the railroad man built in memory of his daughter. According to the notes on the map, she died having a baby at sea. Such a sad story for such a beautiful church, but no sadder than that of his own grandmother — his real grandmother, whom he would never meet. Was his dad anything like her? Was Peyton?

He continued his downtown ramble, and again his nose led him into temptation. He followed the aroma of fresh bread into an old Spanish bakery, where he didn't recognize anything on the menu and had to ask for help. A pretty dark-haired girl behind the counter recommended the empanadas. She selected three for him, which he took in a paper bag, and then he made his way back to the dock and the *Madame Queen.*

Every time he started her up, the sound of her engine made his heart beat a little faster. While he knew it was only his imagination, he liked to think that the old boat was as ready to run as a Thoroughbred coming out of the gate. Soon Peyton and the *Madame* were gliding across shimmering water lit by a late morning sun.

He loved speed and always had — a trait his mother found worrisome. He wasn't reckless by nature, nor was he drawn to danger. It was the movement — the way the world looked different when it was zooming past and the feel of the wind in his face. That's what he loved. Cars and bikes and horses were okay, but speed was always better when it came from a source beyond the ordinary — like the *Madame Queen* or a roller coaster.

The best speed Peyton had ever experienced was in an airplane. His father had bought them both a ride in an open cockpit biplane when he was about ten years old, and he'd been hooked. From then on, he got an airplane ride for his birthday every year. Even now, he couldn't name a better present than the thrill of climbing in, hearing the engine start, and watching the propeller begin to spin, knowing that any minute now, the plane would shoot down the runway and climb into the air.

For now, the waters of St. Augustine would have to be his runway. Since he was still new to them, Peyton retraced the route Aunt Gert had shown him — up the Matanzas River, through the pass, into the Atlantic, and down the coast to Anastasia Island, where he did a fair enough job of backing the *Madame* next to the dock and tying her up.

He decided to leave his food and cooler in the boat and take a walk on the beach. Kicking off his shoes, he rolled up his khakis and walked along the water's edge, letting the waves give him a splash now and then. Every time planes from one of Florida's many bases flew over, he stopped and looked up, shading his eyes to see if he could spot any Mustangs.

Airplanes aside, whenever he let his thoughts drift in their chosen direction, they always carried him straight to Lisa. Though he had given up hope of spending any time at all with her this summer, she was always there, in the back of his mind. He could close his eyes and picture her in the gown she had worn to the spring formal.

Before the dance, Peyton had asked his father to quiz him on all the rules he was supposed to remember: *The young man stands here, the young lady stands there . . .* Halfway through, his dad stopped mid-sentence and said, "Son, they're teaching you everything except what you really need to know." And then he said something Peyton never forgot: "What most boys your age don't understand about girls is that they're not trophies to show off or points to score. They're people. You want to win over a special girl like Lisa? Listen to her. Pay attention to her — what she says and what she does and what she thinks and what she feels. And don't so much as glance at another girl when you're out with her. She deserves better than that. All girls do. Treat Lisa like she's the only person in the room, and I promise you, she won't care whether you bow or curtsy."

The night of the dance, Peyton was allowed one of his grandparents' drivers so he wouldn't have to be taxied to and from a big date by his dad. When the car arrived, his father winked at him and said, "You remember what we talked about. I told Floyd to take you anywhere you like, as long as you behave yourself and get Lisa home on time."

Peyton had never been more grateful for his father's advice than he was that night. Lisa looked so beautiful in the emerald dress that brought out the little green flecks in her blue eyes. And she was like a feather in his arms, so easy to dance with, be it a waltz or a fox-trot. When they were twirling to the music, Lisa seemed happy and content, but between dances, when they were surrounded by all the other couples who had grown up together but were still strangers to her, a lonely cloud would cross her pretty face.

"Would you like to get some air?" Peyton asked her. That brought back her smile. He asked Floyd to drive them to Forsyth Square, where tourists were always posing by the grand old fountain, taking pictures to send home. Peyton laid his jacket on a park bench to protect her dress, and the two of them sat in the moonlight and talked

— really talked — until it was time to take her home. For the first time, Peyton realized what it was like to be with a girl he couldn't bear to part from.

But they *were* parted — had, in fact, been forced apart. And while Peyton knew there were far worse places to be stuck than St. Augustine, stuck was stuck. All he could do now was mentally calculate the distance between here and Miami and get himself ready to take a ride.

THIRTEEN

Peyton had spent the whole day roaming St. Augustine and had secured the *Madame* back at Aunt Gert's dock on the river. He was halfway to the house when he saw it — a gorgeous bike, parked by the back steps.

It looked like a brand-new Western Flyer. Peyton hadn't seen a new bike since before the war. All the factories were too busy helping with the military effort to make them. But this one — it had never touched the road. It was red with cream trim and a brown leather saddle. It had a built-in headlight, a sleek tank, and a rack behind the seat that flowed perfectly with the frame.

"Meet your new companion." Aunt Gert had been watching him from the screened porch and now came outside to join him.

"Aunt Gert, where did this come from?"

"The store."

"Yes, ma'am, I realize that, but what I mean is . . ."

"Peyton, sometimes you're just way too polite for your own good. The bike is yours. I bought it for you and meant to have it here when you got into town, but Western Auto was a little slow gettin' my order delivered. And don't you even think about tellin' me I shouldn't have. I quit worryin' about shoulds and shouldn'ts before you were ever thought of. It's just a bike. Ride it. Enjoy it. Enough said."

"Thank you, Aunt Gert. I've never seen anything like it. What's this?" He pointed to the saddlebag draped over the rack, secured with a buckled strap.

"That's filled with things you'll need to take with you when you make up your mind to do the thing we both know you're eventually gonna do. A couple o' spare inner tubes, money, a water flask — the essentials. I got you a small bike pump too. And one other thing. Finn has an old Navy buddy who slipped him a bottle o' stuff that's s'posed to keep the bugs off. It's just for the military, so don't let anybody know you've got it. Best to be prepared. Now come on inside, supper's ready. You can take your bike out to see the sights when we're done — after you call your mama, that is."

As they went to supper together, Peyton grinned at his aunt and said, "Have I told you how lovely you look, Aunt Gert?"

"Oh, hush."

FOURTEEN

Peyton had taken to riding his bike early each morning, pedaling all over the city and even venturing out on A1A, just to see what it would feel like. Now that he was acclimated to St. Augustine, Aunt Gert decided it was time for him to "embrace the Atlantic" and summoned Finn to teach him how to handle a boat in the ocean. They wouldn't be taking the *Madame,* which wasn't built for rough weather should any arise, but instead headed out in Finn's fishing boat. He had walked Peyton through all the controls and then put him in the captain's seat. Right now they were cruising through the familiar pass from the Matanzas to the Atlantic, but instead of steering toward Anastasia, Peyton would be going straight out to sea.

This morning, a stiff wind was blowing, making the water a little choppy. "Now the thing you want to remember," Finn was saying, "is you gotta work *with* the sea. You're an intruder as far as she's concerned, so you gotta mind your manners and pay attention when she talks."

Peyton grinned at him. "Sounds like a girl."

"Ha! Just like. Only I always found the Atlantic more forgivin' than any o' my women, even in stormy weather. Okay, now look right there. The swells are gettin' bigger an' you gotta learn how to ride 'em. Keep the bow fairly low and aim for a slight angle as you go into it. You don't want to hit a wave straight on 'cause that's kinda like hittin' a buildin' head-on. On the other hand, you don't want to get sideways in the trough, which can roll you. An' remember — the rougher the seas, the slower you go. If it gets really bad, you might have to heave to and ride 'er out, but I don't think we'll be runnin' into anything that bad today."

Peyton followed Finn's instructions and soon was riding the occasional big swell without any problem. When they were just beyond sight of the shore, Finn told him to shut off the engine and showed him how to drop the boat's anchor. Then he pulled a beer and a Coke from an ice chest on deck and handed the Coke to Peyton.

"I'd say you made a fine showin' for your

first lesson," he said. "You keep this up an' you could take on ferryin' jobs pretty soon."

"What's that, Finn?"

"Your rich leisure fishermen that live on the mainland will pay you to ferry their boats down to the Keys or wherever they mean to go for their trophies. Pays good."

"Don't you need some kind o' license?"

"You do," Finn said with a smile, "but that can be handled."

"How long have you had your boat, Finn?"

"Longer'n any woman — 'cept Gert, o' course, but that's different. Gert's my best friend — best one I ever had, man or woman."

"I don't think I've ever had a girl for a friend — not a really close one like you and Aunt Gert."

Finn took a long drink from the bottle in his hand. "Well, it ain't easy at first. Both o' you gotta agree there ain't gonna be any wooin' to it. An' you both gotta mean it, else one o' you's gonna be jealous all the time. But if you both arrive at the same conclusion, why, a woman can make a fine friend. They listen different from men. Plus they smell better and they can cook!"

"I knew you had an angle," Peyton said with a grin.

"Ha! Always do." Finn took a quick sip of

his beer. "How much you know about readin' the weather?"

Peyton ran the icy Coke bottle across his forehead to cool off. "Well . . . I know a ring around the moon means rain's comin'. So do mares' tails and a buttermilk sky. I know the barometric pressure drops before a tornado or a hurricane. And if it thunders in February, it'll frost in April."

Finn nodded. "Red sky at mornin'?"

"Sailor, take warnin'," Peyton answered.

"You know about the full moons — their names an' their meanin's?"

"Just the Flower Moon that Aunt Gert told me about."

"Well, there's an even better one comin' up in June — the Strawberry Moon. That's how the Indians knew it was time to gather the wild berries. An old sailor I used to run with always said it's good luck for the Strawberry Moon to rise on your journey."

"I'll try to remember that."

"Peyton, the thing about livin' on the sea — or by it — is you gotta pay attention to what's happenin' around you. Did the air all of a sudden get cool? Did the wind all of a sudden get still? Is the water white-cappin'? It all matters, my friend — 'specially for anybody thinkin' o' puttin' hisself at the mercy o' the elements, if you know what I mean."

Peyton looked up at the sky and back at Finn. "Would you teach me everything you know, Finn — or at least everything I need to know?"

Finn slapped him on the back. "I'll getcha ready, alright. Today was just the beginnin'."

FIFTEEN

"Peyton, honey, you need to put down that paintbrush and go clean up!" Aunt Gert stepped into the backyard, a dish towel tossed over her shoulder, and examined the final touches he was putting on the trim of her house. "That looks shipshape!" she said as she handed him a glass of water.

He took a long drink and wiped his sweaty face with the tail of his T-shirt. "The ole girl cleans up might nice, don't she?"

Aunt Gert playfully slapped at him with the dish towel. "I have *got* to stop lettin' you spend so much time with Finn on that boat o' his. You're startin' to talk just like him."

Peyton laughed and downed some more water. He had spent the past week going out with Finn in the mornings and repainting the bungalow in the afternoons. It was now "a sunnier shade of purple" that Aunt Gert had chosen, trimmed in white.

"I'm not kiddin' about cleanin' up," she was saying. "You get in that tub, and then I want you to put on your dress pants and a nice shirt."

He frowned at her. "What for?"

"Because Finn twisted his ankle when he got home from the marina and can't dance with me at the VFW tonight. You've got to stand in for him."

"*Me?* On the dance floor? Oh, no. You're not makin' me dance in front o' the whole bloomin' town."

"Don't be a twit about it. They didn't have a dance last week because the roof leaked and soaked the floor, and now Finn's outta commission. I am *not* missing two Saturday night dances in a row just because the men in my life won't cooperate. Get moving."

Peyton offered one last desperate protest. "Aunt Gert, I know the waltz and the fox-trot, which is all they taught us in Miss Helen's cotillion class. I doubt they do much waltzin' at the VFW."

"Now, listen here." Aunt Gert put her hands on her hips. "You're lookin' at the best dancer in this whole burg, and I can teach anybody. I've never missed a Saturday night at the VFW, and I don't intend to start now. Get a move on!"

Peyton groaned and rolled his eyes as he

cleaned his brushes. He knew it was futile to argue with her. He'd just have to accept the fact that he was about to make a total fool of himself in front of the whole town. His mother would call it a "stars-in-your-crown opportunity."

By the time he cleaned up, Aunt Gert had fixed them a supper of jerk chicken with rice and plantains — she said she learned to cook Jamaican food when her late husband was stationed in the Keys and sometimes had a yen for it. Leaving the dishes to soak in the sink, she took off her apron, ready for the dance.

Peyton eyed his aunt's ensemble. She was wearing a bright blue dress with a full skirt, low heels, and a string of pearls. "You look real nice, Aunt Gert," he said with a grin. "Sure you're not, you know, goin' fishin'?"

"Oh, hush!" she said as they made their way outside. "I'll tell you like I told Finn — I got no time for that nonsense. But I do like to let the other old ladies in town know that it's *my* choice to be on my own. I've still got it goin' on. Now, move it!"

Peyton had never set foot in a VFW hall before. The one in St. Augustine was about a ten-minute walk from Aunt Gert's house, and the parking lot was working alive when they got there, with cars, trucks, scooters, and people coming and going in and out of the hall. "In the Mood" was wafting through a screen door at the main entrance.

"They've got a real band?" Peyton asked.

"The real deal," Aunt Gert answered. "They're called Alejandro y Los Nuevos."

"What does *los nuevos* mean?"

"It means 'the new ones.' Alejandro had an orchestra that played with him before the war, but he couldn't get 'em back together after so many of 'em got drafted. I guess he didn't have time to think of a name for his new players, so . . . *los nuevos.*"

Peyton laughed as they found Finn, who had come to the VFW on homemade crutches and was saving them a seat. He had already bought a glass of wine for Aunt Gert and a Coke for Peyton.

"Finn," Peyton said, "what've you done to me? She's gonna make me dance in front o' all these people because o' you. Sure you're not fakin' it?"

Finn slapped the table and laughed. "That'd be just like me, now wouldn't it? But no, my bum ankle is the genuine arti-cle." He caught Aunt Gert talking to one of the other ladies at the table and slipped a flask out of his hip pocket. "Take a swig," he said. "It'll give you courage."

Peyton held up his hand in protest. " 'Preciate it, Finn, but that stuff didn't do my daddy any favors."

"Fair enough." Finn took a quick sip and slipped the flask into his pocket before Aunt Gert turned to Peyton and said, "Shall we?"

"Yes, ma'am." Peyton stood and offered Aunt Gert his arm. He was hoping for a slow song, which would be easier to dance to, but just as they made it onto the floor, Alejandro got a request for "Sing, Sing, Sing." Peyton and Aunt Gert were about to jitterbug.

The dance floor was packed, which actually took some of the pressure off. Nobody was staring at him. They were too busy trying not to step on each other. And Aunt Gert hadn't exaggerated — she really was a great dancer. The steps were coming surprisingly easy to Peyton, who had never jitterbugged in his life. He fumbled a few turns, but Aunt Gert righted him, and before long he was having as much fun as she was.

They danced four straight numbers before Aunt Gert said she needed to rest a bit.

"What's that?" Peyton asked her as they returned to their table, where a line of seven or eight women had formed — all of them old enough to be his grandmother.

"I smell a rat, and his name is Finn," his

aunt said.

"Ah, Gert!" Finn stood up with his crutches. "Welcome back!"

"What's all this?" Gert pointed to the women in line beside the table.

"Why, they all want a dance with the boy!" he said with a big grin.

"No," Aunt Gert said to Finn. "And no to you too," she said to the line of women.

"But we already paid!" one of them objected.

"Paid?" Aunt Gert glared at Finn. "You *sold* my nephew to these women?"

"Of course not!" Finn appeared to be conjuring his best innocent face, but it wasn't playing well with Aunt Gert. "I'm shocked you would suggest such a thing! I only . . . rented him, so to speak."

"Give them their money back, Finn."

"But, Gert, some of 'em were willin' to pay top dollar and —"

"Finn, I swear, if you don't give them back their money right this second, I'm gonna beat you to death with your own crutch."

Now the women had surrounded Finn, who was looking desperate.

"Hold on, ladies," Peyton intervened. "Finn's gonna give you your money back, but I'd be honored to dance with you. When Aunt Gert's ready to spin again, though, you'll have to find another partner. That shouldn't be too hard, because, if you don't mind my sayin', you all look *very* pretty tonight."

Now the women were smiling again.

"There now, see?" Finn said. "Everything worked out, and we're all friends again."

"Not till you pay them," Aunt Gert said. "Cough it up."

Finn reluctantly repaid the women. A plump one at the front of the line pinched Peyton on the cheek and said, "I'm first!"

"Yes, ma'am." He escorted her to the dance floor, the line of women following, as the band played "A String of Pearls" and wondered how on earth he'd gotten from spring dances with Lisa to a VFW with women just this side of the nursing home. But then again, he knew the answer. He got here on a bus by way of a hospital by way of a bottle by way of a war.

SIXTEEN

Peyton and Aunt Gert sang and danced all the way from the VFW hall to her purple bungalow. The breeze was picking up, and they could hear occasional thunder off in the distance. The Atlantic coast could swing from hot and sunny to brisk and stormy in a heartbeat.

They were walking up the driveway, laughing about one of Peyton's missteps, when Aunt Gert suddenly fell silent and stood very still. She was frowning and staring at her house.

"What's the matter, Aunt Gert?" Peyton asked.

She pointed at the dark house. "I never leave the lights off when I'm out at night."

Now Peyton was looking at the bungalow barely visible in the darkness, surrounded as it was by palms and tropical shrubs. "When we left for the VFW, I asked if I should turn off the living room light, and

161

you said no," he reminded her. "I'm sure I left it on."

"I'm sure you did too. Let's get to the toolshed."

Inside the dark shed, Aunt Gert felt her way to a spade, which she handed to Peyton, and a shovel, which she held on to herself. "Follow me," she whispered to Peyton, "and keep quiet."

They tiptoed onto the front porch, stopped, and listened. Nothing. Aunt Gert felt for the key she kept on top of the door frame, but it wasn't there. She looked at Peyton, then slowly turned the doorknob. They both heard it click open. Just inside the living room, Aunt Gert reached for a lamp and switched it on. No one was there. The living room was empty, the lamplight a comfort.

Slowly, they made their way through the small dining room and into the kitchen — both of them empty. Down a short hallway to the bedrooms, they found Aunt Gert's door open, but Peyton's was closed. They crept to it and listened. There was no movement inside, but they both heard a sound, faint but audible. Aunt Gert motioned for Peyton to get his spade ready, then she quickly opened the door to his room and turned on the light. They both gasped and dropped their weapons in a clanging heap on the floor.

"Katie?" Aunt Gert exclaimed, rushing to the bedside, where Peyton's mother lay on top of the covers.

She was fully dressed — including her shoes — and looked like she had been crying forever. Peyton could see her mouth moving but couldn't make out what she was trying to say. Finally, he heard it: "He's gone."

Aunt Gert sat down on the bedside as she took a handkerchief out of the nightstand and handed it to Peyton's mother. "I know you're heartbroken, honey, but remember your child is listenin', and he's gonna remember every word you say."

Peyton's mother looked up and saw him standing in the doorway. He hadn't moved since he saw her there.

She held her arms out to him, and Aunt Gert slid down to make a place for him next to his mother.

"Daddy?" he said.

"Yes, sweetheart."

"How? I mean — I thought — I thought he was getting better."

She reached up and laid her hand against his face, answering in fits and starts as she struggled to breathe. "He *was* getting bet-

163

ter . . . every day. Just this morning . . . we walked out onto the hospital terrace . . . to enjoy a little sunshine . . . We talked about you . . . what we might all do together before school starts back . . . We talked about . . . moving back to Tybee."

Peyton's mother lowered her hand from his face and was no longer looking at him but staring instead at some distant point in space, as if she were replaying a memory to make sure she hadn't imagined it. "While we were talking . . . he leaned his head back against his rocking chair . . . and closed his eyes. I watched him smile into the sun . . . and I remember thinking . . . that there's never been . . . a more beautiful face in the world . . . But then . . . I saw him turn his head just slightly . . . and he frowned . . . like he was trying . . . very hard to hear what somebody was saying to him. And then . . . then he relaxed and smiled again. He was nodding, as if he were . . . answering a voice I couldn't hear . . . He raised his hand to his head, looked at me, and said . . . 'I have to go now, Hoppy.' And then . . . then his head slumped over . . . as if he had dozed off . . . He looked so peaceful . . . like every care he'd ever had . . . suddenly got lifted away . . . all at one time. But he never woke up."

Now she was looking at Peyton again. She sat up in bed and said, "Oh, sweetheart, I'm so sorry." He put his arms around her and held her tight. "I just didn't see another stroke coming, honey. I wish I could've prepared you — but I wasn't ready myself."

Aunt Gert, who had been sitting silently while his mother poured out her grief, finally spoke — but in a quiet voice, not her usual commanding one. "Peyton, let's give your mother this room till we figure out what's what. Everybody's way too tired for any o' that business right now. You like the porch best anyway, so that's all settled. Katie, are you hungry at all?"

Peyton's mother grimaced, as if the thought of food might do her in right now.

"Alright, then. Tomorrow morning we can figure out what happens next, but for right now I think sleep is best. Or at least rest. I doubt any of us will sleep much tonight."

Peyton kissed his mother on the cheek, then walked silently out to the sleeping porch, feeling stunned, numb, and a little nauseated. He lay down on one of the beds, thankful for the cool pillowcase against his face and the breeze coming off the river. It wasn't possible, was it — that his dad could be gone from this earth? Even when he was drinking, at least he was here. Peyton could

165

look at him in the flesh and still see the father he had been before the war. But never again.

"You didn't take time to pack, if I know you," Aunt Gert said. "Not to worry. I still maintain your special drawer."

Kate mustered a weak smile. "When Marshall would take Peyton to UGA for the weekend and I'd come down here, you used to take me shopping every time, but you wouldn't let me wear my new clothes till the next trip."

"My way of keepin' you comin' back," Aunt Gert said, handing her a nightgown from the drawer and sitting down next to her on the bed. They put their arms around each other.

"What on earth am I going to do?" Kate asked.

"Nothing tonight, Katie. Nothing tonight."

SEVENTEEN

On a cloudless May morning, Peyton steered the *Madame Queen* through the pass and into the Atlantic, bound for Anastasia Island. The morning sun threw its golden light onto blue-gray water as a warm breeze blew out of the south. It might rain tonight.

The boat glided past the public beach, where cars and pickups parked right on the sand and a jubilant crowd of locals and vacationing families spread their blankets and set up their volleyball nets. But there was nothing jubilant about the *Madame Queen* this morning. Her passengers were in mourning.

Peyton steered the boat to a now familiar inlet on Anastasia and secured it at the dock. Then he helped the women climb up. His mother was carrying an urn, delivered by messenger. The three of them left their shoes on the dock and made their way over the dunes. Gentle waves washed the shore at low tide.

Peyton's mother took a deep breath, closed her eyes, and turned her face to the sun. A salty breeze blew her blonde hair back, and the warm rays brought roses to her cheeks. Whether she was lifting a silent prayer or saying her final goodbyes, Peyton could only guess. At last, she seemed ready. Cradling the urn like a child, she led Peyton and Aunt Gert through the shallow water and onto a sandbar, which glistened with every salty splash from the Atlantic.

She looked at Peyton. "Do you need to say anything, son?"

He shook his head silently.

She lifted the lid and handed it to Peyton. Then she slowly tilted the urn until the Atlantic winds scattered the ashes across the water. When the urn was empty, she looked down at it, kissed it, and tossed it into the sea. She looked at Peyton, who did the same thing with the lid. Then she took his hand and Aunt Gert's and led them back through the tide.

Staring down at the water and watching it swirl around their legs, Peyton had a flash of memory. He was about four years old, standing between his parents, holding their hands as he jumped the waves on Tybee. It was a happy time, long forgotten until grief called it back.

Standing atop a tall dune, the sea oats dancing in the wind, Peyton, his mother, and Aunt Gert turned to look at the urn, which did not fill immediately with water but instead floated out to sea. Without thinking or even realizing, really, what he was doing, Peyton lifted his hand in a solemn wave goodbye.

Somehow, he believed, his father would make it to another shore.

EIGHTEEN

The night rain was soothing. Peyton's sleeping porch had become his refuge, a place where he could lie in the still, dark hours and try to tame the torrent raging in his head. If only his mind could be as quiet as St. Augustine late at night, where the silencing of cars and trucks and people amplified the peaceful rustle of palms, the nocturnal call of frogs and owls, and the lap of river water against the dock.

He heard the flap of Aunt Gert's cat door and felt Pirate jump into bed with him. The cat had paid him no mind until the night after they scattered his father's ashes. Since then, at the very moment when Peyton thought his head would surely explode with thoughts, Pirate would come onto the porch, climb into bed, and stretch out next to him. Soon after, Peyton would relax and drift off to sleep. In the morning, the cat would be gone.

What was roiling in his head tonight was a phone call. Peyton had called Lisa's house to see if her parents might give him the number of her relatives in Miami so he could tell her what had happened. Instead of her mother or father, Lisa's sister, Judy, answered the phone — and she had plenty to say. Her mother was convinced Peyton and Lisa were too serious and instructed the Miami relatives not to relay any messages from him. But Judy could get through. And she promised to give Lisa Aunt Gert's phone number. Now all Peyton could do was wait.

What first brought hope soon turned to misery as Peyton hung around the bungalow, studying his father's old Florida map and listening for the telephone. It was driving him crazy. It was driving Aunt Gert and his mother crazy. He was pacing back and forth on the sleeping porch when he heard Pirate come through the cat door. The cat did something he had never done before. He rubbed his head against Peyton's leg. Then he pawed at the screen door that led outside. Peyton opened it and watched as Pirate walked calmly down the steps and rubbed his head against the front wheel of the bike. Then he leisurely made his way toward the river and his favorite napping tree. Peyton had never been superstitious, but, man — that was spooky.

"I know what you're thinking."

He turned to see his mother standing behind him on the porch. She smiled at him, but it wasn't her old, happy smile. It was her trying-my-level-best smile.

"Oh yeah?" He grinned at her. "You think you know everything."

She put her arms around him and gave him a hug. "I can't believe I have to look up at you now. Where was I when you grew up?"

"Oh, you were there — tellin' me I needed a haircut."

"Let's go get some air, son."

They walked down to the dock and climbed into the *Madame Queen*. Peyton's mother navigated as he drove them to a shady inlet off the San Sebastian River and shut off the engine. For a time, they sat listening to the water lap against the boat. Now and then a fish would jump, disturbing the river and the quiet.

Finally, she said, "Things will be very different for us now, Peyton."

Unsure of what to say, he just listened.

"With your father and your grandfather gone, I doubt Jimmy will be able to hold on to the purse strings anymore. He secured as much as he could for you and me, but we'll have to be careful how we spend it. Julian will likely sue for executorship, and he'll probably win. Then he'll do everything he can to deprive us of whatever he can. It won't take him long to lose everything your granddaddy built, after all those years of your daddy being such a good steward. We'd be in for nothing but misery if we stayed tied to them, son. I think we have to make it on our own."

Peyton reached over the side of the boat and ran his hand over the water, watching the ripples fan out from the *Madame*. "Where would we go?"

"I think you deserve a say in that. No matter what happens, I want you to finish high school with your friends. I was thinking I might get a job at the hospital in Savannah and rent a little place on Tybee. How do you feel about that?"

Peyton thought it over. Now that he saw the Cabots as his mother always had — how they had both depended on and resented his father — he didn't think he could go back to them, ever. All that money hadn't made any of them happy, and Peyton couldn't see the point in fighting over it.

"I think that's a good idea," he answered.

"And I can get a job too."

"We're not that desperate — yet," his mother said, trying to muster a smile.

"No, I want to," he said. "I want to know I can help. It's important."

His mother nodded. "You're right. It is. You need to know you can stand on your own two feet. I'm so proud of you, Peyton. So was your father. I hope you know that."

River sounds filled the silence between them. Finally, he said, "I know about Daddy's mother — his real mother, I mean. Aunt Gert told me."

His mother rubbed her forehead with her hand, the same way she did whenever Uncle Julian was around. "Oh dear. I'm not sure this was the right time to tell you."

"No, I'm glad she told me. A lot of things make sense now that I know."

"Don't blame your father for keeping you in the dark. That was my doing."

"I know," he said with a grin. "Aunt Gert told on you."

His mother sighed with what Peyton knew was exhaustion of every kind and put her head in her hands.

"Chin up, Katydid!" he said.

His mother had to laugh. "How you turned out the way you did, with all you've had to deal with, I'll never know."

174

"Mama, you make it sound like I was raised by a pack o' wolves."

"No, just Cabots."

They both had a much-needed laugh before she grew serious again. "I really am sorry I kept such a big secret from you, Peyton. It's just . . . well, I saw what it did to your father when he first found out. I'm not sure he ever got over it. I just didn't want that for you. So I lied. Not exactly the example I wanted to set for you."

"I know you were tryin' to do the right thing. But from here on out, you've gotta promise to tell me everything. Even if it's hard. And I'll do the same. Deal?" He offered her a handshake.

"Deal," she said as they shook on it. Then she took a deep breath and said, "Now about that bike and that map . . . ."

"You really don't want me to go, do you?"

"I didn't say that. I don't, of course, but after all you've been through, I think you have a right to ask for something that matters to you. What I need to know is why. Is this just about getting to see Lisa? Because if it is, I'll drive you to Miami."

"No, ma'am, there's more to it than that."

"I thought so." It was peaceful on the river as the *Madame Queen* gently rocked them back to another hard question. Finally, his mother spoke. "You know you've got nothing to prove — to me or your daddy."

"I know. It's just something I need to do. But I don't want to make things harder on you than they already are."

She took his hand and kissed it. "Did you know that the very few disagreements your father and I ever had were about you?"

"Me? Why?"

"Because I thought the most important thing in the world was to protect you, but Marshall thought the most important thing in the world was to protect your freedom. He wanted you to be free to make your own choices and live your own life — provided you didn't try to do something truly off the beam, of course. But that was never an issue with you. You were born with a good head on your shoulders."

"Why was it so important to him — freedom, I mean?"

"You remember how your Uncle Gil always ends that tale about Marshall's bike ride to Key West?"

" 'And *that,* ladies and gentlemen, was the last time Marshall Cabot ever let anybody tell him what to do.' That the part you're talkin' about?"

"That's the biggest lie any Cabot ever told, and they've told some whoppers. Your daddy devoted his whole life to his family — protecting his father's investments and making sure there would always be plenty of money, not just for the family but to keep all the mills going so poor families around there would have jobs. And the thing is, Marshall himself didn't care about money at all. To him, it was just a way to provide for other people. He was bound and determined you would never feel obligated to live your life a particular way. He wanted you to follow your own path."

"What about you?"

She reached over and squeezed his hand. "I want that too."

"Even if my path takes me to Key West?"

"Even then. But I'm not as brave as your daddy. You have to promise to call me collect every Sunday night — maybe a time or two in between when you can manage it."

"I promise."

"And you remember what I told you before — there's more to this bike ride than pedaling."

"I remember."

"I took the liberty of tucking a few things into your saddlebag — things your daddy told me he wished he'd had. I hope you don't mind just a little meddling?"

"I don't mind."

"One more thing, son — I can't watch you ride away. So I guess you'll have to get up early when you go."

NINETEEN

The bungalow was still dark and quiet. Peyton was careful not to make any noise as he eased open the screen door, went into the backyard, and began loading his bike for the trip. He would have to travel light or he'd never make it. Strapping Aunt Gert's saddlebag to the bike rack behind the seat, he laid a small duffel on top of it and used an old belt to secure it.

Peyton was wearing the lightest pair of khaki shorts he had, a cotton T-shirt, his sneakers, and a UGA cap he'd picked up during a lunch break from the hospital in Atlanta. The duffel bag held a change of clothes, his bathing suit, and the small bike pump Aunt Gert had given him.

He had a sudden memory of the Ghost Tree at his grandparents' house and the talk of a bet that he, Winston, and Prentiss had carried on before everything changed. What would they think of him now, setting out

179

for Key West? Maybe he would call them when he got there. Then again, maybe not. After all that had happened, it seemed disrespectful to tie the journey ahead to something as frivolous as a bet.

In fact, such a momentous day should be marked somehow, but Peyton couldn't think of any way to do it. On Aunt Gert's dew-covered step, he wrote the date with his fingertip: May 23, 1947. It was a temporary monument, soon to evaporate, but at least it was something.

"Well, Pirate, I guess this is it," he said to Aunt Gert's enormous cat, which occasionally glanced up at Peyton as it lazily groomed itself in an Adirondack chair on the lawn. "Look after the ladies for me."

Peyton pushed the bike across the yard and down the driveway. Then he climbed on and pedaled down the street toward A1A. Only when he crossed the bridge onto Anastasia Island did it hit him: *I'm really doing this.*

Just below Crescent Beach, where Anastasia narrowed so much that you could just about throw a rock from the Matanzas riverbank on the western side of the highway and hit the Atlantic Ocean to the east, Peyton pulled onto a boardwalk and stopped to take it in. The sun, rising over the sea,

180

was bathing the morning sky in golden light. Boats were already heading downriver, bound for the St. Augustine and Matanzas Inlets and the fishing grounds that lay miles out to sea. What had his father seen when he pedaled this very road? And what was he himself expecting to find on it?

He had no answers — not yet anyway. He wasn't even sure what the questions were. He just knew it was time to go, whether he was ready or not.

TWENTY

Kate lay curled up on Peyton's bed, wishing for a thunderstorm as a light breeze blew across the sleeping porch. Marshall always loved the rain. He said it calmed his mind. That's the thing about quiet people — their minds are often noisy. It's as if their taciturn nature is a way to balance the internal roar.

She reached down and ran a finger over the lid of a shoebox — one of two she had brought with her. Ida Buck, who knew the back way to her house, had slipped in, fetched them for her, and mailed them to Atlanta. By now, Kate knew, Julian would've emptied the lake cottage of anything that belonged to Marshall, claiming what he wanted and destroying the rest. Her brother-in-law was so predictably spiteful. Besides her wedding ring — and Peyton — these boxes were the only physical reminders she had of her husband.

Opening the one closest to her, she took

out a bundle of postcards tied with string. The one on top read, "Meet Our Lovely Mermaid, Sue!" The "y" in "Lovely" was a mermaid tail. On the back, Marshall had written a short note:

I'm pretty sure that was an oxygen tank Sue kept swimming around.

Just came through Daytona and rode my bike by the ocean. It's beautiful — at least it would be if you were here.

Don't forget about me, okay?

Love, Marshall

Don't forget about me.

Forgetting Marshall would be impossible. Living with the memories — with only the memories — that was what Kate couldn't fathom.

She thought back to a special wedding anniversary, when Marshall had taken her to The Olde Pink House in Savannah — such a beautiful restaurant, with immaculate white linens, polished silver, and candlelight. It was hard to say what she remembered most about him that night. His hand cupping a wineglass the same way it cupped her face when he kissed her? Eyes the color of the ocean right before a rain? An unexpected smile on a face often serious?

After dinner, Kate and Marshall had driven back to their house on Tybee and lay together in a big chaise lounge on a little crow's nest that made them feel like they were floating in the night sky, high above the rooftops, with nothing overhead but stars.

Was Marshall looking down from that sky right now? Could he see her somehow?

She longed to go with him, but she had a son to raise, and Peyton deserved the best she could give. Part of her wished she had made him promise to call every day. But Marshall would say that was defeating the purpose of his journey. She would just have to trust them both.

TWENTY-ONE

By lunchtime on the first leg of his trip, Peyton had made it to Flagler Beach, where he had a cheeseburger and a mountain of fries at the restaurant on the fishing pier. The ride through Flagler was especially nice because A1A ran like a ribbon along the ocean, hugging a watery view. After lunch, he had walked onto the pier and watched the surfers for an hour or so before hopping back on his bike — and realizing he had the first flat tire of his journey.

He found a shady spot across the highway from the pier, took out his pump and an inner tube, and soon had his bike road-ready again. He refilled his water flask and was repacking his supplies into the saddlebag when he spotted something he didn't remember seeing in there before — gray leather fingerless gloves. Peyton pulled them out and read the note tucked inside: "To keep those blisters on your hands from getting any worse. Love, Mama."

He turned his palms up and examined the red places already forming at the base of his fingers and the inner sides of his thumbs, where he gripped the handlebars. For whatever reason, the sores on his hands made him think of the watch on Doctor Crenshaw's wrist the day of his father's accident. Peyton remembered how he had studied the watch, wondering whether it had been an heirloom passed down from the doctor's father. Maybe the blisters on his hands were *his* legacy, his inheritance, wounds handed down with no promise of healing. This much Peyton was sure of: He needed to get this journey done. He needed Lisa.

The afternoon ride into Daytona proved much more taxing than his morning travels. Even in late May, which was nowhere near the hottest part of summer, the Florida sun was beating down. He had drained his flask, and his T-shirt felt heavy and sticky, clinging to his body like moss on a rock. While his ball cap protected his face, his exposed arms and thighs were feeling the effects of a full day in the sun, and his eyes were stinging from salty sweat, which found a way to trickle in, no matter how much he swiped at it. His throat felt like sandpaper. Peyton could think of nothing right now but water — water to drink, water to cool his blistering skin, water to wash himself clean.

He followed the signs to the beach. Peyton had heard about Daytona but had never seen anything like it — sand packed so hard that you could drive on it, which everybody did. Fronting the water was a line of parked cars. Another row lined the sand closest to the beachfront hotels. Tourists simply loaded their trunks with snacks, towels, and umbrellas and played in the surf, returning to their Fords and Chevys whenever they were hungry or thirsty. Between the two rows of parked cars was a slow-moving roadway, with cruisers driving up and down the beach, checking out the sights.

Peyton found a public park with bathhouses, where he drank blissfully cold water from a fountain, downing so much of it so fast that he almost made himself sick, before refilling his flask, changing into his bathing suit, and washing his clothes in the sink. More comfortable with his bike in sight, he pushed it across the sand and parked it next to a station wagon where a family was having a picnic. After hanging his wet clothes over the seat and handlebars, he waded into the surf.

Nothing — *nothing* — felt better than bracing ocean water on hot, sweaty skin. Peyton let wave after wave roll over him to wash away the residue of the road — dust, salt, and sweat, all mingled into a sticky grime that coated his whole body, as if A1A wanted to leave a lasting stain on him. Relaxing in water up to his chest, he turned to face the beach.

The picnicking family looked out of place in Daytona. They were all barefoot, but the mother was wearing a dark brown dress, her little girl a navy skirt and white blouse. The boy, who looked about four, had on a dress shirt but had taken off his pants, while his dad had rolled up his trousers along with the sleeves of his shirt, and Peyton could see an undershirt peeking out where he had unbuttoned the collar. They were all very pale and clearly more at home in cooler climates. Focused on her children, the mother was pointing out seagulls and pelicans flying overhead. The father, Peyton thought, looked distracted, as if this sojourn on the beach were something to be endured, not enjoyed.

Down the beach, he heard music coming from an outdoor theater shaped like a castle. The band was playing Benny Goodman's "Sing, Sing, Sing," which made him miss

Aunt Gert and their jitterbugging at the VFW. Strange to think about it now — while he and Aunt Gert were dancing that night, his mother was crying, grief-stricken over a loss he wasn't yet aware of. He had danced when mourning was called for, but he couldn't see it at the time.

Peyton tipped his head back and ran his hands through his wet hair. The ocean air was cool and refreshing, though he knew that if he were to wade out of the surf and walk just a few feet onto the sand, he'd be sweating again in no time. At least the sun was slowly dropping lower in the sky, making its way toward sunset. That would cool things off.

A pickup truck pulled onto the beach a few yards away from Peyton's bike, and a couple who looked somewhere in the neighborhood of sixty got out. Their engine was steaming. The man raised the hood to let the ocean breeze cool the old Ford motor, then took a water can out of the back and struck out for the bathhouses across the beach. The woman stood on the sand, watching a flock of seagulls overhead. She was wearing a dress and heels. It looked so disjointed — a woman in her Sunday best, standing on a beach filled with people in bathing suits. Apparently, something about this drivable sand compelled people who were ill prepared for the beach to venture onto it.

Soon the man returned, filled his radiator, and slammed the hood. Just like that, they were gone — empty space where people had been just moments ago.

Now a sightseeing tram was cruising by, pulled by a golf cart rigged up to look like a locomotive engine. The driver had a train whistle of sorts, which he would blow at every stop along the shore as he shouted, "All aboard!"

The train had just gone by when Peyton heard a man call out, "I can't swim!" His cries quickly grew desperate as he called out again and again, "I can't swim! I can't swim!"

It took Peyton a few seconds to figure out that the cries were coming from the beach, not the waves. They belonged to the man with the rolled-up sleeves and undershirt, from the family with two kids. But where was the little boy? Peyton scanned the water around him. A few yards to his left, he spotted the child bobbing up and down in his white dress shirt. What looked like a rip current was quickly pulling him out. The boy must've gotten caught in it when he was playing close to shore, and it had dragged him into danger so quickly that, once his parents recognized it, they were too late to stop it.

Peyton swam toward the drowning child as hard and fast as he could, catching the boy by the collar just before a swell took them both under. Once it passed, Peyton was able to get a firmer grip, holding the child with one arm while swimming across the riptide to get them free of it. Once they made it to shallow water, Peyton ran to the beach, carrying the boy, who was completely limp, his lips pale blue.

Struggling to remember everything his dad had ever taught him about water safety, Peyton laid the child on the sand and began pressing on his chest. He remained still, but Peyton kept on until at last came the coughing and breathing. It was only then that he realized the family was kneeling on the sand around him, the mother praying out loud, her daughter clinging to her, the father staring hopelessly at his son. The minute the child was breathing again, his mother gathered him in her arms, rocking him back and forth as she knelt on the sand.

"I did the best I could, sir," Peyton said to the father. "But y'all might want to let a doctor look at him."

"I can't swim," the man said again.

"We don't know how to thank you," the mother said, clinging to her child. "If we had any money, we'd give it to you, but that's how come we're down here — lookin' for work. You really think Billy here needs a doctor?"

Peyton thought it over, then went to his bike and took out fifty of the one hundred dollars Aunt Gert had hidden in the saddlebag on his bike. He sat down next to Billy and his mother and handed it to her.

She stared at the money wide-eyed, as if she had never seen anything like it before. "We can't take your money. That'd be a handout. Wouldn't be right."

"Wouldn't be right not to get your boy the help he needs if there's a way to do it," Peyton countered.

Again, she stared at the money he was holding out, finally reaching to take it.

"Good luck to y'all," he said.

He pushed his bike through the cruisers on the beach and changed into dry clothes at the bathhouse. Then he had an early supper — a footlong and fries at a beachfront joint called the Sawlty Dawg. By the time he finished, the sunset was painting the sky with soft blues and corals, and a cool ocean breeze was blowing. He knew he should save his money and look up the local police chief, but he was exhausted, and the little motor court next door had a vacancy sign.

He made his way to the motel office, stepped inside, and felt the blessed chill of an air conditioner. They had been popping up all over the South since the war.

"Welcome to The Sandman!" called the woman behind the front desk. "How can I help you today?" She was probably in her sixties, tall, with reddish-brown hair, which she wore in a twist on the back of her head. Her fingernails were long and red. She had a twinkle in her eye and the kind of smile that made you think she could take the worst situation and make everything alright.

"I was hoping to get a room?" Peyton said.

"Sure, honey. How many nights?"

"Just one, I guess."

"Okay, then. That'll be six dollars for a garden view — that means facing the swimming pool — or ten for an ocean view. What'll it be?"

"Better go with the cheaper one."

"You want to pay twenty-five cents to unlock the phone in your room?"

"No, ma'am. I don't reckon I'll be making any calls."

The woman handed Peyton a form to complete. He filled in all the spaces, gave it back to her, and watched as she reviewed it, wondering if he had done everything right. He had never rented a motel room before.

The woman peered at him over her reading glasses. "Now, honey, I notice right here where it says 'tag number,' you wrote 'bicycle'?"

"Yes, ma'am," Peyton said. "This is the first day of a bike trip I'm taking."

"Where to?"

"Key West."

"Key *West*? You got any idea how far that is?"

"Yes, ma'am."

"And you're gonna ride all the way from — where'd you say you came from again?"

"I didn't, but I started in St. Augustine."

The woman looked Peyton up and down. "How old are you, honey?"

"Fifteen."

"I woulda guessed eighteen or nineteen. Your mama know where you are?"

"Yes, ma'am. She's not thrilled about it, but she let me go. My daddy made this ride when he was my age. I just want to see if I can make it too."

"And what about your daddy, honey — what does he say about this?"

"Well, he's not here anymore. I mean . . . he died. Recently."

The woman laid her hand against her

cheek. "Well, now that just breaks my heart. I'm sorry, honey. You need anything at all, just come and get me. I live over the office here. My name's Jackie, but everybody in Daytona calls me Aunt Jack."

Peyton smiled at her. "Thanks, Aunt Jack."

"Here's your key. And like I said, you let me know if you need help, okay?"

"Yes, ma'am," he said. "And thank you."

Leaving the office, Peyton followed the sidewalk to a rectangular pool behind the oceanfront units. It overflowed with little kids in bright-colored inner tubes. Teenagers showed off for each other on the diving board or flirted on the pool deck. He felt a pang of loneliness as he wondered what Lisa was doing right now.

Peyton circled the pool, reading room numbers until he found one that matched the long wooden tag on his key: 105. It was small but cheery, with turquoise walls and a bright yellow bedspread and curtains. And it was air-conditioned. There was even a tiny bathroom.

He pushed his bike inside, unstrapped his saddlebag and duffel, and tossed them on the floor next to the bed. Then he stripped down to his underwear, pulled back the covers, and fell onto the mattress. He had never been so exhausted. Just outside, he could hear the shouts and laughter of a pool full of strangers. But he had no desire to join them. Right now all he wanted was sleep and — if he were very, very lucky — another dream of Lisa.

TWENTY-TWO

The moment he rolled onto his back, Peyton knew something was wrong — horribly, painfully wrong. Every muscle in his body seized with pain, especially his neck and shoulders. His hips, thighs, and groin felt like one big bruise. Worst of all was a particularly painful spot on his backside. The slightest pressure on his right hip shot him with a searing pain.

Peyton had played sports all his life. He'd had his share of hard knocks, even a broken bone or two. But this . . . nothing he had ever suffered on a ballfield even came close to the throbbing, burning sensations attacking him now. Determined to stay calm, he took some deep breaths, telling himself to relax. He tried sitting up, but it was as if the pain in his body grabbed him by the shoulders and threw him back on the bed. He couldn't move. He couldn't think. All he could do was hurt. And pray. And wish to

197

goodness he were back at Aunt Gert's. His eyes stung, the telltale sign that he might actually cry, something he hadn't done since elementary school — something he hadn't even done when his father died, though he wasn't sure why.

Slowly turning his head toward the window next to his bed, he could see soft rays of morning light streaming through the blinds. The swimming pool, which had buzzed with splashing, squeals, and laughter until midnight, was silent now. It must be early still. The office might not be open yet. Aunt Jack probably wasn't even awake. What difference did it make anyway? He'd never be able to make it to her, and he was cursing his decision to save a quarter on the telephone.

Gripping the edge of the bed, he gritted his teeth and turned onto his right side. He saw the saddlebag on the floor and remembered what his mother had said — that she had packed what he might need. She was right about the gloves. Right now his hands felt better than just about any other part of his body. Taking another deep breath, he reached for the bag, letting a cry escape as he lifted it onto the bed and rolled onto his back, which only aggravated the sore spot on his rear. As quickly as he could move again, he rolled onto his left side to relieve the pressure, opened the saddlebag, and emptied the contents onto the bed. He could tell just by looking at them who had packed what.

From Aunt Gert: spare inner tubes, possibly illegal bug lotion, his water flask, and one hundred dollars, fifty of which he had given to the family on the beach. He had spent another eight or nine on his motel room and supper.

From his mother: Noxzema, talcum powder, lotion, liniment, Band-Aids, and another hundred dollars in small bills. A piece of masking tape was wrapped around the Noxzema. On it, his mother had written "For saddle sores." Peyton found a similar label on the talcum powder: "For chafing."

Now he just had to figure out how to use them when he was too sore to move. Pushing back the covers, he started with the liniment, pouring a little into his hand and massaging it into the opposite shoulder until he could feel the muscles loosening up. That brought at least a little relief. He repeated the liniment rub on the other shoulder. It was like oiling a rusty bike chain.

Peyton could endure some movement in his upper body now. His face, neck, and forearms were sunburned, as were the tops of his thighs. He took his time spreading the cooling lotion onto his red skin.

Now it was time to tackle the painful sore on his backside. He slid off his underwear and then unscrewed the lid on the Noxzema. Scooping out a big dollop, he reached back and gently smeared it where the saddle sore was throbbing. It stung a little at first, but then it cooled and soothed his sore, which wanted padding, Peyton decided. He fished two large Band-Aids out of the box and put one on top of the other, covering the sore on his hip. Looking down at the red rash inside both legs, he reached for the talcum powder and gave it a good shake on his splotchy skin. One application felt so soothing that he decided to give himself another. Just as he raised the tin of powder, he heard a key in the door of his room, and Aunt Jack came bustling in with a tray of food.

"Aunt Jack, wait!" he cried as he grabbed the sheet and jerked it up to cover himself.

She laughed as she set the tray on his nightstand. "Honey, I raised six boys. I've powdered more misters than you ever will. How you feelin' this mornin'?"

"Like a train ran over me."

"I guess you've figured out you won't be ridin' that bike today."

"Yes, ma'am."

"You want to stay here?"

"Yes, ma'am. I've got the money in my bag —"

"Don't worry about that right now. I've been at this long enough to know you're not a bill skipper. When you feel better, come by the office and we'll settle up. I brought you a little breakfast. Figured you wouldn't be able to get out."

"Thank you, Aunt Jack."

She pointed to the tray. "You see that orange juice, honey? I want you to drink every drop. All that vitamin C's good for your skin. It'll help you heal."

"Yes, ma'am. I sure do appreciate it."

"You remind me so much o' my youngest," she said, laying her hand on Peyton's forehead the way his mother always did when she was checking for a fever.

"Does he live here?"

Aunt Jack gently raised him up and fluffed his pillows. "No, he didn't make it home."

"I'm — I'm real sorry," Peyton said as he lay back down.

"It's okay, honey. You didn't have a thing in the world to do with it. Just get some rest. Come and see me when you feel better."

TWENTY-THREE

"Here, honey, I bought you some underwear for the road."

"Aunt Jack!" Peyton felt his face flush with heat as she handed it to him in the motel office.

"Ha! You're a sight, Peyton. How come you get embarrassed so easy?"

"Lady, you just handed me a bundle of underwear right in the middle of a busy motel office!"

She pinched him on the cheek. "You're just as cute as a button, Peyton. I know your mama must be real proud o' you. But now, Aunt Jack's serious about the underwear. You've got to keep yourself dry or you'll be hurtin' again. Understand?"

"Yes, ma'am."

"And Key West ain't goin' anywhere. You need to break up your trip a little better and get some rest."

"Yes, ma'am."

"You really gonna listen to me, or are you just sayin' 'yes, ma'am' to shut me up?"

"I'm really listenin'. I promise. Now hug me goodbye so I can take my new skivvies and hit the road."

Peyton hugged Aunt Jack and thanked her again for getting him well. His extended visit with her had made him ready to ride again.

As he loaded his bike and made his way back to A1A, Peyton had to wonder: Had anybody helped his father? Was there an Aunt Jack in his path, someone to salve his wounds and help him heal? Something about this trip made Peyton feel at war with himself, one minute struggling to piece together his dad's every move, the next wishing he could put the long-cherished map away for good and find his own way, taking the road as it came, on his own terms.

The sound of engines — loud ones — caught his attention. He pulled his bike onto a sidewalk fronting the beach so he could see what was going on.

About twenty or thirty cars with numbers painted on their doors were racing each other on the beach. They would fly down A1A, hang a left into a sand-entrenched curve that banked high, race up the beach, then speed or slide through a second sandy curve and back onto A1A. They formed a big oval loop, driving around and around, passing each other, crowding each other, and fighting for position. Spectators sat on blankets and beach chairs in the center of the oval, which seemed pretty crazy to Peyton, given the way those guys were driving. About the only thing protecting the crowd was the three- or four-foot height of the giant mound of sand.

Peyton found a bike rack and used the lock and chain Aunt Jack had given him to secure it, because "this is Florida, honey, and you've gotta know what's what." He took his money out of the saddlebag and slipped some into each shoe before walking onto the beach and standing at the edge of the spectator mound to watch.

Man, his dad would've loved something like this. Peyton wasn't sure whether he had taken this trip to remember his father or forget him. Thinking about him and knowing there would be no new memories of him — that was almost too much to bear. But trying to forget him or push his memory aside seemed like a coward's way out. Whatever had happened to his father in the Pacific, whatever demons had followed him home, he deserved to be remembered for who he was before the war and who he could've been after it, if only he had lived long enough.

"Hey, neighbor!"

Peyton looked up to see a man standing next to a '39 Ford while a mechanic changed one of his tires. "Me?" he asked.

"Yeah, you! Can you spot me for the last ten laps?"

"I don't know what that means."

"It means you sit in the passenger seat and watch out that side — help me get around." The mechanic was finished, and the man ran to the driver's door. "Well? You in or ain't you?"

Peyton didn't know why he did what he did — years later, he would still try to figure out what made him do it — but he ran to the car and jumped in.

" 'At's more like it!" the man said as he stomped the gas and streaked up the highway. "What's your name?" he shouted.

"Peyton Cabot!" Peyton shouted back, bracing his arms against the dash.

The man headed into the first turn on the beach so fast that the back end of the car skidded to the right. He braked and clutched and steered and accelerated till the car righted itself and went flying up the beach. Peyton felt a rush of adrenaline that came as close to taking flight as anything he had ever experienced.

"I'm Will Fournier!" the man shouted. "Now look out that window and tell me who's out there an' back yonder."

Peyton braced for the next turn and checked out the track. "You've got a Chevy comin' up on this side, but the engine's on fire — '37 Ford on your bumper!"

"Attaboy!" Will eased up as he entered the banked turn, then swept down it and accelerated for the inside lane, leaving the '37 and the now flaming Chevy in the dust.

Peyton soon got the hang of spotting and helped Will move ahead of most cars in the pack. By the time they crossed the finish line, they were in third place, and Daytona Beach was littered with wrecked or otherwise disabled cars. A couple of tow trucks set to work removing them.

Peyton watched as Will accepted his third-place trophy and a hundred dollars. Then he waved to the driver and started walking back to his bike.

"Hey, Peyton! Wait up!"

He turned to see the racer coming toward him.

"You forgot your take." Will took out his wallet and handed Peyton twenty dollars.

"You don't have to do that — I had fun," Peyton said.

"Naw, now, them's the rules. Spotter gets twenty percent. That's fair."

"Most fun I ever had on a summer job," Peyton said with a smile.

"You want to go one more time?"

"Really?"

"There's another race soon as they get the track squared away, an' I sure could use you. Same pay — twenty percent o' whatever I win."

Peyton thought it over. "Just one more?"

"Yep. One more race o' twenty laps, and we're through."

"Okay."

Will slapped him on the back. "We might come outta this one with the whole shebang, me an' you! Meet me at the car in half an hour."

Peyton had skipped breakfast and was starving now that there was no excitement to take his mind off his stomach. He grabbed a cheeseburger and a Coke at a beachside stand and then went to find Will's number 10 car in the line that was forming, two vehicles deep, right on the sand.

He got in just a few minutes before the starting gun fired, and the cars went flying up Daytona Beach and into the first turn. Peyton was especially vigilant in the turns because he quickly figured out that's where a truly heinous crash was most likely. But the thrill of the speed in the straights more than made up for any apprehension he might've felt in the turns. It was the closest you could get to flying on land.

They got bumped and scraped and cut off now and again but somehow made it to the final five laps without major incident. As Will accelerated on the beach straightaway, Peyton noticed that the tide was coming in. Ocean water was now licking at the right-lane cars closest to the sea. But nobody was slowing down. Around and around they kept going, and the water came higher and higher onto shore with every lap until Peyton could actually hear the tires splashing through surf and see ocean spray coming off the car in front of them.

Just as they came out of a turn and onto the beach for the last lap, Peyton saw it — an abnormally large swell very near the shore. Finn had warned him about rogue waves, which could get as tall as a building out at sea. "Will, look out for that wave!"

"Ain't got time to look at the ocean, Peyton — we're in second!"

"It's gonna hit the —" The number 10 car was just passing the swell as it began to crest. "Floor it, Will, floor it!" Peyton shouted.

" 'At's the spirit!" Will said. He cleared the car ahead of him and floored the accelerator, making it safely to the finish line back on A1A just as the wave broke against the shore and swamped all the cars behind them.

Will was so focused on the checkered flag and his first big win that he was completely unaware of what had just happened. Peyton bailed out of the car as soon as he could and ran toward the beach. All the cars behind them were stalled, with ocean water up to their engines. One Chevy had been pulled out by the tide, and Peyton watched as the driver climbed out of the window, then stood helplessly in the water as wave after wave hit his car and pulled it out to sea.

When none of the other drivers showed up to congratulate him, Will joined Peyton on the beach, staring in disbelief at what looked like a lake full of race cars. "What happened?" he said, rubbing his eyes as if that might clear the scene for him.

"They got hit by a wave," Peyton said. "I saw it comin'. That's what I was tellin' you to look out for."

Will frowned, and then a forlorn expression saddened his face. "You mean I didn't really beat them other cars?"

Peyton laid his hand on Will's shoulder. "You didn't just beat the cars, Will, you beat the ocean."

That brought a smile. "You're a good man, Peyton. I sure wish you could ride with me every race."

"I 'preciate that. And I thank you for takin' me along. But I gotta get on down the road."

"I hear ya. Well, I reckon I need to give you your take." He handed Peyton a hundred dollars.

"Dang, Will, are you sure?"

"Fair's fair. You earned every penny."

"Thank you. Guess I better get goin'. You take care, now."

"You too, Peyton. Keep it in the road."

"I'll try," Peyton said with a smile. "You do the same."

They shook hands before Peyton retrieved his bike and asked directions to the police station. He was feeling flush with cash but knew he had a long way to go, so he compromised — he'd have a nice supper at a fish house on the beach but see if he could spend the night in the city jail.

"Thank you, son — thank you so, so much for calling. I love you, sweetheart!" Kate hung up the phone in Aunt Gert's living room and returned to the kitchen, where her aunt and Finn were shucking shrimp for supper. "He's alright!" she told them as she began shredding a head of cabbage for slaw.

" 'Course he is!" Finn said. "I'm tellin' you, Miss Kate, you ain't gotta worry about that one. Peyton's rock-solid. You can count on him to see a thing through."

"Where is he?" Aunt Gert asked as Finn gathered up shrimp shells and carried them to a trash bin outside.

"The Daytona city jail!" Kate said. "Apparently, Herschel — he's our police chief in Savannah — wrote him a letter of introduction so the chiefs would feed him and give him a place to sleep. Can you believe that?"

"Of course!" Aunt Gert said. "Honey, you and Marshall got it right with that boy. He's grade A, a hundred percent. Did you tell him his sweetie called?"

Kate put the shredded cabbage into a mixing bowl, grated onion over it, and added sweet pickle relish and mayonnaise. "I debated it — didn't know if it would make him feel better to know she called or worse because he missed it — but I told him."

"You think she's got it as bad as he does?"

"Yes." Kate smiled at the thought of such

211

a lovely girl being smitten with her son. "She's just not ready to admit it yet. She told me how sorry she was to hear about Marshall and asked me a million questions about how Peyton was doing."

Aunt Gert began heating a Dutch oven filled with oil, then joined Kate at the table, where she started breading the shrimp. "What about you, Katie?" she asked without looking up. "How are you doing?"

Kate mixed the coleslaw with a wooden spoon. "The best I can hope for is numb, Aunt Gert. When I think about Marshall, it's like a raw nerve — like a physical pain that runs through my whole body. And to tell you the truth, if it weren't for Peyton, I would've gladly gone with him."

Aunt Gert stopped breading the shrimp and looked up at her. "But there *is* a Peyton. And he needs you — now more than ever. Best not to even let those thoughts enter your mind."

Kate poured the slaw into a serving bowl, covered it, and put it in the icebox to chill. She poured herself a cup of coffee and sat down at the table. "How did you do it, Aunt Gert? How did you make it through?"

Aunt Gert began dropping shrimp into the hot oil. "Who says I've made it through?"

TWENTY-FOUR

A beach-town jail was no place to get a good night's sleep. Everything was fine till about ten o'clock, when all the carousers had downed enough beer and hard liquor to start causing trouble and get themselves hauled in. After that, the jail was a cacophony of slamming cell doors and ringing telephones and drunk men snoring. Plus it was hot and airless. The minute he saw a hint of sunrise coming through the bars in his cell, Peyton straightened up his cot and pushed his bike out. The police chief had told him it wouldn't be a good idea to leave one that nice outside the jail.

He was thanking a deputy for letting him stay when a voice called his name. And there behind a cell door stood Will.

"What are you doin' here?" the race car driver asked him.

"It's kinda complicated, but the short answer is, the chief let me spend the night here so I wouldn't have to pay for a hotel."

"Same here," Will said with a grin.

Peyton frowned at him. "My cell door stayed open all night. You don't appear to have the key to yours. What happened?"

"Got into a little scrape with one o' the other drivers."

"Will they let you out today?"

"Doubt it. I don't know nobody with that much bail money."

"How much?"

"A hundred and fifty bucks."

Peyton whistled. "That's a lot!"

"Not my first offense," Will said with a shrug. "I get a little 'shine in me after a race, and next thing you know, the fists are a-flyin'. But I done it to myself, so I ain't got nobody to blame but me." He sat down on his cot and put his head in his hands.

Peyton propped his bike against a wall and walked over to the cell door. "Wait a minute, Will — what about all that money you won at the race?"

"Lost it at the casino — all but thirty or forty dollars."

"Oh. Then take back the money you paid me and use it to pay your bail."

"I can't do that, Peyton. Bad enough I blow my own money. You done me a real good turn, and I ain't gonna repay you by blowin' yours."

"Give that one money and he'd prob'ly find a way to gamble it away right here in the jail — wouldn't even make it down the hall to the bail office," said a deputy walking by.

"That true, Will?" Peyton asked.

His friend looked up at him from the cot. Gone was the boyish excitement from the race. Will looked empty and defeated. "Prob'ly," he said.

Peyton thought it over. "Then I won't give it to you. I'll give it to the deputy."

He took the money out of his shoe, and the deputy pointed him to an office down the hall, where he found a desk manned by a skinny little woman typing ninety miles an hour. Her hair, which was pinned into a bun, was an odd shade of fiery red — had to be dyed. She wore round, black-rimmed glasses and a sour expression.

"What?" she said without looking up from her typing.

"Uh, I'm here to pay bail for Will Fournier, ma'am."

"Why?"

"So he can get outta jail."

Now Peyton had her attention. She stopped typing and looked up. "I know that, dimwit. Why do you want to get him outta

215

jail? He your daddy?"

Peyton swallowed his anger. It wouldn't do Will any good, and it might land Peyton himself behind one of those locked cell doors. "No," he said.

"No, what?"

He knew what she wanted. She was demanding a "ma'am," but she didn't deserve one.

"No, we're not related."

"Well, bully for you. Don't just stand there lookin' like you ain't got good sense. Hand me 150."

Peyton gave her the money and waited patiently while she took her time typing up a form, stamping it, and giving him a carbon copy.

"He'll be back," she said with a sneer. "Don't let the door hit you in the backside on the way out."

Peyton got away from her as quickly as he could. Why would anybody be that way — treat people so mean for absolutely no reason? Maybe she hated her job. So get another one. He couldn't wait to free Will and get out of there.

Once they were in the parking lot, he asked his friend, "Why's that woman in the bail office so mean?"

"Hazel?" Will swatted at a mosquito.

"Peyton, you ain't gonna believe this, but me and her's known each other since we was kids. And I'll tell you somethin' else — she was born that way. Yessir, Hazel Scoggins was mean as a snake when she was a toddler, and she's mean as a snake to this very day."

"So I guess there's no chance of a jailhouse romance between you two?" Peyton said with a grin.

"Whoo-ee!" Will whooped. "I'd sooner snuggle up to a big ol' alligator."

They laughed as Peyton reached into his shoe and pulled out his money. "Listen, this is all I've got, but I'll split it with you."

"You done enough — more'n anybody else woulda done. You keep your money. I still got a few greenbacks left. That'll carry me awhile — if I can stay away from the casino."

"You sure?"

"Yeah, I'm sure." Will scratched the stubble on his face. "Guess I better get me a shave somewhere. Can me and the number 10 car give you a ride?"

"No, thanks," Peyton said. "I'm leaving town."

"On that bicycle?"

"Yep."

"Well, where you headed?"

"This might sound a little crazy, but Key West."

"Key *West*? You got any idea how far that is?"

Peyton laid a hand on Will's shoulder and grinned. "Why do people keep asking me that? I guess you might say the distance is kinda the point. Part of it anyway."

"Well, alright then. But you run into any trouble, I work down at the A&R Marina. You remember that — Will Fournier, A&R Marina, Daytona, Florida. I ain't got no phone where I live, but you can call down at the marina and tell 'em to find me if you get in a scrape. Me an' the number 10 car'll come a-runnin'."

"I'll do that." They shook hands as Peyton said, "Good luck to you, Will."

"You too, Peyton."

Pedaling out of the parking lot, Peyton heard Will's '39 firing up. The Florida sun had yet to heat the early morning air, but those hot rays were coming. So was another beach town where he wouldn't know a living soul.

TWENTY-FIVE

Kate sat on an old cotton quilt and slid her bare feet into the sand. When she was about ten years old, Aunt Gert had given her this blue-and-yellow quilt in the Dresden plate pattern, already faded, and told her she could make it her beach quilt. It was a little threadbare now but still holding together. She and Marshall had sat on it and talked for hours the day they met here. And after he left for Key West, she wouldn't let Aunt Gert wash it because it held the faint scent of him.

There was nothing of Marshall left on the quilt now — nothing but the memory of what it had been like to sit here by the ocean with him as a starry-eyed teenage girl. Plenty of boys his age would've taken advantage of the situation, but not Marshall. Even as a boy, he was a hopeless romantic, holding her in his arms and giving her a kiss that she could still feel, ignited by youthful passion yet still gentle — protective even. It was her very first. From the beginning, Marshall didn't so much look *at* her as *into* her, like he could see something even she didn't realize was there. They had over twenty years together, and he'd never stopped looking at her like that. Twenty years when eighty wouldn't have been enough, not nearly enough.

She looked out at the Atlantic, calm now and washed in the cool, dreamy colors of sunset. This was Marshall's favorite time of day. It reminded Kate of the most spectacular sunset they'd ever seen together — on their honeymoon in Key West.

They had spent the morning getting married, twice — once at the courthouse and once at Aunt Gert's church — and then Aunt Gert and Finn took them to a grand old restaurant downtown. That's when Marshall announced that he and his bride would be leaving on their honeymoon right after lunch.

"You mean *today*?" Aunt Gert protested.

"Gert, girl, are you so old that you can't remember why they're in a hurry?" Finn said.

Marshall took Kate's hand and kissed it. "I want you to see it. I want you to see Key West with me."

She couldn't believe it. "We're going there together — today?"

"Yes. Today. As soon as you can pack."

"I can pack fast."

They hurried through lunch and raced back to the purple bungalow while Aunt Gert and Finn were still paying the check.

"What should I take?" Kate asked Marshall, who was sitting on the bed next to her open suitcase.

"Not much — you'll want completely different clothes once we get down there. Key West is something you have to put on — wrap it around you."

She laid her hand against her cheek and stared at him.

"You're looking at me like I'm crazy," he said.

She laughed and sat on his lap with her arms around his neck. "I don't think you're crazy. I just don't understand what you're talking about."

"You will," he'd said, kissing the curve of her neck.

Kate felt a spray of sand hit her leg, bringing her back to the beach.

" 'Scuse me, ma'am. I didn't mean to kick sand on you."

She looked up to see a boy about Peyton's age standing over her. He was holding a

221

fishing rod and a net. Kate blinked at him, sad to leave behind a memory where she was happy and come back to the present, where she was desolate.

"It's 'bout to get dark, ma'am. You need any help?"

"No," she said. "Guess I just lost track of time. But thank you."

As he waved and went on his way, she stood up and held the quilt by one edge, letting it flap in the wind to blow the sand away. Then she folded it and took her time crossing first the dunes and then the bridge, thinking all the while of a distance she could not get over — the great divide between where she was and where she longed to be.

TWENTY-SIX

Over breakfast at a waterfront café in Titus-ville, Peyton unfolded his father's map and reviewed, for what seemed like the hun-dredth time, the neatly written notes, all in pencil, that traced his path out into the blue ocean. Most people wrote in rounded let-ters, but his dad wrote in architectural, boxy letters, sometimes at odd angles, as if he couldn't be confined to a straight line — not so much writing his thoughts, hard and permanent, as sketching them with a fluid-ity that could be reconsidered. Next to a tiny arrow pointing to Merritt Island, he had written, "Could hide away here with Kate forever."

Peyton wondered if his father had ever envisioned himself having a son back then, or did he dream only of being a husband? His father had never done anything to make him feel like an unwelcome addition to the perfect union, but maybe he had been, at least in the beginning. Aunt Gert might have the answer. Then again, maybe he would find it on a Florida island marked by an arrow written in his father's hand.

After paying his tab, Peyton climbed onto his bike, heading south to a bridge that crossed onto Merritt, dense with palms and palmettos. On its western shore, it was separated from the mainland by the Indian River. To the east, the Banana River flowed between the island and Cape Canaveral. It was isolated yet far from quiet, reverberating with the hum of cicadas punctuated by birdcalls. Cranes waded its shallows, while ducks noisily congregated on the island's lakes and ponds. Now and again, the narrow pavement would play out altogether, and Peyton would find himself pedaling across hard-packed sand, gravel, and shells.

At last, he came to the first sign of life — human life, at least — that he had seen here: an unpainted, wood-frame house slightly elevated on low coquina pillars, with tall windows, a metal roof, and a deep front porch. An old woman wearing a cotton dress, tennis shoes, and a wide-brimmed straw hat was sweeping the front yard, which was much too shady for a lawn. She threw up her hand when she saw him. Peyton stopped and waved back.

"You got time to come in?" she called to him.

"Yes, ma'am," he said as he pedaled into her yard.

She propped her broom against a tree and walked out to meet him. "Matilda Jenks," she said, extending her hand.

"Pleased to meet you." He shook her hand. "I'm Peyton Cabot."

Her eyes grew wide as she stepped closer to him. "Cabot?"

"Yes, ma'am."

"Well, if that don't beat all."

"Ma'am?"

"I've lived on this island all my life — outlived my mama and my daddy and my husband — and in eighty years, I've seen exactly two boys on fancy bicycles passin' through — had to be twenty or thirty years apart — that was both named Cabot."

Peyton's heart jumped into his throat. "You met Daddy — Marshall Cabot, I mean?"

Matilda's mouth flew open. "That boy Marshall — he growed up to be your daddy?"

"Yes, ma'am. But, well . . . he passed away not too long ago."

Matilda covered her mouth with her hand,

sadly shaking her head. "Bless his sweet heart."

"Did you spend much time with him?"

"No, can't say that I did. But I fixed him some lemonade and we had a nice talk in my kitchen. He spent the night here before he went on his way. You want some lemonade?"

"Sure — thank you."

Peyton followed his host onto her porch, down a wide center hallway, and into the kitchen on the back of the house. It was painted a cheery shade of yellow, with white wooden cabinets and a small table with ladder-back chairs.

"Have a seat," Matilda directed him. She went to her icebox and retrieved a pitcher of lemonade along with two glasses. "Would you like something to eat?" she asked as she poured.

"No, ma'am, I just had lunch, but thank you." Peyton took a sip of his lemonade, which was cold and tart-sweet. "Sure is good."

"Mama's recipe," Matilda said with a smile as she laid her hat on the table and had some lemonade herself. "Tell me about your daddy. He was 'bout your age when he came through here — couldn't be more'n forty by now. What on earth happened to him?"

That was the question Peyton was trying to answer himself — one of them, anyway. "He had a horseback riding accident and hit his head," he explained, making the choice to begin his father's story with Bootlegger, not the bourbon.

"Well, now, that's just a pure tragedy. Such a sweet, quiet boy."

"Mrs. Jenks, did Daddy tell you anything about why he was ridin' to Key West?"

Matilda leaned back in her chair, tilting her head to one side. "You appear willin' and able to take in the truth. Do I judge you right?"

"Yes, ma'am, I think so — hope so anyway," Peyton answered.

"Well and good." Matilda nodded and smoothed a pulled thread on her checked tablecloth. "I've thought about Marshall Cabot many times over the years. And like I told my husband — he passed in '39 — it always seemed to me that young man was a house divided. Part of him wanted to get as far away from home as he could, and part of him wanted to turn around an' go right back the way he came. One minute he was tellin' me how he loved this wild ol' island, and the next he was askin' me reckon how

227

long it would take him to get back to St. Augustine if he was to light out right away. You got any idea what that was all about?"

"Yes, ma'am. He left Georgia to get some distance from his family and figure some stuff out, but then he met my mama in St. Augustine and didn't want to leave her. I guess he had trouble sortin' that out."

"Makes sense," Matilda said, fanning herself with her straw hat.

"What was Daddy like back then — if you don't mind saying?"

"Well, like I said, he was a sweet, quiet boy. But there was somethin' else goin' on. Couldn't quite put my finger on it. He said somethin' that stuck in my mind. I told him I thought it took a awful lotta courage for a boy his age to ride all the way from Georgia to the Keys. And he said, 'It didn't take courage to come to Florida; what'll take courage is goin' back to Georgia.' I asked him was he scared o' gettin' in hot water with his folks, but he said 'no ma'am.' I started to ask him more but decided that would be pryin' an' ill-mannered, so I just let it go. But I never forgot about Marshall Cabot. An' I never quit wonderin' what that sweet boy was facin' in Georgia."

Peyton gazed out the kitchen window, overwhelmed with sadness and regret for his father. He felt Matilda's hand on his arm.

"Was it wrong in me to tell you, Peyton?"

"No, ma'am," he said. "I think I already knew. But it helps to hear it from somebody else. Guess Daddy realized he'd never get to make his own choices if he went back to Georgia, but he figured he'd be letting his daddy down if he didn't. That's a lot to put on somebody the same age as me. Don't know how I'd handle it. I guess part of him just wanted to hide from it — make it go away."

"Islands ain't for ever'body," Matilda said. "Some of us needs one and some of us don't. Somethin' tells me you might be somewhere in the middle. Marshall, though — I never seen nobody need an island the way he did."

"Makes me feel so sad for him."

"Well, now, it wasn't all bad, was it?" Matilda asked. "Sounds like he was pretty taken with your mama."

"They were happy together."

"And where do you figure in?"

"I reckon I'll have to sort that out somehow."

Matilda took a sip of her lemonade. "You been loved, Peyton. I can tell. It just shows in a person. You coulda been off havin' all kinda adventures, but here you are takin' the time to talk to a old lady in her kitchen."

Peyton pointed a finger at her and grinned. "You bribed me with lemonade."

"Ha!" Matilda gleefully slapped the table with her hand. "That I did."

Matilda's clock on the wall ticked away before she said, "Your daddy stayed the night with us — with my husband and me — back then. He wasn't goin' to till we told him about a little fishin' shack on Sykes Creek back here behind us. I reckon he wasn't comfortable stayin' in the house with strangers. You in a big hurry, or you want to have supper with me and stay the night out there like he did?"

Peyton thought it over. He was anxious to find Lisa and then get to Key West, but he knew if he kept riding hard, he'd just end up sidelined for several days, doctoring sores and rashes. "Yes, ma'am. I think I do. Thank you."

Matilda clapped her hands together. "Well, that's just wonderful. I can't remember when I've had comp'ny from the mainland. Let's go get you settled in, and you can rest yourself until supper. Oh, this is just a *treat*!"

Matilda's fishing shack was a tiny cracker-style house made of cypress — just one room and no electricity. A sink on the front porch held a hand pump for water from the creek just a few yards away. Tall screened windows offered cooling cross breezes and kept the bugs out.

He and Matilda shared a supper of pan-fried trout, fresh greens, new potatoes, and cornbread before he helped her with the dishes and retired to the shack, where he sat on the end of an old pier that jutted out into Sykes Creek. The sun had already set, and the sky was quickly growing dark. Peyton could see the rising moon reflected in the water below. A few minutes more and that's all there was — dark sky above, dark water below, and a lone traveler suspended like the moon between the two.

His father likely loved this place — the quiet and the solitude. But Peyton had realized something on his coastal odyssey: Unlike his dad, he wasn't escaping but seeking — riding *to* something, not away from it. He was making his way to answers about his father for sure, but just as important, he was closing the distance that separated him from Lisa. If she were here, Merritt Island would be heaven on earth. But she wasn't. So it wasn't. And he couldn't wait for morning.

TWENTY-SEVEN

Peyton awoke with a painful cramp in his right calf. It gripped him with such excruciating pain that all he could do was thrash about in bed, barely able to catch his breath till it subsided at last and he could rub it with liniment and walk off the soreness, pacing back and forth in Matilda's fishing shack.

He left just after daylight, dousing himself with the last of Aunt Gert's bug lotion and putting new inner tubes in his tires before slipping a hastily scribbled thank-you note under Matilda's kitchen door. Then he put on the leather gloves that were saving his hands and pedaled down the highway.

Even as the sun climbed high and the scattering of small Florida towns dotting A1A began to wake up, this stretch of highway was quiet. It threaded the waters of the Atlantic on one side and the Indian River on the other. Looking to the ocean, Peyton could see nothing but dunes, water, and sky. On the river side, he saw the weather-worn docks of marinas that had been here forever, where sport fishermen loaded coolers of ice onto their boats and prepared for a day on the water. Tonight they would gather in pubs, swapping tall tales about the one that got away.

The rhythms of coastal life had become so natural to Peyton that scenes like these no longer registered with him. They were just in the background. But right after lunch, he saw something that did get his attention — a man whose build was identical to his father's, standing on top of a dune, holding the hand of a little boy who looked to be three or four. The angle of the sun blocked any detail so that the pair were silhouetted against the blue sky. The man even had the same haircut as Peyton's father, evident in the shapes and shadows around his head when the wind blew.

Without realizing it, Peyton had stopped dead still in the middle of the highway, watching intently as the man knelt beside the boy, pointing up at the sky and a flock of pelicans flying overhead. The child clapped his hands in delight as the man picked him up and carried him down the dune, disappearing on the other side. Peyton was jolted into action by the blare of a horn and squealing tires as a car swerved around him, the driver shaking his fist out the window.

Heart pounding, he hastily pushed his bike over to the ocean side of the highway, then ran to the top of the dune where the man and boy had stood. He felt suddenly and irrationally frantic, looking this way and that, searching the beach for any sign of them. He cupped his hands around his mouth and called up the beach, "Are you there?" And then down the beach: "I said, are you there?" Looking down, he saw the man's footprints leading off the dune and followed them, placing his own feet into the indentations all the way down the beach and into the water, where they ended in yet another question mark.

The Atlantic soaked his sneakers and drenched his shorts, but it yielded nothing. And what had he expected it to give him? Some explanation from the breakers? Not just a reason why his father's life had to be cut short, but some justification for the dreams he'd sacrificed and the joy he'd surrendered, all in the name of family? What about *their* family — Peyton, his mother, and his father? Had his dad sacrificed what they might've had together for what the

234

Cabots demanded of him? Did he even have a choice? There had to be a choice. There was always a choice. Right?

His eyes were stinging, his hands trembling, and he felt both foolish and nauseated — foolish for chasing a complete stranger onto the beach and sickened by the sadness that had made him do it. He reached down, picked up a seashell, and threw it into the waves. Then another. And another. Again and again until the simple rhythm of physical motion helped him regain control of his emotions. You had to keep your wits about you out here on the road.

Peyton closed his eyes and turned his face to the sky, feeling the warmth of the sun and the salty breeze coming off the water — the healing power of the Atlantic. He breathed in the space where he imagined his father once stood until he was filled with it. And then he knew that he was strong enough to go on.

About four o'clock in the afternoon, Peyton arrived at a place he had seen circled on his dad's map — Cubano's Fish Camp in St. Lucie, Florida.

The camp sat on the east bank of the Indian River, with a spit of land protecting it from the Atlantic. Cubano's consisted of a marina with docks and four or five small cottages made of heart pine, resting on coquina pillars to lift them above the floods. There were stacks of aluminum boats and kayaks for rent, a two-story house where the owners likely lived, and a waterside café with a porch facing the river.

It was too early for supper under normal circumstances, but Peyton was hot, tired, and hungry. He rode to the café, which sat higher than the other buildings, parked his bike behind a tall flight of wide steps leading to the entrance, and chained it.

The café was dark and cool inside, its walls, floor, and ceiling made of unpainted cypress. Shutter-flanked windows, each one about six feet tall and all of them open, rimmed the café, which had a bar in the center, booths lining the outer walls, and tables and chairs sprinkled in between. Ceiling fans were spinning above, and more large fans were scattered around the place.

"Sit where you like," called a girl with skin the color of caramel and a long braid of black hair hanging down her back. She was drying glasses behind the bar but stopped when she saw Peyton, then brought a menu and a glass of ice water to the booth he chose overlooking the back porch and the river beyond. She looked a few years older than him. "You want anything besides water to drink — a beer or a Coke maybe?" Her accent was Spanish, like the girl who'd sold empanadas at the bakery in St. Augustine.

"A Coke would be great — thank you," Peyton said. "Y'all make a good cheese-burger?"

She glanced around before she answered. "No. The beef is one day from bad and the cheese is not fresh. The cook does the best he can, but there is only so much he can manage with the poor quality."

" 'Preciate the tip," Peyton said. "What do you recommend?"

"The fish jumps out of the river and into the skillet, so it cannot help but taste good. Get the grouper sandwich and some fries. You will be happy with your choice."

"Alright then. Grouper it is." He handed her the menu.

"The place will start to fill up soon when all the boats come in. If I get busy and forget to check on you, my name is Gina."

"Thanks, Gina — mine's Peyton."

Gina stood beside his table, tapping her pen against her ticket pad as if she were making up her mind about something. Finally, she said, "Do not take this the wrong way, because I am engaged, but do you have a girl? Because my baby sister, she cannot find nobody good."

"I do have a girl. If I didn't, though, I'd be honored to meet your sister."

"All the good ones are taken," Gina said with a shrug.

"How do you know I'm a good one?"

"I work in a fish camp," she said, rolling her eyes. "I know. I will be back with your Coke and your food."

Peyton looked out the window toward the river and could see fishing boats beginning to make their way in. Watching them dock made him oddly homesick — not for Savannah or any other place in particular, but for the sense of being home, of being right where he belonged. Turning his palms up, he studied his hands, where early blisters had now become calluses. Finn would say he finally had fisherman's hands.

He wondered why there was a small bowl of thumbtacks and a pen on his table but then noticed all the dollar bills people had signed and tacked to the wall. He was reading the ones next to his booth when something on a dollar about three feet above the table caught his eye — the neat, almost architectural handwriting. He climbed onto his knees in the booth so he could see the dollar better. And there it was: "Marshall

Loves Kate."

He ran his fingers over the signature. Even scattering his father's ashes hadn't delivered the gut punch he felt from this penciled declaration of love on a worn dollar bill tacked to the wall of a fish house. Maybe riding his father's road had made him appreciate both the adventure and the loneliness of it. His dad had sat in this very booth, thinking of his mother. And now here Peyton was, thinking of Lisa. He pulled out the tack and took down the dollar bill, then slid back into his seat just before Gina arrived with his food and a bottle of Coke.

"What are you doing?" Gina frowned and pointed at the dollar he had taken down.

How would he ever explain — that his parents fell in love at first sight, that they would've given their lives for each other, that family dragged them off of their idyllic island and a war drove a bottle between them, that his father had suffered in silence and his mother never gave up on him . . .

"My parents," he said, pointing at the names on the bill.

Gina looked at the dollar, then back at Peyton. "They still alive?" she asked.

"My mother is. Not my father. Not anymore."

Gina kept looking at him. "You keep it.

You need anything?"

"No thanks," he said as Gina backed away from his table. He carefully tucked the dollar into his pocket, took another from the money roll tucked inside his shoe, and wrote "Peyton Loves Lisa" on it. He tacked it to the wall where his father's dollar had been. Then he ate the food Gina brought and waited for her to come back with his check.

He had been so preoccupied with the dollar — and so shaken by it — that he hadn't noticed the café filling up. Every booth, table, and barstool was occupied, and there appeared to be only one other waitress helping Gina, who was waiting tables and tending bar, practically running back and forth between the two.

She looked up and saw him watching her. Hurrying to his table, she tore a ticket off her pad and laid it on his table. "I am sorry to leave you sitting there so long, Peyton," she said, "but the bartender called in sick, one waitress didn't show, and the cook slipped in grease on the floor and twisted his ankle. The manager is in the kitchen frying fish, and I am covering the bar. Just leave your money on the table and I will get it later, unless you need change?"

"No," he said, "I don't need change. But do you need help?"

"What?"

"I don't have to be anywhere. Can I help you?"

"You are serious?"

"Yeah. Like I said, I've got nowhere to be."

She seemed to think it over, then exclaimed, "Bless you, Peyton! You can tend bar. Come with me."

"But I never tended bar. I'm only fif—"

"Do not worry." She had him by the hand and didn't appear willing to change course. "These people are fishermen. They never order anything but beer and whiskey. Neither do their women." She took him behind the bar and showed him the bottle opener, the taps, and the shot glasses. Then she gave him a quick lesson on the cash register and pointed out a list with the prices of everything tacked to the wall behind the bar. "Anybody gets rough with you, come and get me."

With that, Gina was gone. He watched her disappear into the kitchen before someone at the end of the bar called out, "Barkeep!"

Peyton had no idea what he was doing, so he decided to imitate every bartender he had ever seen in the movies. He tossed a bar towel over his shoulder, walked down to face his customer, and said with a smile, "What's your pleasure, my friend?"

"Take a pint an' a shot."

"Comin' right up." Peyton's height and build made him look older than he actually was, so nobody questioned why a kid was running a fish camp bar. He followed Gina's instructions and soon had served his first customer and collected his first nickel tip, which he dropped into a glass beneath the bar.

As the night wore on, food orders slowed down and drink orders picked up. Peyton helped Gina and the other waitress, another Cuban girl named Leya, load their trays and collect their tabs. And he found that the more he talked to the people at the bar — rather, the more he let them talk to him — the bigger they tipped. His mother would probably call that doing a good thing for a bad reason.

Maybe so. But Peyton had decided something: Any new thing you try, from spotting race cars to tending bar, has its own rhythm. And once you tap into the rhythm of a thing, you can get the hang of it.

"*Santo cielo,* here they go again," Gina said as she returned to the bar from the kitchen, where she had loaded a tray with clean beer mugs. She nodded toward the jukebox, where a couple had just begun to dance. The woman was tall and wiry with bleached hair cut short. She wore a tight lemon-yellow dress, white high-heeled shoes, and way too much jewelry. The man was wearing trousers and what looked like a bowling shirt, only it was covered with a loud parrot print. His hair was slicked back with tonic, and he wore a thick gold chain bracelet on his left wrist.

At first, they attempted a swing dance to "Ac-Cent-Tchu-Ate the Positive," but the woman's tight dress encumbered her movement. As a slow version of "Sentimental Journey" followed, she went to her purse, which was lying on a nearby table, and took out two cigarettes. The man pulled a lighter out of his pocket and lit them both. They each took a puff and then wrapped their arms around each other — cigarettes still glowing. The dancing couple looked like two people who had been thrown overboard, each holding on to the other for dear life. Peyton marveled at the way they both instinctively stopped at the exact same spots in the music and released each other long enough to take a long drag off their cigarettes and flick the ashes onto the floor before embracing again and continuing their sad dance.

243

"Now that's something I've never seen before," he said.

Gina laughed and put her arm around his shoulders. "Peyton, I am willing to bet there are many things you have never seen before."

"You're prob'ly right. Still, I'm pretty sure this is gonna stay at the top o' the list for a while."

Gina started wiping the bar with a wet cloth. "Where you come from anyway?"

"Savannah, Georgia — by way o' my aunt's house up in St. Augustine. I've been stayin' with her some."

"You said your mother is still with us, thank God," Gina said, crossing herself. "But your papa is not. And you have been living with an aunt away from them both. He has been sick, your papa?"

"He had an accident and he was in the hospital. We thought he was gettin' better, but, well . . . he all of a sudden . . . left us."

"And now you are all the way down here far from all of them, alone. There is a reason. But you do not have to tell me. What you need tonight is family. You will come to my house."

"Gina, I can't come to your house —"

"Not *my* house. My mama's house. My family's house. You do not belong here in this fish camp." She opened the register and took out five dollars. "Here is your pay. Help me clean up and we will go."

Peyton helped Gina and Leya put the chairs up on the tables and mop the floor while the café manager worked in the kitchen. Gina told Peyton that the waitresses and bartender kept their own tips, so he poured his into a paper bag. His mother would have a fit if she knew where he was and what he was thinking: Bartending would make a great part-time job once he got to UGA.

Peyton walked Gina out and pulled his bike from behind the steps. "You came here on that?" she asked as they crossed the parking lot together.

"Yeah."

"From where?"

"St. Augustine."

Gina stopped walking and stared at him. "You got to be kidding me."

Peyton held up his right hand. "Promise. I'm tryin' to ride all the way to Key West."

"Key *West*? Do you have any idea how far that is?"

"Do you have any idea how many people have asked me that question?"

Gina gave him a dismissive wave of her hand. "Well, it is impossible."

"Actually, my dad did it when he was my age."

"I see." Gina walked along beside him for a little way and then asked, "You are honoring your papa with this ride?"

"Something like that."

"Then I will say you are doing a brave thing. You may kill yourself on that bicycle, but you will do it with courage."

They walked silently down a side street that ran parallel to the main river road. Gina suddenly stopped walking and turned to face him. "Hey, how old are you?" she asked.

"Fifteen — sixteen in June."

"*What?* I thought you were just shy of the draft!"

"Not quite."

"Never tell your mama I had you tending bar as a *bebé*," she said as they continued on their way. "You know that June starts tomorrow, right?"

"Seriously? Well then, I'll be sixteen next month — the seventeenth, to be exact."

"Fine. I will think good thoughts for you on June the seventeenth."

"I'd appreciate that. How old are you?"

Gina gave him a light smack on the back of the head. "Now you are showing your youth. Never ask a woman her age."

"Oh. Sorry."

"I forgive you. And I am nineteen."

"Where's your fiancé? He's not gonna beat me up for coming to your house, is he?"

"He most definitely would," Gina said, shadowboxing in Peyton's direction. "If he were here. But he is in the Navy. And do you want to know how crazy that Navy is? There is a huge base in Key West. But do they send Rolando there when he signs up for another hitch? No. They send him to the Philippines. That is just the kind of silly thing men do. I will bet you there is some woman in the Philippines wondering why on earth they sent her man to Key West."

"When does he get out?"

"Four more years. We are getting married on his next leave in August, and then I can go with him wherever they send him. I am saving to buy a wedding dress."

"You excited about traveling?"

She looked up at the night sky, thinking it over. "Not really. I am excited about making a home for Rolando and starting a family together. I would be happy doing that anyplace, I guess."

"You really don't care where?"

"I really don't. I will miss my family if we stay in the Philippines. But once you find the right person, you know your place is with them."

"If you don't mind my asking, how did you know — that Rolando was the one, I mean?"

"Mama always told us girls, 'The world is full of men who expect you to put them first. You find the *one* who will always put *you* first.' Most guys, they see a girl, they think she's pretty — right away, they wonder what can they get from her. Maybe a kiss, maybe more . . . When we first met, Rolando says to me, 'What would make you the happiest girl in the world right this second?' I thought he was joking, but no. I told him I loved the water, so he rented a boat and took me on a picnic to a tiny little key not far from here. And while we are there, all he wants to talk about is me — my family, my job, what I dream of . . . and I could tell he was genuine. He was real. He put me first from the very beginning. That is how I knew. That is what makes me want to put him first. Now tell me about your Lisa."

Peyton was surprised. "How'd you know her name?"

"I read your dollar, silly."

"Oh. Right. Well . . . I don't have much to say. I'm not a hundred percent sure she's *my* Lisa — not yet anyway, but I'm working on it."

"Is she tall or short?" Gina prompted him.

"Somewhere in the middle."

"What color is her hair?"

"It's this dark shade o' red like I've never seen before, and it's long and thick and wavy and shiny. I guess Rita Hayworth comes the closest to having hair that pretty."

"What color are her eyes?"

"They're blue, but they've got these little bits of green in them. Reminds me of the ocean down here."

"I see. Does she have pretty skin?"

"Like ice cream."

"And is she smart?"

"Very smart. And not just book smart either. Lisa thinks about things. She has opinions."

"Forgive me for saying so, Peyton, but she sounds a little stuffy and serious."

"Oh, no! She's lots o' fun. Lisa's a great dancer. She's easy to talk to — has a way of making you feel like you're the most interesting person in the room, which must take some effort when she's talking to me. And she's got a great sense o' humor."

Now Gina was laughing. "For someone with nothing to say about this girl, you have told me quite a lot!"

Peyton had to smile. "You tricked me."

"Why are you apart from your Lisa?"

"Well, first my dad got sick and I had to stay at the hospital with my mother, and then Lisa's folks decided we got too serious too fast and sent her to Miami to stay with some of her kinfolks this summer."

"Ah, I see!" Gina said. "Suddenly this trip to Key West makes more sense. Miami is on the way there, is it not?"

"Is it really?" Peyton said with a grin. "I had no idea."

"But that is not all, is it? I saw the way you looked at your father's dollar bill."

"I guess not. You ever gone looking for answers when you weren't even sure what the questions were?"

"That sounds more like something a man would do," Gina said with a frown.

Peyton laughed. "Maybe so."

"This is Mama's driveway." Gina led Peyton to a two-story wood-frame house glowing with light and overflowing with people. They were everywhere — on the porch, in the yard — there were even a couple of kids sitting on the flat part of the roof above the porch, their legs dangling over the edge.

"It's cool up there at night," Gina said, following his gaze to the roof. "We all come to Mama's on Saturday nights."

They were soon swarmed by the Gonzalez family, who seemed to be asking Gina questions, but Peyton couldn't be sure because they were all speaking Spanish. Eventually, the flood of relatives swept them into the house and to the kitchen in back, where a petite woman in a red floral apron stood at the stove, dishing out yellow rice, beans, and something that looked like stew and smelled unbelievable. She turned when she saw Gina and Peyton.

"Gina, *quien es este joven?*" the woman asked.

"*Su nombre es* Peyton, Mama," Gina answered.

What followed was a long back-and-forth conversation, all in Spanish, between Gina and her mother, who at first looked concerned but then began nodding in agreement as Gina went on. Finally, Peyton heard his friend say, "Key West."

Her mother put a hand to her forehead and exclaimed, "Key West?"

"*Sí,* Mama," Gina said. "*Su forma de honrar a su padre — que está muerto.*"

Gina's mother clutched the string of pearls around her neck. Then she came to Peyton, reached up to hold his face in her hands, and said, "I thought you a man up

251

to no good, but you a boy with no papa. You all alone."

Peyton smiled down at her. "Not anymore."

She kissed him on each cheek. "You right, Peyton. You not alone anymore. Tonight you sit at Mama Eva's table."

"Thank you very much."

The others made room for Peyton and Gina at the kitchen table, and Mama Eva served them steaming bowls of stew with Cuban bread.

Peyton tasted a spoonful. "Oh, man, this is good!"

"*Gracias,* Peyton." She kissed him on top of his head as she ladled more into his bowl.

"It is her *ropa vieja,*" Gina explained. "She starts cooking it early Saturday morning and lets it simmer all day. Then we all come here after our jobs so we can spend some time together."

Peyton copied Gina as she took a piece of warm, crusty bread and dipped it into the meaty stew, the richest he had ever tasted.

Mama Eva's kitchen could have used a revolving door, given all the relatives who were constantly moving through it, dipping food from huge pots on the stove, pulling pieces of bread from the loaves in the center of the table, pouring wine, laughing, and talking. Then they went into the living room to listen to Cuban music on the record player or moved outside to the porch so they could enjoy the night air.

Except for Gina's grandparents, everyone could speak English and did so now that they had decided Peyton came in friendship.

Out of the blue, a young woman who looked about Gina's age sat down across the table from them and plopped a small notebook down. "I would like to interview you," she said to Peyton.

"*Interview* me?" he said as he pulled another piece of bread from a loaf on the table.

"Rosa, that is a wonderful idea!" Gina said. "Peyton, this is my sister Rosa. She just got a job with the local newspaper and needs a good story. You would make a wonderful story!"

"Me? But I haven't done anything interesting — not till this week anyway."

"You think all the other people with their stories in the newspaper do interesting things all day long?" Gina countered. "No. They do interesting things now and then. Or maybe once in their whole life. Last week, there was a story about a mailman who rescued a cat from a rooftop. You think he saves cats all day every day? No. Just that once. But it made a good story, mostly because the mailman is allergic to cats. You are far more interesting than the sneezing mailman."

"Okay, then," Peyton said with a shrug.

Rosa settled in and began her interview, asking what he was doing, where he had come from, who he had met along the way, and what he had learned from his journey. He told her about Finn and Aunt Gert, who had been preparing him for this trip all along, though he didn't know it at the time. He described Will and the races in Daytona and the jail he had slept in. But then his mind drifted back to the hospital in Atlanta and the two hungry children he had fed. He told Rosa about Bonnie — how fearless and smart and selfless she was, and how he hoped she and her little brother were alright. Rosa hung on his every word, her pen flying across her notebook.

At last, she asked him what was becoming a familiar question: "Why are you doing this?"

He became very still and considered his answer. He wanted to be truthful, not just with Rosa but with himself. Finally, he said, "Because I'm hoping I'll find what my father did when he took this ride — and because it's the last thing I'll ever share with him."

Rosa stopped writing. Mama Eva put down her soup ladle. Gina stopped tearing bread from a loaf. All three women looked at each other and then burst into tears. Next, they were all over Peyton, hugging him and kissing him on the cheek.

"Ladies, ladies!" he cried. "It's okay. I didn't mean to make you sad."

The women all sat down at the table, blotting their eyes with dish towels and napkins.

"Peyton, you are going to make a wonderful story," Rosa said, sniffing as she talked. "And I will tell it right, you just wait and see. I will use my thesaurus and everything. By the way, I need to take your picture tomorrow morning. I am out of flashbulbs for my camera, so I need the daylight."

The kitchen grew quiet as the women kept dabbing their eyes and shaking their heads.

"Does this mean I don't get any more stew?" Peyton said with a grin.

Now the women were laughing again. "Bring your bowl to me, sweet Peyton, and I will fill it as many times as you like," Mama Eva said as she went to the stove. "And before you leave my house, you gonna call you mama and tell her you safe, *sí*?"

"*Sí,* Mama Eva."

Twenty-Eight

Sunday morning turned Mama Eva's house into a beehive, everyone gathering first around her breakfast table, then scattering to get dressed for mass before reconvening on the front porch. She insisted that Peyton come to church with her family and spend one more night under her roof before moving on. So he borrowed church clothes from one of Gina's brothers. Rosa took his picture next to his bike before they all walked together toward the church bells ringing out through the palm trees.

St. Joseph's was a beautiful old stone church with a bell tower and massive iron-hinged doors made of heart pine. Peyton's family had been members of Independent Presbyterian in Savannah as long as anybody could remember. He had never been inside a Catholic church.

This one echoed with silence. No one spoke once they entered. St Joseph's was a seafaring church, with an inscribed roll of sailors and fishermen who had died at sea hanging on a wall just inside the entrance. The font of holy water was shaped like a seashell, and the murals over the altar included the apostle Paul at sea in stormy waters. Stained-glass windows depicted seafaring scenes from the Bible — Moses parting the Red Sea, the disciples casting their nets, Christ walking on water.

Sitting next to Gina on what she called "Mama's pew," Peyton looked up at the series of carvings that lined the walls of the church — fourteen in all — depicting Jesus from the time he was tried, through carrying the cross to the crucifixion, to the empty tomb. They were beautiful and horrifying at the same time, crushing and triumphant. Peyton was feeling something in this old Catholic church that he couldn't verbalize. He just let the Latin and Spanish flow through him, allowing himself to feel what he couldn't understand.

After church, even as the family laughed and talked on their way home, Peyton couldn't stop thinking about those carvings.

"You are very quiet, Peyton," Gina said. "What message did St. Joseph send you?"

Peyton frowned. "I'm not sure. I just know I can't stop thinking about those carvings

257

around the church."

"Ah," Gina said. "The stations of the cross. They moved you, no?"

"Yes. And I'm not sure what to do about it."

"Receive it, Peyton. That is all."

On Monday morning, it was time to say goodbye. Peyton made his bed, wrote "For your wedding dress" on his bag of tips, and left it on his pillow.

After breakfast, he hugged Rosa and Mama Eva, who had wrapped him a bundle of tostadas in tinfoil. He secured it in Aunt Gert's pouch on the back of his bike. Then Mama Eva hung a small medal around his neck. "St. Christopher protects all travelers," she said. "But I have prayed special mercies on you."

"Thank you, Mama Eva," Peyton said, looking down at the medal. Then he turned to Gina.

"You remember everything I told you," she said.

"I will."

"You don't trust nobody. Who knows where those people on that highway come from?"

"I promise."

"And you change your mind, you come

back here. I will drive you to find your Lisa myself if I have to."

Peyton kissed her on the cheek. "I wish you were my big sister."

"I am — and don't you forget it." Gina hung a more delicate St. Christopher medal around his neck. "For good measure. And if you start to feel alone on that highway, you remember the carvings. You are not the only one who has felt forsaken. That is how you know you are not." She hugged him good-bye. "Now go before I cry."

Peyton set off, waving one more time at the end of Mama Eva's driveway. As her house full of family faded into the distance, Peyton felt as lonely as he had ever felt in his life. Except for Prentiss and Winston, he rarely thought about the Cabots — his blood relatives — and yet he knew he would carry Gina and her kin with him always. They were a real family, the kind everybody was meant to have, and now that he saw what one looked like, he couldn't go back to pretending that's what he had in Savannah. His mother, Aunt Gert, Finn, and Gina — they were his family now. He could only hope Lisa would want to be part of it.

TWENTY-NINE

Kate dug through the clothes in her special drawer at Aunt Gert's until her hand landed on a memory — the white dress shirt Marshall had worn to the courthouse the day they married. She had forgotten about it until now.

On the day they left for Key West and the beginning of their life together, he had taken off the dress shirt and put on something cooler. Kate tucked the discarded garment into a drawer. Over the years, Aunt Gert's purchases of shorts and kerchiefs and sailor blouses buried it, but last night, Kate had dreamed of her wedding day — of two young people so in love they couldn't see anything but each other — and she remembered the shirt.

Pulling it out, she held it to her face and took a deep breath, hoping that Marshall might somehow linger in the threads. Too many years had passed for the shirt to retain his scent, but Kate didn't need any physical traces to conjure it. Marshall had always smelled clean, with just the slightest hint of sandalwood.

Kate took off her blouse and put on the shirt. She knew Aunt Gert would disapprove, calling such an indulgence "wallowing in sorrow." But her aunt had ridden with Finn to Jacksonville to buy parts for his fishing boat and would be gone all day. That gave Kate something she had been longing for — uninterrupted time alone with Marshall.

She knew how crazy that sounded. And it wasn't as though she believed her husband would actually appear. She just needed time alone with his memory. Something told her that, until she retraced the steps they took together, she wouldn't be able to stand on her own.

Kate packed herself a lunch of cold chicken and biscuits and a cooler of Cokes, then loaded the food, her quilt, and the box that held Marshall's postcards from Key West into the *Madame Queen* and set off for Anastasia Island.

Once she had docked and settled into her usual spot on the beach, she opened the box. All these years, she had kept the postcards in order, the ones from the beginning of his bike ride on top, all the way through to the ones from the end of his journey on the bottom.

She remembered how the appearance of each card in Aunt Gert's mailbox had both thrilled and tormented her. As happy as she was to hear from Marshall and to know that he was thinking of her, she had no way to answer as he traveled from one coastal town to the next. Kate had been trapped in a one-way conversation that allowed her to receive from Marshall but give nothing back. Her only salvation was that he called her at least twice a week — but he mailed a card every single day.

The earliest ones were quirky and fun — from the Lovely Mermaid Sue to a kitschy Wild West show right by the ocean. But the farther he traveled, the more thoughtful he became about the sights along coastal Florida.

Kate read her way through pictures of beaches and palm trees, orange groves and sailboats, until she came to one that showed a smiling family of tourists posing next to a large alligator with its mouth muzzled shut. It made her sick to think of Marshall actually seeing something like that. As a teenage boy, he found it disturbing; as a man, he would consider it unacceptable and do whatever he could to stop it.

I hated this place. Any creature that's
too dangerous to be around people ought
to be left alone.
I'd give anything to be with you right now.
I'm so in love with you,
beautiful Kate,
Marshall

Next, she picked up a postcard that had
always made her want to wrap her arms
around Marshall and shield him from the
world. It was a watercolor of Florida marshlands.

I wish the two of us could steal away to
a place like this. No one would find us on
Merritt Island. It's so quiet and peaceful
and away. The only thing missing is you.
Longing for you,
beautiful Kate,
Marshall

Well into the stack, Kate read his neatly
written message on the back of a postcard
featuring Cubano's Fish Camp.

People write messages on dollar bills
and tack them to the wall of the café here.
I wrote "Marshall Loves Kate" on one last

263

night. Because I do.

> I miss you so much,
> beautiful Kate,
> Marshall

Finally came the postcard she had only read once because it broke her heart. It was a picture of Seven Mile Bridge on the old railroad Marshall had somehow pedaled across.

> Can you even imagine pedaling across such beautiful water? I've never felt so free. The water and the sky made a tunnel of color where nothing could touch me. Nothing but you.

> I love you, beautiful Kate,
> Marshall

The extremity of it — of needing a solitary ride over the ocean to breathe free — what must that have been like? How ensnared Marshall must've felt, even at fifteen, even before the burden of family obligation overtook him.

Kate put the cards back in the box and folded part of her quilt over it to protect it from the ocean breeze while she took a walk along the shore. She said a silent prayer of thanks for sunny weather and asked God to watch over her son as he pedaled his way to some kind of understanding of his father. And then she prayed that Peyton would never feel as detached from the world as Marshall so often had.

That was the critical difference between them, really. Her son could touch the world in a way that her husband couldn't. Part of Marshall was always observing, always standing at a distance, in a perpetual state of contemplation. But Peyton could reach out and dive in. He could look at a thing, make a decision, engage, and move on. Marshall always struggled with the moving on. Strangely enough, that's one of many things that made her love him so much — how deeply he felt.

Kate looked out at the morning waves curling and breaking against the shore. They made her think of very different waters, the mystic expanse she and Marshall had crossed together on their honeymoon in the Keys.

She had wanted to drive the whole way, but there was no road to Key West back then — just a railroad track that cars bumped across between trains, and Marshall said it had just about beaten him to death when he crossed it on his bike. So they drove to Miami and caught the train there. Actually, they didn't make it to Miami right away. They were just outside of St. Augustine when Marshall pulled over and they ran into the dunes with Aunt Gert's quilt. They stopped again in Daytona and rented a room at a little beachfront inn with a Hawaiian name that Kate couldn't remember, then spent another night in Coconut Grove before catching the train from Miami to Key West.

Kate would never forget how the rail cars appeared to fly across the water, which was neither blue nor gray but a shade of turquoise so brilliant that it looked illuminated from below.

Marshall took her to the platform outside the coach so she could see the whole of it as they crossed Seven Mile Bridge. "Doesn't it make you feel so free — like you're just sailing over the water?" he said.

"Is that what you want, Marshall — to be free?" she said.

"Yes. I want to be free with you."

He put his arms around her and held her tight as they glided over the ocean, bound for a place as far removed from Savannah as Marshall could get back then.

Kate would give anything to feel his arms around her right now. She shaded her eyes with her hand and looked out to sea, knowing there would be no sign of her husband on the horizon, yet she couldn't help longing for one. And she knew she always would.

THIRTY

June 4, 1947
"BIKE BOY" MAKES DARING RIDE
BY ROSA GONZALEZ

SEBASTIAN, FLA. — Alone he rides. Through the wind and the rain and the scorching heat of the Florida sun, which beats down on him with each and every circuitous turn of his bicycle wheels. Where is he going? Key West. Why? To honor his gallant, courageous father.

A veteran who served his country in the Pacific, recently and tragically deceased; a brave boy retracing his father's long-ago journey to honor his memory — it is a story of family, of honor, of remembrance.

It all began in St. Augustine, Florida. Early on the morning of May 23, as his grieving mother and beloved aunt slept, Peyton Cabot quietly, stealthily pushed his bicycle down the driveway of a charming

268

bungalow — his temporary home during his father's illness — and said goodbye to all he knew, all that was familiar, all he loved and held dear in his fifteen-year-old heart.

Now, he was alone, solitary, singular. Just a boy, a bike, and a highway. And he remains so, pedaling through the pain — in his body and his heart. Will he make it? Will he turn back? No one knows. Not even young Cabot. And yet he rides. Why? He says it best: "Because it's the last thing I'll ever share with [my father]."

For all who see him as he travels mile after mile beside the vast, majestic Atlantic Ocean, wave to him. Cheer him on. Do anything you can to help the Bike Boy triumph — over the inexorable trials of the highway, over the heart-wrenching pain of his grief.

"Mama! Mama, where are you?" Rosa ran to her mother's kitchen, waving the local newspaper in the air.

"Rosa! What is all this fuss?" Mama Eva was at her stove, turning plantains in a cast-iron skillet pooled with butter.

"Look, Mama, it's out! My story about Peyton."

"Oh! Let me see." Mama Eva took the

paper from her daughter, absently tending her plantains as she read. She pulled the hem of her apron up to her face and dabbed at her eyes. "Such a dear boy — and such a beautiful story, Rosa." She hugged her daughter and kissed her on the forehead. "I am so proud of you. Be sure you buy many copies of that paper for me to keep."

"I will. Oh — I forgot the best part! Some of the reporters at the paper — they think it might get picked up by a wire service like the Associated Press. They would edit it, of course."

"Edit *this*? What on earth for? You call that Associated Press on the telephone and tell them this story is perfect!"

Rosa laughed and hugged her mother. "I'll tell them, Mama. Can you just imagine? If the AP picks up my story, it will go everywhere!"

Mama Eva raised an eyebrow. "Whose story?"

Rosa nodded. "You're right. I'm getting full of myself. It's really Peyton's story. *His* story will go everywhere."

THIRTY-ONE

By the time he finally made it to Palm Beach, Peyton had changed more flat tires and slept in more firehouses than he could count. Rosa's story made little towns like Jensen Beach and Hobe Sound all the more welcoming as his "Bike Boy" fame spread down the coast. The Palm Beach firehouse was especially hospitable, giving him a comfortable cot and inviting him to the table with all the firemen. The chief helped Peyton get a job filling in for one of the pool boys for a couple of days at a swanky resort called The Breakers. Peyton hoped to earn enough money to take Lisa out for a special dinner in Miami — and he was making the most of the free-meal-a-day that came with his job.

It was the end of his Saturday afternoon shift, and he had just found an empty poolside table, taking a seat with a cheeseburger and fries, when he saw another member of the staff pointing him out to a woman wearing a dress and heels and carrying one of those little reporter notebooks. She looked out of place by a swimming pool.

"Would you be the Bike Boy?" the woman asked with a smile as she approached his table.

"Yes, ma'am, I reckon that's me," Peyton said, standing to offer her a chair.

"I'm Peggy Martell," the woman said as she took a seat. "I write feature stories for the *Miami Herald.* Please — finish your lunch."

"Can I get you anything?"

"Well, aren't you sweet! But no, thank you."

Peggy Martell looked like a model or a movie star. She was tall and thin, with blonde hair done up in a French twist. Her skin was tan, her nails manicured, her makeup flawless. Peyton had a feeling Gina wouldn't like her one bit.

Tapping her notebook with a pen, Peggy stared at Peyton and said, "Now — tell me the *real* story."

"Ma'am?"

She grinned and winked as she reached across the table to touch his arm. "I don't look that old, do I?"

"Oh — I didn't mean —"

"I'm just having a little fun with you," Peggy said as she leaned back in her chair. "But seriously, Peyton, I've read that piece on the wire service, and I have to tell you, I'm not buying it."

"Not buying what?"

"That this whole thing is just you paying tribute to your dad. There must be another reason why you're riding a bicycle the whole length of Florida. What's her name?"

"Who?"

"The girl!"

"I never said there was a girl."

"You didn't have to. Is she pretty?"

"She's beaut— now, wait a minute. I can't bring her into this."

"You're not! We're just talking. So you have a girl in Florida and you're so madly in love with her that you just had to see her. Is that about it?"

"Well, no, ma'am, it's not like that —"

"And she's a blonde. Like me. I can feel it."

"Her hair's dark red, but that doesn't —"

"How romantic! An alluring ginger siren to rival Titian's Venus! Does she live here in Palm Beach?"

"No, ma'am."

"Miami, then — or Key West? Does she live there?"

273

"Neither one — but ma'am, you've got this all wrong."

"Perhaps she's just visiting . . . Miami?"

"Well, I'm not sure if she's there . . ."

Peggy leaned forward and fixed Peyton with a stare. "Tell me her name, Peyton. You know you want to."

There was a time when he probably would've blurted it out, but Peggy had finally managed to conjure the image of Gina shaking her head and rolling her eyes. "No, ma'am," he said. "I can't do that."

"Of course you can."

"But I won't."

Peggy leaned back in her chair and stared him up and down, as if she were making some sort of calculation. "Well then, I guess we're finished here." She snapped her notebook shut.

"I guess so." Peyton stood when she did.

She started to go but then turned and said, "You do realize I could make you famous, don't you? I could make *both* of you famous."

"Thank you, but I kinda am already, and she doesn't want to be."

Peggy hurried to the pool gate as if she had someplace far more important to be. Peyton finished his burger and looked across the deck to the ocean just beyond it.

The sight of the surf made him think of Finn and Will. He wondered if his friend had won any more races in the number 10 car and if he was staying away from the casino and out of jail. Sometimes Peyton felt like all he did now was say goodbye — first to Lisa, then his father, then Aunt Gert, Finn, and his mother; then Will, Gina, and her family . . . All the goodbyes were beginning to wear on him. He found himself longing for reunion — not the artificial kind the Cabots orchestrated at their picnics, but the genuine reunion that Gina and her family enjoyed around Mama Eva's kitchen table every Saturday night. He imagined what it would be like to have a family like that with Lisa — everybody laughing and gathering around the table, nobody worrying about which fork to use.

Now Peyton was preparing to say goodbye again, this time to the firemen who had been so kind to him. Tonight he would tally up his money and pack the couple of extra shirts he had bought in the hotel gift shop. Then he would leave another piece of his father's journey — another fragment of his story — behind.

THIRTY-TWO

June 8, 1947
LOVESTRUCK BIKE BOY SEARCHES FOR HIS VENUS
BY PEGGY MARTELL

MIAMI — Peyton Cabot pedals his bicycle through "wind and rain and darkness of night" for the oldest reason of them all — love. You can hear it in his voice when he talks about her, see it in his eyes when he envisions her, the nameless, mysterious, alabaster-skinned, auburn-tressed beauty of his dreams, his own Titian's Venus.

One can imagine the legendary painting as he describes his young paramour, the two of them separated by fate — and, no doubt, watchful parents — as their youthful passion flames with a white-hot heat.

Early reports suggested he rode for family honor. Now we know better. We heard it from his own mouth. He rides for a girl.

276

What is her name? Cabot will not say. Where is she? Somewhere on this lonely highway he travels, with only the ocean for company.

Make no mistake — he will find her. In Miami? In Key West? Only time will tell. This much is certain: Their tender lips will meet again; they will share a longed-for embrace. Love does indeed conquer all. Even on this long, lonely highway the Bike Boy must travel.

THIRTY-THREE

Peyton had intended to get an early start, but between working his shift and making all the preparations to leave, he was exhausted and slept late. It was nine o'clock in the morning when he pedaled out of Palm Beach, determined to close in on Miami by nightfall. Early on in his trip, he had been excited by the experience, savoring every dot on the map. The longer he traveled, however, the more road weary he grew, eager for his final destination and the hope of seeing Lisa. By the time he rode into Fort Lauderdale, his clothes and hair were drenched with sweat, and he thought he might keel over if he traveled one more mile.

A group of teenagers spotted him parking his bike on the beach and draping his sink-washed clothes over the handlebars to dry. Shouts of "Hey, it's the Bike Boy!" went up, and they followed him into the water, peppering him with questions about his adventures. After that, they insisted on treating him to supper at a burger shack before he introduced himself at the local firehouse, where he was invited to stay for the night.

But sleep wouldn't come. He thought about Bonnie and Jasper, wondering how their family was doing in Fort Lauderdale and hoping they had found more prosperous circumstances. Should he try to check on them? Or would their parents take offense? He thought about his mother and Aunt Gert and Finn and Pirate. But what he thought about most, lying wide awake on a cot with a cross breeze that would have lulled him to sleep in St. Augustine, was how much cooler it would be to ride at night and how he was only thirty or so miles from Miami — thirty or so miles away from Lisa.

He slipped out of his cot, grabbed his small duffel bag, and tiptoed out, being careful not to wake the handful of firemen sleeping in the room with him. He tossed his duffel through the opening for the firemen's pole and then slid down it. His bike was parked with the fire trucks. Unzipping his bag, he took out a pair of hand-me-down Army shorts that one of the pool boys at The Breakers had given him and put them on, along with his sneakers and a clean T-shirt. Then he strapped the duffel on top of his saddlebag, put on his gloves, and made his way out of the firehouse.

Back on A1A, Peyton was ready to head south for Miami, but the sight of the ocean arrested him, as it so often did. The Atlantic was spellbinding tonight, with a soft silver moonglow shimmering on the water.

Up ahead, he saw a neon sign advertising a roadside attraction his father had marked on the map — not with a circle or arrow but with a heavy *X* as if he had crossed it out over and over, trying to make it go away. It was the Gatorama. Peyton was traveling a relatively empty stretch of highway, where occasional roadside attractions like this one were the only bridge from one town to the next. Had the sky been cloudy, he wouldn't have seen the odd shadows ahead that made him stop in the middle of the deserted highway. Even aided by moonlight, he rubbed his eyes to make sure he was seeing clearly and not imagining the unbelievable sight in front of him.

A parade of alligators was crossing the highway, apparently moving from the beach-front Gatorama to someplace inland. The four in front were each somewhere between four and six feet long, but the one in back was a monster — at least fifteen feet from his snout to the tip of his tail. Every now and then, one of the reptiles would stop and have to be coaxed along by whoever was following behind. Peyton could see the shadow of a person holding what looked like a long staff and gently tapping at a gator's tail to try to get it moving again. Then he heard a girl's voice: "C'mon now, Le Roi, just a little farther and you'll all be free o' that awful place."

Making as little noise as possible, Peyton pulled off the road and laid his bike down in the sea oats so it wouldn't attract attention from anybody traveling this late at night. Then he walked toward the alligators, which had made it across the highway and were now following a narrow, sandy path that wound through scrub pine and sea oats. Hiding behind a tall pine, Peyton watched their movements. Occasionally, one of the gators would snap its tail back and forth, as if it suddenly felt the need to smack the daylights out of something and was flailing about in the darkness, searching for a target.

Peyton could see moonlight reflected off what looked like a river or canal up ahead. The girl with the staff held a pair of garden shears in one hand. She laid down her staff, took the shears, and tried to cut something

off the lead alligator's snout. All of the gators were starting to appear agitated, but
the four smaller ones were traveling in a
pack while the monstrous creature bringing
up the rear kept to himself.

"Now, hold on, fellas, and don't go all
jeepers on me. This is gonna work. Just trust
me."

Apparently, she wasn't strong enough to
do whatever it was she was trying to do.
Peyton stepped from behind the tree and
walked toward her.

"You need some help?" he asked calmly.

The girl gasped and dropped the shears.
"You the game warden?"

"No. I was just passing through when I
saw a girl and a bunch o' alligators crossin'
the highway. I don't think you can fault me
for being a little curious."

The four alligators in front had broken
formation and were starting to slowly
wander toward the river.

"You gonna call the police?"

"Why? What are you doin'?"

"You see the Gatorama on the beach?"

"Yeah."

"My daddy bought that place for the sole
reason o' celebratin' the gators. Never once
made 'em suffer. Kept 'em healthy. Never
muzzled 'em. Folks were plenty content to

pose by the fenced-in pond he dug for 'em and listen to Daddy tell 'em why Florida gators were the most majestic creatures on earth. And after a while, he'd turn a-loose the ones he had an' catch some more so none of 'em stayed outta the swamp for very long. But then he died back in the spring, and Mama sold the business. New owner keeps the gators muzzled with a band around their snouts except when he feeds 'em so the stupid tourists can sit on 'em and get their picture made — and because he's got no idea how to handle 'em or catch more. It's cruel. And it don't respect the gators' dignity. So I'm tryin' to unmuzzle 'em and let 'em smell their way to the river up yonder. They can follow it to the 'Glades. In case you didn't notice, they're about to figure out where the water is, so if we don't quit runnin' our traps and get these muzzles off, one of 'em's liable to get away from us and starve to death with that thing on. What's it gonna be?"

Peyton had to walk behind the monster gator to get to the girl, dodging a flapping tail from one of the smaller ones as he picked up the shears. "Tell me what to do," he said.

The girl looked relieved. "Just clip one side o' the band and then get back as quick as you can."

Peyton started with the small alligator farthest in front, which was moving slowly but steadily toward the water. It snapped its head up when he slipped the shears under the muzzling band, but he held on and quickly squeezed the handles together. As the muzzle fell off and the gator opened its mouth wide, Peyton realized that he had just given a mighty predator the liberty to eat him. But the gator was focused on the scent of water and began moving swiftly away.

One by one, Peyton clipped the gators free, wondering each time if he would have to shimmy up a pine tree to escape their powerful jaws. His palms were sweating at the thought of what he had to do next: free the monster gator that could easily swallow him in one bite. Slowly circling around behind it, Peyton could see that he could lie down on the ancient-looking creature's back and still have its tail to spare. Its feet looked like a cross between a giant bird's foot and a lion's paw, and it had an odd scar shaped like a crescent moon right between its eyes. The alligator's back was as high as Peyton's waist, and he could see its sharp teeth peeking out from fearsome jaws, locked down at the moment but soon to be freed by his own hand.

As he tentatively approached its snout, the girl called out in a loud whisper, "Wait!" He stopped as she walked up to the imposing reptile and laid her hand on its back. "You made Daddy real proud, Le Roi. Safe journey to you. And remember what I told you — grocery store chickens ain't native to the 'Glades, so if you see a bird in the water and it ain't got no feathers on it, promise me you won't bite it, okay? Well . . . I guess this is goodbye."

Then she gave Peyton a nod. Amazed that his hands didn't shake like crazy, he somehow managed to stay steady enough to slip the shears under the great alligator's muzzle band and cut it in one swift, determined motion before jumping back as fast as he could. Le Roi stretched his jaws open wide, then turned his head just a little to the left, as if to acknowledge his liberator. Or maybe eat his liberator. But then he, like the others, followed the water's call and stalked slowly to the river, swishing through the tall grass, no doubt bidding good riddance to all humanity with its muzzles and fences.

Peyton handed the shears back to the girl, who was wiping her eyes with the collar of her shirt. "I'd offer you a handkerchief if I had one, but I'm traveling kind o' light," he said.

"That's okay." She was sniffling and blotting her eyes.

"Listen, that new guy that bought the Gatorama — won't he figure out who turned his stock loose?" Peyton asked.

She shook her head. "Our family don't live here no more. Mama said the beach made her sad without Daddy, so she bought a marina on Okeechobee. She thinks I'm visitin' my cousins in Fort Lauderdale. My truck's parked in a pine thicket right up the road. You better get on outta here too. Say, I didn't hear a truck or anything when you came up."

"That's 'cause I was on a bicycle," Peyton said with a smile.

"You need a ride?"

"No, I'm good. Be careful going home."

"You too," she said. "And listen — thank you."

"You're welcome. You did a good thing."

Peyton was about ten miles down the road, pedaling in solitude and moonlight, when it dawned on him: He didn't even know the name of the girl from Okeechobee. He knew Le Roi's, but not the name of the girl brave enough to free him. Peyton had stumbled onto a total stranger in the middle of the night and, without thinking too much about it, helped her rustle alligators. And then he had climbed back on his bike and gone about his business without even asking her name.

It wasn't normal, this road he was on.

Like everything else on it, captive alligators conjured memories of his father, who never could abide pens and fences. He always kept his horses in sweeping pastures with plenty of room to run, even for Thoroughbreds. Whenever Peyton's elementary school classes took their obligatory field trips to the zoo, Peyton's dad would ditch work and keep him out of school. They would go on a field trip of their own — fishing or kayaking or spending a day on Daufuskie Island, where his father knew an old Gullah woman who ran a little café off her back porch. Best food Peyton ever put in his mouth.

No pens, no fences. Ever.

THIRTY-FOUR

Not since he'd picked up Lisa for their very first date had Peyton been this nervous. He had spent so much time getting ready at the Miami firehouse that the whole company was giving him grief. They had already loaded his bike onto one of the trucks and offered to drop him off a couple of blocks from Lisa's relatives. His mother had passed along the address — relayed by Lisa — and now he was ready to go.

"Get the lead out, Romeo, or she'll be married to somebody else before you get there!" Captain Sanchez called.

All the other firemen laughed and made catcalls when he joined them.

"Lookin' snappy, Bike Boy!"

"Go get 'em, Georgia!"

"Might as well take a preacher with you!"

"Gimme a break," Peyton said, rolling his eyes.

"You won't get any mercy from this crew."

Captain Sanchez laughed. "Climb aboard, Peyton. Your hour of reckoning is at hand."

As promised, the captain dropped him near Lisa's aunt and uncle and helped him unload his bike. "Good luck to you, my friend," he said as he shook Peyton's hand.

"Thank you, Captain. Somethin' tells me I'm gonna need it in a few minutes."

"Don't let those people rattle you. Get on in there and show 'em what you're made of."

They waved goodbye, and Peyton pushed his bike a couple of blocks to a Mediterranean-style house surrounded by palm trees. He smoothed his shirt and ran his fingers through his hair before parking his bike on the sidewalk near an iron gate that led to the front entrance. His hands felt sweaty as he rang the bell.

A housekeeper in uniform came to the gate. "May I help you, sir?" she asked.

"Yes, please. My name is Peyton Cabot, and I'm a friend of Miss Lisa Wallace. I wondered if I might see her?"

"Won't you come in?" The housekeeper escorted him to a sunroom that looked like it was lifted from some island hotel. Everything was new and color coordinated, as if all the furniture and every picture on the walls had been bought from the same store

289

on the same day.

Peyton tried not to fidget, but it was hard, after all the time he'd spent waiting to see Lisa. He couldn't believe it was about to happen.

"So you're Peyton Cabot."

He turned to see a woman who looked older than his mother standing in the doorway. "Yes, ma'am. I'm pleased to meet you." Standing to greet her, he offered his hand, then awkwardly lowered it as she didn't let go of the book and newspaper she was holding.

The woman was dressed the same way her house was furnished — as if she had opened a catalog, turned to the Miami section, and ordered everything there. She was wearing slim pants that hit above the ankles and high heels, both in a bright shade of coral, with an ankle-length, coral-and-blue, sleeveless coat sort of thing over them. Big jewelry, big hair that looked dyed black. Lipstick and long fingernails — both the exact color of her pants. She had what Peyton's mother called a "nothing-better-to-do tan" — a dark hue that could only be achieved by doing little else besides sunbathing.

"Have a seat," she said.

Peyton sat back down on palm-print cushions as the woman took a seat in a matching chair across from him.

"I gather you've seen this?" She laid a newspaper on the glass-topped coffee table between them. It was a copy of the *Miami Herald* with a big picture of Peyton on the front page. He was sitting at a table by the pool at The Breakers. No doubt Peggy Martell had snapped it when he wasn't looking.

"I don't understand," Peyton said.

"Oh, I think it's pretty clear. You told this reporter that you were making this journey in hopes of a rendezvous with a mystery girl you call your very own Venus."

"Beggin' your pardon, ma'am, but I didn't say that. She said it — the reporter, I mean."

"I'm curious as to when and how a boy your age would have seen a painting of Venus, Mr. Cabot?"

"I haven't, ma'am. That's what I'm tryin' to tell you. All I said was that Lisa — I didn't call her by name — was a beautiful girl with red hair. The reporter called her that — that Venus."

"Well, just so you know, here is the image that my young, innocent niece apparently conjures in your lascivious brain." She opened the book she had been holding — some kind of art encyclopedia — and turned it around.

"Good grief!" Peyton stood up in shock

291

as he saw the painting of a woman with long red hair — and not a stitch of clothing — reclining on a bed. "I'd never talk about Lisa like that! Especially in a newspaper!"

"But you *think* about her like that all the time — don't you?"

"Is Lisa here?"

"No. Once I told her about this article so she'd know what you're made of, I sent her home where her parents could keep her safe."

"Look, I don't know you, ma'am. And you don't know me. If you did, you wouldn't think so ill of me. I care a lot about Lisa. And I have a lotta respect for her. You got the wrong idea. And you're listenin' to a newspaper reporter who'd prob'ly lie about her own mama to get a headline. I'll be goin' now."

Lisa's aunt stood up. "I'm not through with you."

"Yes, ma'am, I b'lieve you are."

Peyton hurried out of the house, grabbed his bike, and feverishly pedaled to get as far away from that awful house as he could. He stopped at a gas station to get directions back to A1A, changed into his shorts and a T-shirt, and grabbed a quick sandwich from a little lunch counter in back before getting change for the phone.

His heart pounded faster with each coin he dropped into the slot. He dialed Lisa's number and counted the rings. *One . . . two . . . three . . .*

"Hello?"

"Judy? Is that you?"

"Peyton? Where on earth are you?"

"I'm in Miami. I came to see Lisa, but your aunt said she sent her home."

"My aunt lied. And in case you haven't figured it out, she's an evil troll, but you'll never convince Mama of that. Lisa's not here. Get this — she's in Key West."

"What? You gotta be kiddin' me!"

"Nope. That's probably why Aunt Marilyn told you they sent her home. They don't want you looking for her down there. But dear Auntie did tell Lisa about that article, and said she put it in the mail to my parents. Sis was pretty sore, but she was too embarrassed to tell me why. What on earth did you say?"

Peyton fed more coins into the slot. "Listen, Judy, that reporter put words in my mouth. And now your aunt thinks I described Lisa like this painting called *Venus*. But I swear I didn't. That reporter did. Judy? Are you laughing?"

Judy was laughing so hard she couldn't talk. "Peyton, honey, you can get yourself into some scrapes! I studied that painting in art class. Ol' Venus is as naked as a jaybird!"

"I know! The reporter tricked me into sayin' I had a special girl and that she's beautiful and has red hair. That's when she came up with that Venus business, and now your aunt thinks I'm sittin' around picturin' Lisa . . ."

Judy was laughing again.

"You've just gotta stop laughin', Judy, this is serious!"

"I'm sorry," she said. "I'll straighten up. But one o' these days, I promise you'll laugh pretty hard yourself. Meantime, I can't help you much with Key West because I don't know where they are. Our great-aunt owns a vacation house on the island and invited Lisa and our cousin Bobbie Ann to come down. I don't remember where it is, but I'll see if I can find out."

"Thanks. And promise me you'll set your parents straight about that article. Please?"

"I can't do that right away because I can't let them know we're talking. But I'll straighten it out as soon as I can."

"Thanks, Judy. I owe you. Guess I better get goin'. You take care."

"No, you take care. Heavens to Betsy, Peyton, I'm in your corner, but your luck needs to change. You and Lisa are wearin' me out. Call me if I can help you."

Emotionally drained but determined to put Miami behind him physically, at least, Peyton mounted his bike and returned to the highway that would take him to his last stop on the mainland — Homestead.

THIRTY-FIVE

Kate took the *Madame Queen* up the San
Sebastian to a tiny, tucked-away cove surrounded by palms and mangroves, then
dropped anchor right in the center of it.
Spreading her quilt on the mahogany-
decked bow of the boat, she lay down and
let the river gently rock her.

In the early morning hours, the air was
still cool, the sky a soft, hazy blue-gray not
yet splashed with sunshine. Kate wasn't in
the mood for sun. Part of her wished it
would rain and rain from morning to night
— rain so much that she could climb into
the *Madame* and let the floodwaters carry
her out to sea.

It was a selfish wish, one she kept to
herself, though she imagined Aunt Gert
knew. Kate wondered how much longer her
aunt would indulge her sorrow and solitude.
Eventually, Aunt Gert would say, "Enough,
Katie — now get on with it," but so far, she

296

had exercised remarkable restraint.

With the exception of waves breaking on the shore, there was no more peaceful sound on earth than water lapping against a boat. Marshall always loved it. On their honeymoon, he had rented a spare little cottage with gingerbread porch bannisters wrapping all the way around it. The house sat high on stilts that lifted it into the palms, and it had a dock and a small sailboat. They took the boat out almost every day. Marshall was born to be on the water. He probably would have been happier as a fisherman than a lawyer.

Kate and Marshall had shared a hammock on the porch one stormy afternoon, looking out at nothing but palm fronds swaying in the wind and turquoise water rippling under the pelting rain. The air smelled of citrus and sea salt. Her face nestled perfectly into Marshall's warm shoulder as the hammock swayed with the rhythm of the wind and the rumble of thunder.

Now Kate could hear the flapping of wings above and opened her eyes to see pelicans flying down the river. They looked like feathered airplanes. Maybe Marshall should've enlisted in the Army Air Force, which he'd thought about, instead of waiting to be drafted as his father had insisted.

She knew George Cabot meant well. He was hoping against hope that the war would end before the Army came for his eldest son, who was then in his thirties. The other two had let their father arrange cushy appointments stateside, but Marshall would never do that. He said it wasn't fair to those lacking his means. And so he took his chances on the draft — a gamble that he lost.

If only . . .

Kate knew she was drowning herself in "if onlys," and it had to stop. Her nursing days had taught her that grieving people could second-guess themselves straight into Milledgeville. What happened to Marshall happened. Her husband had made his choices and accepted the consequences. And she loved him with her whole heart, always, no matter what. He knew that. Love shared and remembered would have to be enough.

Now it was Kate who had choices to make — for herself and her son. As she did every morning and every night, she said a silent prayer for Peyton's protection, asking God to guide him down the road he traveled. And then she prayed rest for Marshall's soul, asking that his tender spirit feel only peace and love, now and always.

THIRTY-SIX

The sky was getting dark as Peyton pedaled down A1A. He stopped to watch a squadron of Mustangs fly overhead — practicing night maneuvers, he guessed. What that must feel like, to pilot such a machine. He'd gotten to sit in the cockpit once at an air show during the war. So many dials and switches, all needing a pilot's attention as enemy planes buzzed in every direction and artillery fired from below.

"Hey, buddy, where ya headed?"

Peyton turned to see a couple of Army guys in a Jeep stopped in the road. "Key West," he said.

"Say, are you that Bike Boy from Georgia?"

"Yes, sir."

"You ain't gotta 'sir' me — I ain't no officer. Want a ride somewhere? It's gonna be night soon — the mosquitoes'll eat you alive and sell your bike for scrap."

"Well, yeah, if you don't mind."

"Pitch your bike in the back and climb in."

Peyton hurried aboard, and soon they were speeding down the highway toward Homestead, enjoying the cool early evening air.

"I'm Ezell and our chauffeur here is Le-Blanc."

"Peyton Cabot. Pleased to meet y'all. And thanks for picking me up."

"You lookin' for anyplace in particular, Cabot?" Ezell asked.

"I've been stayin' in firehouses mostly. Jails are too noisy."

"Wanna stay at the base?"

"You serious? They'd let me do that?"

"Most of us are already sick o' you," Le-Blanc said with a grin. "Sarge keeps all o' your newspaper articles tacked up in the trainin' room. And every time he drills us, he hollers, 'If a boy from Georgia can ride a bike to Key West, you lazy sons o' — 'scuse me, Peyton — you lazy so-and-so's oughta be able to run another mile!' We kinda hate you, Cabot."

"Reckon I better sleep with one eye open," Peyton said.

On base, the sarge did indeed make a fuss

over Peyton and wanted to see if the officers would allow him to stay in their quarters. But Peyton insisted on a bunk in the barracks. He didn't want the guys to think he was full of himself. After chow in the mess hall, he crashed on his bunk and never heard another sound.

Early the next morning, Ezell and LeBlanc were showing him the airfield when they spotted a pilot headed for one of the planes. At a distance, the pilot looked a lot like Peyton's father — tall with sandy hair bordering on blond, his eyes hidden behind aviator sunglasses. Ezell jogged out to catch him before he boarded the plane. Over the roar of engines, Peyton couldn't hear what they were saying, but he saw Ezell salute the pilot and point in his direction. Then Ezell motioned for him to join them.

"I hear you're a wing nut," the pilot said with a smile.

"Yes, sir," Peyton said.

"This one's been out for repairs. I'm just taking her up to make sure she's good to go. Want to come along?"

"Yes, sir!"

"Climb in and I'll give you a little preview of the island you're heading for."

The pilot showed Peyton how to strap in.

301

As the buckles clicked shut, one after another, whatever barrier had existed between boy and machine melted away. The plane felt like an appendage, an extension of himself that he didn't know he had. It was exhilarating. Before long, the engine fired, the props whirled, and they were taxiing down the runway, faster and faster until the ground fell below them, the base diminishing as they climbed ever higher. Peyton looked up through the clear canopy that covered the cockpit at a brilliant blue sky and an occasional drift of clouds, which looked like the cotton he used to pull straight from its bolls and stretch through his fingers when he was a little boy.

They had been flying probably less than an hour when the pilot dropped his altitude, tapped on the canopy to get Peyton's attention, and pointed down.

"Oh, man!" Peyton couldn't believe what he saw — a string of islands floating in a sea of turquoise. They must be over the Florida Keys. The pilot tipped his wings over the largest island farthest south. Key West. At this very moment, Peyton thought, Lisa was somewhere down below while he was high above. They occupied the very same dot on the map, yet they were a world apart, unable to touch each other. If it was the last thing he ever did, he meant to cross that divide.

The plane banked at the southern tip of Key West and turned back to base. Peyton could feel the mechanics of a landing in play and wondered what it would be like to have the knowledge and skill to bring a flying machine down onto a precise strip of earth without a scratch.

Once on the ground, he and the pilot climbed out of the plane, and Peyton shook his hand. "I can't thank you enough, sir."

The pilot looked up at the sky. "Think you might climb into the cockpit one day?"

"Sure hope so. I mean to try. Won't ever be as good as you, but maybe I'll be good enough."

"You never know. You might turn out to be the best there is. Here — you'll need these." The pilot took off his aviator sunglasses and handed them to Peyton. "If you're going to fly, you need to see where you're going." Then he winked and walked away.

Peyton stared down at the sunglasses, which had an irresistible pull. He slowly raised them to his face and slipped them on. Instantly, they tamed the sun's glare and made his way clear. One day, he was going to fly.

Some of the guys on base had helped him tune up his bike and put on new tires before he set off, and now he had left the mainland behind. Once on the Keys, Peyton expected to see ocean all the way but was surprised to find palms and mangroves blocking the view. It was a strange feeling. Pedaling through small island villages, past fishing camps and little motels, he would forget that he was in the middle of the ocean until a bridge pulled back the curtain, revealing the vast waters beyond the highway and redefining the supposedly solid ground he traveled: It was nothing more than a string of tiny stepping-stones floating in the deep.

Fish camps were his home as he stopped over in Islamorada and Marathon, finally closing in on Key West. Just as the sunrise pierced the darkness, he packed his bike and pedaled out to the one leg of his journey that gave him trepidation — Seven Mile Bridge, seven miles of two-lane highway surrounded by water. If he encountered any kind of trouble, there would be nowhere to go. He would literally be at sea. He felt for the St. Christopher medals hanging around his neck and turned them over and over between his fingers. If his dad could muster the courage to pedal a railroad track across the very same water — and trust the train wouldn't change its schedule — surely Peyton could manage a smooth highway.

As he started across, the sun lit the sky enough for him to see the water. It took his breath away. Neither blue nor gray — the shades of the Atlantic — the water here was turquoise, more green than blue but not quite either. With the sun growing brighter, the water lit up, as if a fire were burning beneath it someplace far below the surface.

A passing fisherman pulling a boat waved and gave his horn a friendly tap as someone leaned out the passenger window to shout, "We'll tell 'em you're almost there, Bike Boy!" Peyton gave them a thumbs-up.

By the time he was midway across the bridge, the Florida sun was high and bright, and he found himself squinting. Pulling over and getting as close to the guardrail as he could, Peyton reached into his saddlebag and pulled out the aviator sunglasses. His view of the world immediately changed as he slipped them on, just like the first time he wore them. The shadows were gone, the glare dissolved, the roadway clear. He wasn't afraid of Seven Mile Bridge anymore.

It was taking him where he wanted to go, across a watery divide to Lisa.

THIRTY-SEVEN

LeBlanc and Ezell had advised Peyton to ditch A1A when it split from the Overseas Highway on Stock Island, a few miles east of Key West, and follow US 1, unless he had a burning desire to pedal a whole lot more than necessary. If he didn't turn off, it would take him straight to Duval Street, which LeBlanc called "the dadgum main artery of Key West."

An expansive bridge between Boca Chica and Stock Island gave Peyton another infinity view of the most beautiful water he had ever seen. Fishing boats dotted the horizon in both directions, and seabirds were gliding overhead. He saw ospreys, herons, and even one brilliantly plumed roseate spoonbill.

Once he made it across, with marshland as far as he could see to one side of the highway and not much else on the other, Peyton became acutely aware of his solitude.

He was pedaling through a coastal wilderness, without a soul in sight and nothing to get him across but two wheels and his own two feet. It made him feel not just alone but lonesome. And he had to wonder if his quiet-natured father, who always needed more time to himself than most, had felt the same way. Or had he relished his time in the marshlands?

With no traffic in sight, Peyton stopped in the middle of the highway and looked around. Cicadas were singing in the Florida heat. A slight breeze stirred the palms now and again, but not nearly enough to offer a cool respite from the sun. The occasional flap of wings overhead would draw his attention to a pelican or an egret in flight. He could hear much more than he could see: croaking frogs and the occasional *plop-splash* of one hopping through mud and into the water. The call of an ibis, which was part quack, part caw, and part old man complaining. Seagulls filled any break in the conversation. Peyton had the unshakable sense that something was about to show itself, but what?

He got his answer soon enough. Out of the swamps and marshlands they came, a swarm of mosquitoes thick as a cloud, biting Peyton with such frenzied ferocity that he almost lost his balance trying to swat them away. Bloodthirsty and relentless, they showed no pity as he pedaled as fast as he could while swatting madly at his crazed attackers, cursing himself for using all of Aunt Gert's contraband bug lotion before he reached the one place where he needed it most.

As he made the crossing onto Key West, still flailing one arm while steering with the other, he followed the split LeBlanc and Ezell advised and soon could see open water. He sped off the highway and into the sea oats, dropped his bike without thinking about his belongings, and ripped his shirt off as he sprinted to the sand. Quickly kicking off his shoes, he laid the aviators inside one of them and jumped into the translucent water. Even when he came up for air, he kept his whole body beneath the surface as he clawed at mosquito bites. Peyton had sense enough to know that scratching bites only turns them into welts, but he couldn't help it.

Just as he was about to climb out, a pickup truck pulled over. It was covered — every inch of it — in seashells. A scraggly man who looked about Finn's age got out of the truck and, without saying a word, unfastened Peyton's duffel and saddlebag, tossed them aside, and loaded the bike onto his truck.

"Hey!" Peyton shouted. "Hey, mister, that's my bike!"

"Finders keepers, losers weepers!" the man shouted back. Before Peyton could get out of the water, the shell-covered pickup drove away. He ran to the highway to see which direction the truck went, but it turned and disappeared onto a side street. For all Peyton knew, it could be on its way back to the mainland.

He felt abandoned — barefoot and bare-chested, covered with itching, painful bites, his shorts dripping saltwater, stuck on an island in the middle of nowhere. Peyton sat down by the highway and put his head in his hands, battling his emotions so fiercely that he was trembling all over. He had worked so hard, and this was all he had to show for it?

A mosquito buzzed around his head, and as he looked up to swat it, he realized he was sitting next to a brightly painted sign that read "Welcome to Key West." *Welcome? WELCOME? To what? A miserable, spiteful, mosquito-ridden island at the end of the world?* He picked up a rock and threw it as hard as he could at the sign, which stood steadfast and unfazed as the St. Christopher medals softly jingled around his neck.

The rock thrown in anger immediately conjured an image of Uncle Julian. A tantrum was exactly how his uncle would react to Peyton's situation. He would lay blame on anybody and everybody but himself, howling in anger at the sand and the sea. And if there was one human being on earth Peyton refused to emulate, it was his despicable uncle.

He wrapped his hand around the St. Christopher medals, which brought Gina back to him. What was it she had said? *You are not the only one who has felt forsaken. That is how you know you are not.* Peyton imagined Gina and Mama Eva standing on either side of him. And he pictured his father in this situation. What would he do? He would take stock of what he had to work with and move forward. Peyton still had his clothes and his tennis shoes, with what money he had left tucked inside one of them. He still had his father's map. And he still had the aviators, which, for whatever reason, mattered more to him than the money and almost as much as the map.

Returning to the water's edge, he picked up the sunglasses and slipped them on, then put on his shoes, grabbed his bags, and started walking down the highway.

He couldn't imagine what he must look like — shirtless, covered in bites and welts, walking down an island road carrying everything he owned as he fought the urge to scratch. Even in the Florida heat, with his mosquito bites itching and throbbing like crazy, Peyton could see that Key West was a different kettle of fish from all the other islands. There was just something about it. Maybe it was knowing you had reached the end of the line — or that nobody from your real life could touch you here. It was just an island like all the other keys, floating in the same turquoise water, connected by the same highway, yet it was nothing like the rest.

Turning his face to the cool breeze coming off the water, Peyton felt oddly comforted by Key West, by the rustling of palms and the call of seabirds flying overhead. It was relief that washed over him now. He was hot and tired and a little bit dizzy, but most of all, he was relieved. Finally, after all this time, he had reached his father's island.

"Where you headed, son?"

To Peyton's astonishment, a fisherman pulling his boat behind a black Ford pickup had stopped to see about him.

"I was on my way downtown when an old man stole my bike."

"You that Bike Boy?" the fisherman asked with a grin.

"Yes, sir. Got covered up with mosquitoes a ways back and jumped in the water to get away from 'em, so I'm kind of a mess."

"Well, you're in luck 'cause I know just where to take you. Hop in."

Peyton climbed into the truck, grateful to be out of the sun and off his feet. "I'm Peyton Cabot," he said, shaking hands with the fisherman, "and I sure do appreciate your help."

"Wally Whitehead," the fisherman said. "Pleased to meet you. Now tell me about that missin' bike."

Peyton described the scraggly man as Wally drove down the highway. "And he said the weirdest thing when I tried to stop him."

"Lemme guess," Wally said. " 'Finders keepers, losers weepers'?"

"How'd you know?"

"That's what he always says. Peyton, you just had an encounter with Luther Bunch, the Key West Collector. He takes stuff all the time and arranges it into what he calls vision works in his front yard. But we all know where he lives, so if something we really need turns up missing, we just go to his house and get it. Luther's strange as they come but harmless. We'll swing by there and

313

get your bike, and then I'm taking you out to the Navy base near Fort Zach."

"But I need to get downtown."

"And you will. But you're not lookin' at what I'm lookin' at. You're covered up in bites and you need to get 'em doctored. Heat and mosquitoes will get you quicker'n anything else down here. Let's get you fixed up, and then you can be about your business."

"I 'preciate the advice — and your help," Peyton said. "Now that you mention it, I don't feel so good."

"Well, you just hang in there a few minutes, and I'll get you fixed up."

Wally zigzagged down a few side streets until they came to a tiny, unpainted house with the craziest arrangement in the front yard — pots and pans, an old motor, several oars, rusted metal chairs . . . but no bike.

"Guess he hasn't had a vision for your bike just yet," Wally said. "But he will. And then you can get it back. Just remember corner o' Thomas and Amelia. You need a ride, ask somebody at the base to call me and I'll carry you over there."

Wally pulled into the base entrance, where a young guard greeted him at the gate. "Mornin', Mr. Whitehead!"

"Mornin', Robbie! Ginger on duty today?"

"Yes, sir! Waved her in about an hour ago."

"I got a young man here that needs tendin' to. You read about the Bike Boy bound for Key West?"

"Sure have."

"Well, this is him. Peyton Cabot, meet Robbie Sykes."

"Hey, Peyton!" Robbie said with a smile, stepping up to the truck window.

"Pleased to meet you," Peyton said.

Robbie frowned as he got a closer look. "If you don't mind my askin', what on earth happened to you?"

"Came through a marsh a ways back and the mosquitoes ate me for breakfast," Peyton said.

Robbie whistled and shook his head. "Man, that's tough. Thought for a minute there you had the chicken pox. Don't worry. Ginger's the best nurse on the whole base. Y'all head on over to the sick bay, and I'll call up there to let her know you're comin'."

"Thank you much," Wally said as they passed through the gate.

Peyton was about to experience his second stay on a military base — a place where he was starting to feel very much at home. Something about the entrance gates, guarded by soldiers in uniform, gave a promise of protection that you just didn't find everywhere. There seemed to be a sense of shared pride and purpose. Most of all, Peyton was drawn to the clarity of military life — the certainty of knowing exactly what you were supposed to do and how you were supposed to do it.

Wally escorted him into the sick bay, where a nurse with warm brown eyes and a dimpled smile was waiting for him. "Peyton, this is Ginger, best nurse in the whole Navy."

She looked over his bites. "Boy howdy, when you make up your mind to get bit, you don't mess around, do you?"

"No, ma'am, I reckon not," Peyton said.

"Do they hurt, sugar, or just itch like crazy?"

"Little o' both. The really bad ones kinda hurt."

"Bless your heart. Come on back and we'll see what we can do about that. Step into examining room number 1 and take off your clothes, underwear and all. There's a sheet on the examining table you can cover yourself with."

Peyton hesitated. "Take off *everything*?"

Ginger lightly pinched his cheek. "Don't be embarrassed, honey. If I see anything that looks suspicious, I'll alert the Pentagon."

■ ■ ■

Peyton awoke to see a Navy nurse he didn't recognize standing over him, blotting his face with a cold cloth.

"It's okay," she was saying, but her voice sounded far away. "You're running a fever, but the doctor says it's not malaria. Just a reaction to all those bites. Can I get you anything?"

Peyton couldn't answer. His ears were ringing, and he felt as if he were floating somewhere above the bed. He tried to tell the nurse, but no words would come.

"Don't try to talk. Just get some rest. I'll be right here."

Peyton couldn't stay awake anymore. He felt himself drifting away — from the nurse's voice and the sick bay and Key West . . .

The next time he opened his eyes, he was standing on a rapidly vanishing sandbar, surrounded by rising water. A boy who looked about his age, tall with blondish hair, was walking toward him through the surf. Once they stood together on the damp sand and Peyton could see the boy eye to eye, he recognized him right away.

"Dad?" he said.

The boy nodded.

"Have I lost it?"

The boy smiled. "Maybe."

"What are we doing here?"

"Don't be afraid," the boy said. "It's just a little water."

Then he turned and waded back into the waves. He was looking over his shoulder as if he were about to say something when a familiar voice brought Peyton around.

"See? I told you you'd make it!"

He opened his eyes to see Ginger standing over him.

"What happened?" Peyton asked. He felt groggy and confused. "Did you see my dad?"

"No, honey, there's nobody else here. You ran a scorcher of a fever. And I'll bet you've been dreaming because you've been mumbling for hours. Do you remember anything?"

Peyton didn't have the energy to tell her about the conversation with his dead father, so he just shook his head.

"Are you thirsty?"

"Yes, ma'am."

"Here, take a little sip of this." Ginger gave him some ice water from a cup — the best water he had ever tasted. "Easy now — just a little bit at a time."

He tried to pace himself, but his mouth

318

was completely dry. Ginger stayed with him until he'd had all the water he wanted.

"I don't think solid food would be a good idea just yet," she said as she fluffed his pillows. "But I'll bring you a little homemade broth from the kitchen and maybe some saltines. Does that sound like it might stay down?"

"I think so. Hey, Ginger — I'm sorry for takin' up your time when you've got real sailors to look after."

She gave him a dimpled smile. "Honey, you're a welcome break from the swabbies. Don't you worry about me. I'm here to get you well. Then we'll get you some clothes and put you up for a few days, and you'll be shipshape."

"Thank you."

"You're welcome, honey. I'd like to think somebody would help one of my boys if they got into a pickle out there all alone. That's what women do — we keep you men patched up."

THIRTY-EIGHT

Peyton made up his bunk like the sailors taught him, tucked his money into his shoe, and stored his belongings in his footlocker. The base commander told him he was welcome to stay as long as he needed a bed. Peyton gave Robbie a little salute at the guard shack before walking into town for his first real look at Key West.

Duval Street was a marvel — two long, straight lanes of pavement stretching from the Gulf to the Atlantic. And it was lined with shops and restaurants, all behind storefronts that reminded Peyton of New Orleans, with their gingerbread balconies and double porches. But instead of plaster and wrought iron, everything was made of wood. Everywhere, palm trees swayed in the warm tropical wind.

About midway down Duval, a "Welcome, Bike Boy" banner was stretched across the street, fastened to the upper balconies of two facing restaurants. Some Bike Boy. He didn't even know where his bike was.

Everywhere he looked, tourists were ducking in and out of shops, restaurants, and bars, with bikers weaving through the parade of slow-moving cars coming down the street. LeBlanc had prepared him for what he called "the Duval crawl." Ducking into a shop with tropical-colored shirts and panama hats in the window, Peyton felt a blast of air from an enormous fan near the front door. He slid his aviators on top of his head and was letting his eyes adjust to the dim indoor light when he heard a female voice say, "Well, now you've gone and done it."

He looked up to see a tall, thin girl with a dark tan and short blonde hair standing with her arms crossed, openly sizing him up. She looked about Gina's age.

"What do you mean?" he asked.

"I mean those sunglasses were the only thing that made you look halfway conch, and now you went and took 'em off."

"What's that mean — conch?"

"It means you're a local and know what's what, unlike the busloads o' clueless tourists that show up every day."

"I look like a tourist?"

"Oh, yeah."

"I reckon you're plannin' on sellin' me something to correct my situation?"

"You better hope so."

"I might oughta tell you I'm not exactly a tycoon. And I've gotta get back to Georgia on what money I've got."

The girl's mouth flew open. "Are you that Bike Boy?"

"Yes, I'm the Bike Boy. Sure hope that don't end up on my tombstone."

They both laughed.

"Peyton Cabot," he said, offering his hand.

"Millie Whitehead," she said as she shook it.

"Everybody around here named Whitehead? You're the second person I've met with that name."

"There's enough of us." Millie shrugged. "Now back to those clothes. You're gonna die of a heat stroke in a heavy cotton T-shirt. It's too thick to breathe. Here, try this on." She pulled down a feather-light aqua shirt with a collar, short sleeves, and buttons down the front. "This one's cool as a cucumber and looks good on guys with dark coloring. You need some lightweight Bermudas and low-top sneaks. Skip the hats — they're for old men. And for heaven's sake, wear the shades." Millie had gathered merchandise as she talked. "Go back there and try all this on, then come out and let me have a look."

"How much is all this gonna set me back?"

"Try it on first and then we'll talk."

Peyton followed orders and looked at himself in the mirror. He already felt cooler in the lightweight clothes. And he thought he looked older, but maybe that was just wishful thinking.

"Hurry up already!" Millie shouted. "Sheesh, my grandma can get dressed faster than you!"

Peyton came out and showed her his outfit.

Millie nodded her approval. "Nice. You're lucky I know what I'm doin'. You need to buy every bit o' that."

"How much?"

"Price is relative."

"Not when you're as broke as I am."

"Okay. Normally, I'd say ten bucks for all of it. But for you, the famous Bike Boy, seven."

"Sounds like a deal."

"It is. But once you wear that shirt for a day, you'll be back to buy another one. Plus I just can't stand to see you plastered all over our newspaper lookin' like a Georgia cracker."

"Well, I 'preciate that, Millie."

"I'll put your other clothes in the charity bin," she said as she rang him up.

"But . . . I thought I might take 'em with me."

"For what? You sure ain't gonna wear 'em on the island. You'll look like a —"

"I know, I know. A Georgia cracker."

"Exactly. Trust me. You'll be back in here to thank me before you leave the Keys."

"Alright then. Give my personal effects to the needy."

"Not sure anybody's *that* needy."

"Hey! Don't go besmirchin' my wardrobe."

Millie laughed with him. "I don't know about besmirch-in' — I'm just saying you oughtn' to be caught dead in that getup."

"You're just out for a sale." He put the aviators back on and grinned at her. "But I do look good."

Millie threw a small bag of peanuts at him. "Get outta here, hotshot. Take some complimentary peanuts and be about your business. Hey, lemme see your bike."

"I don't have it anymore. Fella named Luther took it."

"You gotta be kiddin' me. All the bikes he coulda stolen on this island and he picked yours?"

" 'Fraid so."

Millie sighed and shook her head. "Guess I'll have to fix this like I fixed your pitiful wardrobe. Follow me."

Peyton fell into step behind her as she walked two doors down and came out of a cigar shop with a bullhorn. "Carlos says we can borrow it," she said. She walked down the center of Duval, ignoring the cars coming and going, with Peyton following. Once they stood beneath the "Welcome, Bike Boy" sign stretched high above, Millie raised the bullhorn and called out, "Hey, Duval Street!"

Some of the noise abated, but the tourists kept coming and going.

Again, Millie called out, "I said, hey, Duval Street! Stop in your tracks and hush up!"

The whole street grew quiet as all the shopkeepers came out to stand in their doorways and see what Millie was up to.

"Luther stole the Bike Boy's bike. Everybody keep an eye out and lemme know soon as you see it in his yard. And this — this is the Bike Boy!"

Immediately, they were swarmed as the crowd cheered and a Cuban band stepped onto the balcony of a restaurant nearby, launching into a rumba. Two men hoisted Peyton onto their shoulders and carried him to Mallory Square, with a whole parade of people and restaurant bands following. It didn't take long for the crowd to forget what they were celebrating and just celebrate. A reporter from the island's newspaper took Peyton's picture and interviewed him. Somebody handed him a drink that tasted like coconuts, and all the girls wanted to dance with him, cutting in again and again.

He must've danced for a solid hour before the line of would-be partners finally dwindled and he could sit down. A guy and his trained chimpanzee were juggling together for tips. Another fellow, wearing a striped coat with tails and an orange top hat, was riding a unicycle around the square. Girls who didn't have partners danced with each other, and a group of old men had started a game of dominoes on a café table by the street. Part of Peyton enjoyed the festive spirit of Key West, but there was always that voice in the back of his head: *This can't be real.*

The party was still going strong when he said his goodbyes and slipped away. He had never liked being the center of attention and preferred to just go about his business. In that respect, he imagined, he was very much like his father. How miserable his dad must've been to have the whole family staring at him the day Granddaddy Cabot passed the torch and handed him the estate. How miserable he must've been every gathering thereafter, when Peyton's grandfather would proudly remind everyone how grateful they should be for "Marshall's wise stewardship."

Wandering down a palm-shaded street, he found that he could step just a block or two off Duval and feel completely removed from its carnival-like atmosphere. Wood-frame cottages and two-story Victorians with elaborate double porches and verandas were painted white or faded shades of pink, purple, and green. Others, made of cypress, weren't painted at all but still had the gingerbread woodwork. The houses were tucked into lush palms and banana plants, their fronds sighing in the island breeze.

Something about Key West made Peyton feel transformed, as if he were no longer the same person because he had made it to a place like no other. The island was completely removed from all things ordinary on the mainland, living a life of its own, undetected and unrepentant.

Peyton could understand why Key West would make the perfect escape, especially for somebody like his father. The island was so accepting that literally anybody could feel at home here. Nobody stared at anything — not the chickens wandering in and out of stores and restaurants or the man walking down Duval with a lime-green parrot sitting on top of his head. Any other place, a bike thief would be arrested, but in Key West, well, just give ol' Luther a little time, and we'll figure out what he did with your bicycle. No need to get all worked up about it.

Wandering first one street and then another, Peyton eventually followed a narrow lane that ended about a hundred feet from the water, where a cottage sat high above on tall pilings. There were no cars or other signs of life. The cottage appeared to be abandoned, but something about it took hold of Peyton.

The tall flight of steps leading up into the trees was worn but solid, taking him onto a deep porch that encircled it, framed with gingerbread bannisters. Between the water and the edge of the yard, if you could call it that, was a stand of mangroves so thick and tall that they would likely block the water view eventually, but for now they just made the house feel protected. He could hear Finn advising him: *If there ain't no other shelter, why, head for the mangroves. They'll hold back the tide.*

Walking the circumference of the cottage,

Peyton could see that it was more porch than house. On the porch ceiling, he spotted two sturdy hooks about five feet apart. They likely had held a swing or a hammock at one time — long gone now. The whole structure from floor to ceiling was built of cypress. Its tall windows were all shuttered. Peyton unfastened the shutters covering one of them and peered inside. The place looked empty. He tried the front door, which immediately creaked open into a large room with a little kitchen built into one end and an oversized wicker chaise, apparently pulled in from the porch, sitting in the middle of the floor. A sole interior door led to a tiny bathroom. The rest of the one-room house was empty.

Every front-facing window had a mate on the back of the house. Its cross breezes must be amazing when those windows were all open. Finn had told him how important it was to get your windows right in a Florida house because they could save it from the pressure of a hurricane — let the storm blow through instead of blowing you away.

Peyton heard the wind kick up a bit, and the palms and bananas were now in constant motion, making a sound that was part sigh, part click as the stiff fronds swayed up, down, and around. Returning to the porch, he looked out and saw that the turquoise water, usually smooth as glass, was getting choppy. Nothing major, just a slight motion — the kind of thing Finn had taught him to pay attention to.

Peyton had the strangest feeling that his father had been here, primarily because it was exactly the kind of place his dad loved — simple, authentic, quiet, and private. Private most of all. Peyton knew that he would be oddly homesick for this little house once he left it, but his better instincts told him to get back into town before the weather broke. He took one more look around in hopes of spotting something that might connect the cottage to his dad. But the house kept its secrets.

After closing the shutters and securing the front door, Peyton climbed down the steps and headed toward Duval. Now he heard distant thunder, and the wind was blowing at a steady clip. He had traveled only a couple of blocks when something stopped him. Slowly, he slid the aviators on top of his head and stood very still, as if the slightest movement might turn his vision to a vapor.

On the corner up ahead was a girl with long, auburn hair blowing in the wind. She was standing with her back to him, looking up and down the street as if she couldn't figure out which way to go. Nobody else had hair like that. Nobody. He recognized the white cotton dress with the wide belt that had clusters of strawberries all around it.

Peyton took a few tentative steps. "Lisa?" he called out.

She immediately whirled around. "Peyton?" The wind lifted her hair away from her face and swirled the skirt of her dress around her legs. He couldn't quite read her face — was it joy or shock that he saw there? Maybe a little of both?

Slowly, they took a few tentative steps toward each other before Peyton broke into a run. Without saying another word, he lifted her off the sidewalk and buried his face in her hair. Lisa was holding onto him as if she feared the tropical winds might take her. They were indeed getting stronger. Peyton felt a few pelts of rain hitting his back as he reluctantly lowered Lisa, still holding her tight against him, and kissed her forehead.

"We have to go or we're gonna get drenched," he said with a smile.

She nodded.

"Feel like takin' a little run?"

Lisa's eyes were glistening as she looked

up at Peyton and nodded again.

"C'mon. I know a place that's real close." He took her by the hand, and they ran back to the empty cottage, making it up the steps and onto the porch just as the bottom fell out. Peyton had never seen such a rain, not even on Tybee.

Lisa's eyes were wide as she stared out at the scene — a treehouse view of tropical green swaying under torrential rain, the darkening sky above them, white-capping turquoise water just beyond the mangroves out front. Peyton wasn't paying much attention to the weather. After all this time and everything he had been through, he was actually in Key West with the girl he had dreamed of day and night, through mile after mile of heat and sweat and firehouses and strangers.

"You don't think it's a hurricane, do you?" she asked him.

"No," he said. "Just a storm."

Now they were both silently looking out at the water.

Finally, she turned to face him, staring at him with those blue eyes flecked with green — a whole ocean in Lisa's eyes. They were teary as she softly said, "This is the first time I've felt safe since I got here."

Peyton frowned and took her face in his

hands. "Did somebody hurt you?"

She laid her hands over his. "No, nothing like that. It's just that Bobbie Ann — my cousin — she's a horrible human being." Now the tears were streaming. "I can't believe I was so stupid."

"There's nothing stupid about you, Lisa." Peyton put his arms around her and held her close as the wind grew stronger, making a whistling noise in the trees. "Let's go inside. We'll sit out the storm, and you can tell me all about it."

He opened the door for her and then unfastened some of the shutters on the front and back of the house, raising those windows to let the wind blow through.

Lisa was standing beside the chaise, looking a little hesitant. Peyton realized the back was folded all the way down and quickly raised it. "It's not a bed," he said. "It's just a really big chair — with a really long seat."

Lisa smiled and sat down with him on the lounger.

"Can you tell me what happened?" he asked.

She laid her head against his shoulder, and he put his arms around her as she told him what her cousin had done. "Bobbie Ann told her mother — and me — that our Great-Aunt Maude had invited us down.

The truth was that when Aunt Maude telephoned to say she was going to Cuba for two weeks, Bobbie Ann took the call and volunteered the two of us to housesit. And Aunt Maude's so senile that she never thought to check with Aunt Marilyn — that's Bobbie Ann's mother."

"I've met Aunt Marilyn," Peyton said with a grin.

"Oh, I forgot! Was she mean to you?"

"That's one scary lady — no offense. Did Judy explain that whole newspaper business?"

"Yes. And I'm sorry I got mad. I should've had a little faith in you."

"That's okay. Back to Bobbie Ann."

"Well, Aunt Marilyn seemed glad to get rid of us. Just between us, I don't believe she's the person Mama thinks she is. I had no idea my cousin was bringing me down here, just the two of us. She's wild as a buck — goes in bars and everything — and tries to drag me into her nonsense. Last night, I walked to a little café for supper, and when I got back to Aunt Maude's, the house was overflowing with people I didn't know — including a few sailors — and music was blaring on the radio. I turned right around and went to a boardinghouse I had seen on Caroline Street. The lady that runs it

334

showed me how to rent a room for the night, and that's where I stayed."

Peyton stroked her hair. "All by yourself?"

"Yes."

"Were you scared?"

"Yes."

He wanted like everything to make her smile. "You don't have to be scared anymore because you've got the mighty Bike Boy looking after you."

It worked. He could still make Lisa laugh — and he had never realized until now that it was one of his favorite things to do, because her laugh was the best sound in the whole world.

"I want to go home, Peyton," she said, the anxiety back in her voice. "I have no idea how to get back to Savannah because I don't have much money left. If I call home, Mama will just wire me money to get back to Miami, but that would create a big mess because of Bobbie Ann. I don't want to stay with them anymore. And I don't know what to do."

"Well," Peyton said, "you're in luck because there's a highway back to Savannah, and I happen to know it fairly well."

"So I hear. Did you know you've been in a whole bunch of papers all along the coast?" Lisa asked, looking up at him.

"I did — but only because I have connections with the press." Peyton told Lisa all about Gina and her family. Then he traced his trip backward, from Will and Aunt Jack to Aunt Gert and Finn to the two children from the hospital, Bonnie and Jasper, who had lingered with him — more like something he wasn't supposed to forget than something he wanted to remember.

"There's a reason why you met those children," Lisa said. "I really believe that. Maybe it was just to feed them that one time. Maybe not. You'll just have to wait to find out, I guess. Sure wish I could meet them — all of them. Especially Gina."

"She gave me this," he said, pulling Gina's medal out of his shirt so Lisa could see it. "Her mother gave me one too — see?"

Lisa sat up and held the medals in her hand.

"That's St. Christopher, patron saint of travelers," Peyton said. He took off Gina's medal, which was smaller than Mama Eva's, and put it around Lisa's neck, letting his fingers linger against her neck as he lifted her hair and slipped the silver chain over her head. "There," he said, looking into her eyes, "now you're protected too."

Lisa was smiling, but something about her seemed apprehensive, as if she couldn't shake the image of those sailors who had scared her away from her aunt's house. Peyton remembered something Gina had told him — something he believed Lisa needed right now. "Tell me, Miss Lisa Wallace, what would make you the happiest girl in the world right this second — besides getting back to Savannah, I mean? That's a given. But what else?"

She looked out at the rain, which was beginning to slacken. "Can I only pick one?"

"Pick as many as you like."

"Well . . . I'd like to see Key West with you, I'd like to take a boat ride, and I'd like to go dancing."

"Any particular order?"

"Doesn't matter. Also, I'm starving."

"Me too. How 'bout we start with lunch and take it from there?"

"Deal."

Peyton helped her off the chaise and began closing windows and shutters as the rain slowed to a drizzle, then joined her on the porch, where she was watching seabirds fly over the water and alight in the mangroves. He reached out and took her hand. "Everything's gonna be okay, Lisa. I promise."

"Peyton," she said, taking a timid step closer to him, "I want you to know — I've missed you. I mean I've really missed you, and — and —"

He took Lisa's face in his hands and kissed her the way he had dreamed of kissing her for months now, pulling her close and holding her in his arms as he felt her breath on his face and her hands against his back. Her hair felt like silk, she smelled like gardenias, and she tasted like a cool rain in the summertime. She wasn't afraid anymore. Peyton could feel it. And there was something else, something he knew as surely as he had ever known anything in his life. He looked into those blue eyes and said it out loud: "I love you."

THIRTY-NINE

"Peyton, look — what's that?" Lisa was pointing at what appeared to be a canvas tarp splayed against the mangroves at the water's edge.

He closed the last of the shutters. "I don't know. It wasn't there before. Maybe the wind blew it off of whatever it was covering. Want to have a look?"

They held hands as they made their way down the stairs, which glistened with sunlit rainwater puddled on the old boards, and crossed the small yard. Peyton pulled the tarp out of the trees.

"I'll bet it was covering that boat," Lisa said.

He followed her gaze to a small sailboat sheltered under the house. "I didn't even notice that when I came here by myself!"

"Well, that's because it was covered up. Let's put the tarp back on it."

Lisa led the way, with Peyton pulling the

heavy canvas behind him. Underneath the cottage, he grinned at Lisa and said, "Want to go for a sail?"

"Definitely."

They climbed into the old boat, its mast long gone, its white paint faded and peeling. Peyton and Lisa sat next to each other on the only remaining seat, facing the water.

"Where to?" he asked.

"I've always wanted to see Italy. Take me to Rome, and step on it."

"Yes, ma'am. Is that Rome I see up ahead?"

Lisa peered at the water. "No, that's a sandbar. But it'll do."

They laughed as Peyton surveyed the hull. "To tell you the truth, I'm not sure this boat would make it to that sandbar. And it sure wouldn't make it back."

"Well, now, that's a problem," Lisa said. "I guess we'll just have to build our own boat. We'll need a good name for it."

"*Madame Queen* is taken — that's Aunt Gert's boat."

"Hey, I wonder what this one's called." Lisa climbed out of the boat and walked around to the stern.

"See anything?" Peyton asked. He turned around to see Lisa staring at the stern of the boat, her eyes wide, her mouth open.

"Lisa? What's the matter?"

"Come here and look," she said.

Climbing out of the boat and joining her at the stern, he read the boat's nameplate, chipped and faded but still legible: *Peyton.*

Slowly, he knelt on the ground and ran his hand over the letters.

"Do you think this boat was named after you somehow?" Lisa wondered.

Peyton rested his hand on his knee. "No, the boat wasn't named for me. But I think maybe I was named for the boat. I never even wondered about my name until Bonnie said she thought it was strange. And it is. It's not a family name. It's not a common name. So where did it come from?"

Lisa knelt down beside him and put her hand on his shoulder. "Maybe the boat was really special to your dad. And so were you. I think that's why he wanted you to share its name."

Peyton felt it again, the telltale stinging of his eyes. Only this time, he didn't hold back. His eyes welled, and he let the tears rain down as he put his arms around Lisa and held on tight.

FORTY

Peyton and Lisa needed a way to lift the heavy weight of the cottage — the questions it raised and the secrets it held. After lunch, he took her to meet Millie, who picked out an emerald-green, palm-print sundress for Lisa, along with a pair of sandals, sunglasses, and a wide-brimmed hat to match her dress. Millie also recommended a blue-green bathing suit "just in case." Peyton happily bought it all, with no thought to budgeting his funds.

"Millie, do you know if there's any ferryin' work down here?" he asked his new friend while Lisa put her other dress and shoes into a bag.

"You know how to handle a fishing boat?" Millie asked.

"Not the really big trawlers, but I know what to do on a decent-sized boat."

"Got a license?"

"Yep. But . . . between you and me, I had

a little . . . help getting —"

Millie held up her hand. "I don't wanna know." She reached under the counter, pulled out a paper map of downtown Key West, and drew the path Peyton needed to follow. "Once you get to the marina, ask for Captain Wally Whitehead and tell him I sent you."

"Hey, he's the other Whitehead I told you about — the one who gave me a ride to the base," Peyton said.

"Whole island would sink right into the ocean without us. If he thought you were worth helpin' once, he'll help you again."

Outside, Peyton slipped on the aviators and took Lisa by the hand. "Where to, ma'am?"

"No place in particular," she said. "Can we just ramble?"

They wandered both sides of Duval Street, in and out of shops selling everything from hats and sunglasses to books and Cuban cigars, stopping now and then for a Coke or a limeade or a scoop of mango ice cream.

Lisa drifted toward an open-air restaurant where a Cuban band was playing to a packed dance floor. "Never saw moves like that before," Peyton said as he stood behind her, looking over her shoulder. "Wonder if Aunt Gert knows how to do that."

"From what you've told me, I'll bet Aunt Gert knows how to do everything."

"Want to give it a try?" Peyton suggested.

"You mean dance like that?"

"Well, we're here . . ."

Lisa peered through the entryway, watching the dancers, then tried to help Peyton mimic the steps. "Okay, your left hand goes on my waist and mine goes on your shoulder . . ."

They were taking their first awkward steps on the sidewalk outside the restaurant when they heard a voice behind them. "The danzón is not about counting. It is about courting."

They turned to see an older man, probably in his seventies, watching them from a few yards away. His skin looked like fine leather aged to a rich brown, and his hair was white as a cloud. He wore white linen trousers and a pale blue shirt with short sleeves, a panama hat with a black band, and black leather sandals.

"Sir?" Peyton said.

"You are counting," the man repeated. "You should be courting."

"What do you mean?" Peyton asked.

The man took an imaginary partner in his arms and danced his way to Peyton and Lisa. His steps were smooth and easy, his eyes never leaving the invisible woman dancing with him. When he stopped, he gave them a little bow and said, "I am Silvio."

"Pleased to meet you." Peyton shook the stranger's hand. "I'm Peyton and this is Lisa."

"You are not conch?" Silvio said.

"No, sir," Peyton said. "Kinda wish we were, though."

"What's conch?" Lisa asked Peyton.

"It means local."

Silvio took a few more dance steps with his imaginary partner. "You wish to dance *como un Cubano*?" he asked them.

Peyton looked at Lisa, who shrugged and said, "We're here, like you said."

"Will you teach us?" Peyton asked Silvio.

The man gave them a little bow. "It would be my pleasure."

"Is there — I mean — we don't have a lot of money . . ."

"No, no, no," Silvio insisted. "I do not teach for money. I teach for . . . well, for love, I suppose. Now we begin. How would the two of you be standing if you were about to kiss?"

Lisa blushed.

"Do not be embarrassed," Silvio went on. "It is the most natural thing in the world

345

for a man to kiss a woman. Now. How would you stand?"

Peyton and Lisa turned to face each other, almost touching. "Like this, I guess," Peyton said to Silvio, who rolled his eyes.

"And would you be looking at me — an old man — if you were about to kiss this beautiful girl?"

"No offense, Silvio, but if I were about to kiss Lisa, you wouldn't be here."

"Ha! Now we are getting somewhere. You would wish to be alone in the moonlight at such a time, yes?"

Peyton looked down at Lisa. "Yes. I would want to be alone in the moonlight."

"Well then, let us prepare you for the moon. Put your arm around her waist . . . Yes, very good. Now take her hand . . . Yes, like that. Señorita Lisa, put your free arm around his shoulder . . . No, not against it but around it. You want to embrace him, not push him away. Yes, that's it! Now, you walk toward your Peyton and then you back away, but he comes with you because he cannot bear to be apart from you . . . Yes! Now you walk to the side . . . Very good. And now you walk back . . . *Excelente!* And now you pause to think only of each other . . . Yes! And now you walk again. There. You have learned the danzón. Now go inside and let the music take the place of the moon."

"What about you?" Peyton asked, still holding Lisa in his arms.

"My dance partner is waiting for me at home." Silvio tipped his hat. *"Adios."*

"Adios — and *gracias!"* Peyton called after him. He looked at Lisa and gave a little nod toward the dance floor. "What do you think?"

"Como un Cubano," she said with a smile.

They stepped inside the restaurant, which was dim and cool compared to the sun-drenched street. All the couples on the dance floor, moving in unison to the slow back-and-forth of the danzón, reminded Peyton of palm trees swaying in a tropical storm. Each couple had eyes only for each other, and yet they were all moving together — each pair oblivious to all the others yet dancing to the same rhythm.

Peyton and Lisa found a small empty spot, held each other close, and began the danzón. The music was slow and languid, the rhythm so entrancing that Peyton lost all sense of his own movements and could see only Lisa, her slender arm wrapped around his shoulder, her hand grazing his neck, her breath on his face as she looked up at him in a way that made his heart stop.

But then the music changed. The tempo accelerated to a heated, driving rhythm, and the movements of the older dancers around them grew faster and more passionate. Lisa's dreamy smile vanished, and her face was overcast with the same look of fear and uncertainty that she'd had at the spring formal, surrounded by strangers on unfamiliar territory.

Peyton bent down and spoke into her ear so she could hear him over the music. "Miss Wallace," he said, "we are in over our heads." He grinned and winked at her, which made her laugh. Peyton put his arm around her, guiding her through the other dancers and back outside.

"You think I'm being silly?" Lisa asked, squinting in the bright sunlight as she looked up at him.

"I was just starting to get the hang of it when you bailed," he said, doing an exaggerated hip swivel.

"Stop!" Lisa said, laughing. "You're really not mad?"

"Of course not. How about we do something a little more Americano? Want to rent a scooter and see the sights?"

"Yes! That sounds entirely tame. Right down my alley."

Peyton found a rental stand, and Lisa

chose a bright red scooter. They zipped up and down streets, her arms wrapped around him, stopping whenever she spotted something she wanted to see or do. The first time Peyton forgot himself and really hit the throttle, he was about to slow down and apologize when he realized Lisa was giggling uncontrollably. He pulled over and asked her, "What's so funny, Miss Wallace?"

"Nothing," she said, still laughing. "It's just so much fun to go fast!"

"That seals it," Peyton said over his shoulder. "You're officially perfect."

They took off for Fort Zach and the beach just beyond the guard shack. It was nothing like Daytona, with its broad sandy beach and big waves. This narrow strip of sand fronting calm turquoise water was bordered with grass and palm trees, an occasional picnic table here and there.

Peyton and Lisa sat on one of the tables, resting their feet on the bench, and watched sailboats drift by on the glassy water.

"It's so strange," Lisa said. "Yesterday I hated this place, and today I absolutely love it. Guess I've got you to thank for that."

Peyton kissed her on the cheek. "And I've got you to thank for makin' this whole bloomin' bike ride worth every blister and mosquito bite."

He mimed scratching himself all over, which made Lisa laugh. But then her smile faded and she looked into his eyes. "Were you ever scared — out there on the road all by yourself, I mean?"

He brushed her windblown hair away from her face. "Not really — a little anxious sometimes, but not Rawhead's-after-me scared."

"Rawhead?" Now Lisa was laughing again. "I haven't thought about him since I was about ten!"

"Well, you better watch out, little missy, 'cause he'll gobble you up if he catches you out at night."

They both giggled at the memory of the childhood bogeyman. Then Lisa sighed and slowly twisted a strand of her hair through her fingers. "Remember when I told you about the night I came back from dinner and all those people were at Aunt Maude's?"

Peyton felt like a wave was coming at him, as if something he couldn't dodge or prepare for was about to hit him. "Yes . . . Did something happen, Lisa?"

"No. But it could have if I'd stayed — if those sailors had seen me before I saw them. They all had beer bottles in their hands, and there were empty ones all over the yard. They were loud and rowdy, shoving each

350

other around and staggering. Scared me to death. And I've just been wondering . . . was it like that for you — with your daddy, I mean? Was it scary for you when he drank? Have you been scared like I was all this time?"

"Yes and no," he said, looking at her. "I was scared, but for him, not for me. I knew if Daddy ever hurt anybody it would be himself. Mostly I was just sad for him. And for Mama. It was like this person we didn't know had kidnapped Daddy, and we couldn't figure out where he was or how to get him out o' there. It's just hard for me to believe that neither one of us could help him. I keep thinking if I had done just one more thing . . . but I have no idea what that would've been."

Lisa's beautiful eyes were getting misty.

Peyton laid his hand against her face and kissed her. "I'm makin' you sad. I don't ever want to do that." He put his arm around her as they looked out at the water. "Tell you what. Let's ride by the marina and see if I can get a job — that'll cover your boat ride — and then swing by crazy Luther's house to look for my bike. After that, we'll head down to Mallory Square for the sunset. Then, well . . . we'll figure out how to get home."

Peyton's luck had definitely taken a turn for the better. Millie's cousin Wally gave him a job ferrying a fishing boat to Fort Lauderdale. And now he and Lisa had found the bike. They parked the scooter at the corner and stood together, speechless, facing Luther's yard.

"It's — it's just so — so *beautiful*," Lisa finally said. "Why is it beautiful?"

Luther had completely cleared his little patch of front yard, removing all the other vision works Peyton had seen there before. In their place, in the center of the lawn, was a singular work of art, a giant abstract peacock with a red bicycle at the center — the body of the bird — and a fan of tail feathers. Each one was at least twelve feet tall and made of every conceivable scrap of metal, from pipes to skillets, all welded together. Luther had used fishing line to attach pieces of colored glass, which caught the light and glistened in the sun.

So stunned were they that Peyton barely noticed someone walking up the street. By the time he realized it was Luther himself, the artist was standing right next to them. "Finders keepers?" Luther said timidly to

Peyton, who couldn't stop staring at the incredible sculpture — scraps of metal and glass transformed into a breathtaking bird.

He turned to Luther and nodded. "Finders keepers."

FORTY-ONE

Mallory Square was like a daily Mardi Gras. The whole island, it seemed, gathered there to watch the sunset, and street performers took advantage of the crowd, miming, dancing, swallowing fire — anything and everything to get attention and tips. Peyton held Lisa's hand and escorted her to the edge of the square, finding an empty spot on the waterfront. He put his arm around her as they took a seat and dangled their feet over the ocean.

The sun looked like a giant coral balloon they could reach out and touch as it slowly drifted down from the sky. Its orange glow was casting light on the turquoise water, making colors Peyton had never seen before. Lisa, as she so often did, seemed to read his mind when she said, "Those colors aren't in my crayon box."

As the sun dropped lower, the water changed colors from luminescent turquoise to deep blue, and the whole sky dissolved into shades of pink and coral. Now the big orange globe looked as if it were only a foot or so from the water.

"I half expect it to splash when it hits the ocean," Lisa said.

"It just looks so close," Peyton agreed. "Somebody told me there's a green flash on the water right when the sun disappears."

They kept their eyes on the sun, now slipping faster and faster into the ocean. Just as it fell below the horizon, a split-second flash of green kissed the water and the whole crowd gasped and applauded.

"Did you see that?" Lisa exclaimed.

"I did," Peyton said. He was about to kiss her when he felt a tap on his shoulder.

An older woman who reminded him of Aunt Gert smiled and handed him a sketch. "You two made my sunset," she said. "This one's on the house." Then she disappeared into the crowd.

The woman had drawn Peyton and Lisa from behind, not in any detail but with well-placed lines and curves that let the viewer's imagination fill in what was missing: A boy and a girl sat very close, dangling their feet off the edge of Mallory Square, his arm wrapped around her. An island wind was blowing her long red hair. Both were silhouetted against a giant orange sun, the turquoise sea before them.

"We look happy," Lisa said.

"How can you tell from the back of our heads?" Peyton teased her.

"I just can."

Behind them, the crowd was celebrating the sunset with laughter and music and every kind of revelry. But Peyton could barely hear them as he laid his hand against Lisa's face, leaned over, and softly kissed her. "I owe you a dance, don't I?" he asked her.

"Yes," she said, so quietly that he could barely hear her. He helped her up, then took the drawing and put it in the bag with her clothes, which he had strapped to the scooter.

They heard music coming from somewhere nearby and followed it to a bandstand at the end of a wide pier just off the square. Peyton heard the familiar drumbeat of "Sing, Sing, Sing" and turned to Lisa. "Miss Wallace, may I have this jitterbug?"

"I don't know how!"

"You're the best dancer in the whole school! If Aunt Gert can teach me, I can teach you."

Lisa was light on her feet, quickly mastering every step, twirl, and kick.

When the music stopped, Peyton found two barstools beside the pier railing and bought them limeades from the concession stand. "You could've at least made it look hard," he said.

"Hard to breathe, with you making me laugh the whole time. Oh, Peyton, look!" Lisa pointed to the sky, where a gorgeous moon was raining light on the water. "It's just a little sliver of moon in the sky, but it's so bright. Isn't it beautiful?"

"I got to see the Strawberry Moon right after I left Gina and Mama Eva. Finn said it would bring me good luck. And it has."

"Was it any prettier than this one?"

Peyton turned his attention to the night sky. "No. Because this one's shining on you. Hey, wait a minute. I saw the Strawberry Moon — so this is June."

Lisa frowned at him. "Yes. This is June."

"What day?"

"The seventeenth, why?"

Peyton slapped his knee. "Now *this* has got to mean something. June the seventeenth is my birthday. I got you and a perfect slice o' moon for my birthday. Not bad, Miss Wallace. Not bad at all. You should probably dance with me or something. Listen — they're playing our song."

"I didn't know we had one."

"Sure we do. It's . . . that song playing on the jukebox."

Lisa listened intently till she could make out the tune. " 'Dream a Little Dream of Me.' That's a good one. Let's claim it before somebody else does."

They walked onto the dance floor, which had thinned out with the band on break and a jukebox filling in. "You mind dancing to an ol' jukebox?" he asked as he took her in his arms.

"I'm not dancing to a jukebox," Lisa said, looking up at him and smiling. "I'm dancing to Ella and Louis, with you, over the ocean."

Satch and Ella Fitzgerald crooned about the stars and the night breezes and little kisses as Peyton felt the graceful curve of Lisa's back beneath one hand, her soft palm in the other. He bent down and gave her a lingering kiss he hoped would never end. She looked up at him and said, almost in a whisper, "Happy birthday . . . And Peyton . . . I love you too."

FORTY-TWO

Kate sipped her morning coffee and watched Aunt Gert crumble two strips of bacon into Pirate's bowl. The clouds were thick in the sky, giving hope for a rain.

Aunt Gert filled two plates with scrambled eggs, bacon, and fried plantains — Kate's childhood favorite — then joined her at the table. "You'd already gone to bed when Finn brought me back last night," Aunt Gert said. "Did Peyton call?"

Kate nodded, picking at her eggs with her fork.

"Anything wrong, Katie?"

Again, Kate only nodded as she kept fidgeting with her fork, staring at her plate.

"Well, honey, is he hurt? Is he in trouble?"

Kate shook her head. Finally looking up at her aunt, she put down her fork and flatly said, "I'm a terrible mother." Tears were streaming down her face, though she didn't make a sound.

"Come with me," Aunt Gert said, leading Kate outside, down to the river dock, and into the *Madame Queen*. She untied the boat and drove them to the slough that had always been Kate's favorite, then dropped anchor in the center of it and shut off the engine. They sat together, listening to the water slap against the boat and letting the river soothe them with its rocking.

At last, Aunt Gert looked up at the sky and said, "Now tell me, Katie, what's all this 'terrible mother' business? You're a wonderful mother and always have been."

"What kind of mother lies to her son?"

"I imagine most of 'em at one time or another. You'd walk in front of a train for Peyton, and you know it."

Kate pulled her feet up in the seat and rested her chin on her knees. "He found Lisa, and I've never heard so much happiness in his voice." She smiled at the memory of it. "He's so in love with her, Aunt Gert."

"And you're afraid there won't be room for you? Because that's not true."

"No, that's not it. He found the cottage — the one where Marshall and I stayed on our honeymoon. The sailboat was still there. Peyton said it was beached, but he could still make out the name. He said he knew right away Marshall had been there and had named him for that sailboat. He wanted to know why. I made up something vague — that it had been special to him and he wanted to share it with Peyton. I never even told him we spent our honeymoon there."

"What's the truth of it, Katie?"

"That we never wanted to share that moment in our lives with anybody. That we wanted it to be ours and ours alone. We named Peyton after the sailboat because we wanted to remember it always — and remember to protect him from anything that might deny him a whole life of sailing, if that makes any sense."

"So you wanted a little moment as a couple, and you wished for your child a whole lifetime of moments that special? You're right. You're a terrible person. I don't see how you live with yourself."

Kate looked up to see Aunt Gert smiling at her.

"Katie, do you think you and Marshall are the only husband and wife to wrestle with the dividin' line between bein' a couple and bein' parents? Because you're not. So you wanted to keep something for yourselves — that's true of every man and woman who ever loved each other. Doesn't mean you love Peyton any less. Marshall would've died for him, same as you."

"But Aunt Gert, when I realized he had found Lisa and they had spent a rainy afternoon in the exact place where Marshall and I had been so happy . . . I felt . . . I felt jealous. What kind of mother is jealous of her own child?"

"You're not jealous of Peyton. You just feel cheated, and not by him. Right now he's feelin' for the first time something you remember all too well and weren't ready to give up when it was taken from you. That's normal, Katie. Answer me this: If Peyton had called and told you he couldn't find Lisa and was lyin' miserable and alone in some Key West firehouse, would you be happy about that?"

"Of course not. I can't stand it when he's unhappy, and I'd never ever want him to be lonely."

"Well then? You don't want to deny him any happiness, and you don't want what he has. You just miss what you had. That's not jealousy. That's grief."

Kate stretched her legs out and leaned back in her seat, looking up at the gray sky overhead. "I don't know how to do this, Aunt Gert — how to get to a place where I can carry Marshall with me without crying all the time."

"Every widow who truly loved her husband has wondered the exact same thing. That includes me. Some days, I still wonder it. Look, Katie, I know you've been waitin' for me to tell you enough is enough and get on with it and all that, but it's not gonna happen. You have to come to terms with losin' Marshall in your own way. I'm here to give you all the time and space you need — and to help Peyton through it so the burden's not all on you. There's no dodgin' this one, honey. And there are no shortcuts. It has to be gotten through, one day at a time, one memory at a time, before you can move on. Grievin' ain't for lightweights, Katie. But you're no lightweight."

Kate and Aunt Gert were enjoying their evening glass of sherry when the doorbell startled them both. "Who on earth is ringin' that thing?" Aunt Gert asked, leaving the table to answer the door.

Kate listened as her aunt said, "Oh, yes! Of course I remember you. He's not with you, is he?"

The screen door opened and shut before footsteps approached the kitchen and Aunt Gert walked in with Julian's wife.

"Eileen?" Stunned, Kate stood up to greet her sister-in-law. "What are you doing here?"

"May I sit down?" Eileen asked.

"Of course! Please forgive me. It's just — I'm so surprised to see you."

Aunt Gert poured a glass of sherry for Eileen and joined them at the table.

Eileen was a petite brunette with pale skin and gray eyes. Though she was an attractive woman, she had a strange air about her that suggested what she wanted more than anything was to be invisible. Kate had never seen her wear anything but a simple dress in a muted color. Tonight, however, she was in white capris, sandals, and a bright pink blouse.

"I guess you're wondering where Julian is," Eileen began.

"Not so much," Aunt Gert said.

"The short answer is, I don't know where he is and I don't care. The long answer is, I finally left him, which I should've done the day after I married him — maybe during the reception."

"Left him?" Kate couldn't believe what she was hearing. Eileen was the quintessential subservient wife. Julian treated her like the help and talked to her like she didn't have sense enough to get in out of the rain.

"Good for you," Aunt Gert said. "Smartest thing you ever did."

Kate tried to intervene. "Aunt Gert —"

"Well, it's the truth! She knows it — don't you, Eileen, honey?"

Eileen nodded and took a sip of her drink. "I came here, Kate, because I wanted to tell you how sorry I am about Marshall — and how sorry I am that I wasn't there for you when he died. I wanted to be. Julian wouldn't have it."

Kate reached over and squeezed Eileen's hand. "I know what you were up against."

Eileen looked at her with empty eyes. "Some kinds of abuse don't leave bruises — not the kind you can see anyway. Julian doesn't love me and never did. I don't think he's ever loved anybody but himself. He wouldn't know how. I'm just thankful we never had kids. I don't think I could live with myself if I had subjected children to him."

"This isn't your fault, Eileen," Kate said. "Julian's to blame — entirely."

"Is he?" Eileen asked.

Kate expected tears but saw none. Normally eager to please and placate, Eileen was now blunt and resolute.

"I let myself be fooled for ten long years. And then after I finally opened my eyes, it took me two more to muster the courage to leave him. He told me I was nothing, and I believed him."

"You're far from nothing," Kate said.

"I know — deep down, I know. I just need some time to remember who I am — who I used to be."

"Honey, if you don't mind my asking, what set off the alarm clock?" Aunt Gert asked. "After all this time, I mean?"

Eileen's fingers were lightly wrapped around the stem of the sherry glass. She was slowly turning it back and forth.

"Aunt Gert," Kate said, "Eileen might not feel like talking."

"No, it's okay," Eileen said, looking up. "It was the way he treated Marshall — after he died, I mean. You and Marshall were the only members of that whole Cabot clan who were ever kind to me. The first time Julian cut me off at the knees and absolutely humiliated me in front of all of them — it was the Christmas right after we married — I went running into the kitchen in tears. You and Marshall followed me out and took me to your house to recover. Marshall promised to set up a trust fund for me so I'd have some security if I ever left Julian. He did it too. Did you know that, Kate?"

"Yes."

"Of course, back then, I never dreamed of leaving my husband. But Marshall knew I'd have to one day. Over and over, I told myself

Julian hadn't meant to be hurtful and would be so sorry when he realized what he'd done. How stupid."

Kate laid her hand on her sister-in-law's arm. "You were never stupid," she said. "You just assumed he had a heart. Turns out he doesn't."

"After Marshall died, Julian started giving me all kinds of orders, things he wanted me to do at your house — mostly destroying everything that meant anything to you and Marshall. I'm sure it doubled the thrill for him — making me hurt you, knowing how much I hated doing it."

"Eileen, I know you would never —"

"No, please, Kate — let me get through this. I stalled him for the longest time by sorting and stacking and organizing. He saw through that, of course. A couple of days ago, as he was leaving for work, he gave me this big smile, kissed me on the cheek, and said, 'My dear, you've done a fabulous job organizing everything at Marshall's. Before I get home tonight, I want you to take each and every one of your neatly organized stacks and set it on fire.' And then he walked out the door as if he'd just told me not to forget to buy milk at the Winn Dixie."

Aunt Gert retrieved the sherry and refilled their glasses. "Land o' Goshen," she said.

"What on earth did you do?"

"I went to your house, Kate, and I filled a suitcase with all the jewelry and pictures and letters I could fit into it — anything sentimental I thought might mean something. That's actually how I knew where to find you — there were so many letters from this address. And then I carried the suitcase to the post office on Tybee where nobody knows me and had it shipped here. It should get here any day. I wasn't sure I was leaving right then. I don't have any friends in Savannah — Julian saw to that — so I thought I might just check in to a hotel in Charleston. But then once I got started, all I wanted to do was get as far away from him as I could. I drove over to Marshall's law office and asked his partner to help me move the trust fund someplace overseas where Julian couldn't touch it, which he did, and get me plenty of cash to travel on, which he also did, and draw up divorce papers, which he'll present to Julian next week. Then I chartered a boat from St. Augustine to the Bahamas — it leaves tomorrow morning. I spent last night in a little beach cottage at Fernandina — just needed a little time to collect myself, I guess. And now I'm here."

"Honey, do you mean to tell me you're

fixin' to up and move to those islands with nothin' but the clothes on your back?" Aunt Gert couldn't believe it.

"The clothes on my back and plenty of money," Eileen said. "Julian will contest the divorce, but I don't care. I'm going to a place where it won't matter what's on paper."

Aunt Gert stood up and clapped her hands together. "Well, Eileen, honey, I glory in your spunk! Let's celebrate your liberation." She raised her glass. "To liberty and happiness!"

Eileen smiled for the first time since she'd arrived as she and Kate raised their glasses. "To liberty and happiness."

FORTY-THREE

Peyton waited patiently in a porch swing, watching the island wake up. In the pinkish-gray light of early morning, he could see the occasional bicycle cruising down the street or a milk truck heading out for its rounds. Now and then, a few chickens crossed the small square lawn of the boardinghouse where Lisa was staying. It was women only, and the owner, Miss Flossie, wouldn't even let Peyton inside the front parlor. When he rang the bell, she eyed him suspiciously, snatched Lisa's hand-washed sundress hanging from a hook on the front porch, and told Peyton to take a seat in the swing. He was relieved to see the green dress come back through the doorway, this time worn by Lisa, the blue-green straps of her new bathing suit peeking out just a bit. He had worn a T-shirt over his swimming trunks.

"Morning," he said with a smile, giving

her a kiss on the cheek. "Just in case Miss Flossie's watchin', I'll give you a churchyard kiss."

"Oh, she's watching," Lisa said.

They hopped on the scooter and drove to a beach the guys on base had told Peyton about. It now seemed like the most natural thing in the world to have Lisa's arms around him, a tropical breeze in his face, and turquoise water all around. They parked and found a couple of empty beach chairs. Peyton covered them with towels he had borrowed from the base while Lisa, who was not comfortable taking her dress off in front of all the sunbathers, went to one of the bathhouses.

Watching her walk back across the beach in a bathing suit the color of the ocean, her long red hair blown back by the wind, Peyton thought he might actually faint.

Lisa carefully folded her dress and slipped it into a beach bag she had brought along. "Ready?" she said.

"Yes, ma'am."

Peyton and Lisa held hands and waded into the water, which was smooth as glass, lit by the sun in amazing shades of ocean. Key West was known for shallow waters around its beaches. By the time Peyton and Lisa were in deep enough to swim, they were distant from the families with children happily splashing in ankle-deep water. They swam to a huge sandbar, part of it barely submerged, and lay down on the dry end, letting the cool water wash over their legs.

"Miss Wallace, you are gonna have a ton o' sand in your hair," Peyton said lazily as he gazed at her face glistening from the sun and water, her eyes closed, her red hair salted with sand.

"Yes, I am going to have a ton of sand in my hair," she said with a sigh, "but I don't care." She opened her eyes and stared into his. "You know what's so wonderful about being here, Peyton?"

"I'm looking at her."

Lisa smiled and took his hand. "What's wonderful about being here is that we only have to think about what we're doing — not what other people think we're *going* to do. Back home, if all our friends were out there on the beach, we couldn't lie here alone together on a sandbar because everybody would say it doesn't look right. I feel like I hear that every day of my life: 'You can't do this and you can't do that because it wouldn't look right.' Shouldn't you be judged by what you actually do — not what other people think you *might* do?"

"I don't think it makes sense to spend a

lotta time worryin' about what other people think as long as you do what you believe is right. Everybody has a true *them* that they're meant to be. I think that's why Daddy came down here. He was lookin' for his."

"Do you think he found it?"

Peyton propped on his elbow, looking down at Lisa. "Yeah. I think he did. But the sad thing is, he left it here. I don't want to do that, Lisa. Because there's something else I've figured out. You can't follow anybody else's path, like I tried to do with Daddy — like Daddy thought he had to do with Granddaddy. Somewhere along the way, you gotta draw your own map."

Staring into her blue eyes, he traced the lines of her face with his fingertip, then bent down and kissed her. He was holding her in his arms, their faces almost touching, when he smiled and said, "What do you think we'd look like to a plane flyin' low overhead, me and my beautiful mermaid on a sandbar in the sea?"

Lisa ran her fingers through his damp hair. "Like we found our island and we're never leaving it — no matter where we go."

FORTY-FOUR

"Good morning." On the porch of the boardinghouse, Peyton put his arms around Lisa and gave her a soft, slow kiss.

"Good morning to you too," she said with a happy sigh. "Aren't you worried about Miss Flossie?"

"Not anymore. We're fixing to make tracks. Ready?"

"I am *so* ready!" Lisa said as they left the boardinghouse for the last time and climbed onto the scooter.

"Do we need to go by your aunt's house and get your things?" Peyton said over his shoulder as he started the engine.

"I don't know where they are. Bobbie Ann said my clothes were too old-lady and would scare all the boys away, so she hid everything except the dress I had on — this one." She held up the bag where they had stored her dress and shoes.

"Well then, I reckon we better do a little

shopping in Fort Lauderdale. Let's go say goodbye to Duval Street."

As they passed Millie's shop, they were surprised to see her standing in the doorway. "Hey, Millie!" Peyton called as he pulled up to the curb. "What are you doing here so early?"

"Lookin' out to see who's ridin' a scooter on Duval at this hour — and gettin' ready for a big sale. You headed to the marina?"

"Yep. Looks like we're gonna start making our way home this morning. Any chance you could sell us another shirt and dress for the road? We won't even take up your time trying 'em on. Your reputation speaks for itself."

"Sure, come on in."

Millie riffled through the racks and quickly pulled out a light coral-colored shirt for Peyton and a sundress with deep purple flowers on a white background for Lisa. "Never saw a redhead who didn't look good in purple or white, and this dress has both," she said.

"Thanks, Millie," Lisa said. "We sure do appreciate it."

"No problem, honey. Pay up, Peyton."

"Yes, ma'am," he said with a grin. "Oh, wait — what am I thinking?" He smacked himself on the forehead and slipped on the aviators. "I almost turned myself back into a Georgia cracker."

"Don't let it happen again," Millie said.

"I won't. I promise. You take care — and seriously, Millie, thanks for everything."

Peyton and Lisa returned their scooter to the rental stand and walked the rest of the way to the marina, where they found Millie's cousin Wally hosing down the docks. "Mornin', Peyton!" he called out. "I see from that bag in your hand that Millie separated you from your money before you got here."

"Not too much. I don't know what we woulda done without her help."

"Millie's grade A, that's for sure," Wally said. "Ready to shove off?"

"You bet."

Wally led them down the dock, with Peyton watching out for ropes and tackle that might trip Lisa. They stopped at a Chris-Craft that looked brand-new.

"Man alive!" Peyton said. "She's a beauty."

"Yes, she is," Wally agreed. "Now, Peyton, I'll give it to you straight. Ordinarily, I'd never hire a ferryman as young as you for a boat this pricey. And I sure wouldn't let you travel with a girl on board — no offense, miss. But the owner's one o' my best customers, and it's so busy around here that I can't find anybody else that wouldn't break my bank. Millie ain't never steered me wrong, so if she says you're the man for the job, I believe it. Don't let me down."

"No, sir, I sure won't. You can depend on me."

"I believe I can. Here's half your fee. You'll get the other half from the dock manager on delivery to the A&R Marina in Fort Lauderdale."

"A&R? Isn't there one of those in Daytona?"

"There's five of 'em. Big operation. You want the one in Fort Lauderdale. It's marked on the map — can't miss it. Dock manager's name is Mack McGee. You're fueled up. Ice chest and water cooler are full. You can get your provisions at the marina grocery right over there. All good?"

"All good. Thank you very much for the work. I won't let you down."

Wally smiled and waved as he walked down the dock and climbed aboard a wooden schooner.

Peyton and Lisa dropped their bags from Millie's store, along with Peyton's saddlebag and duffel, into the boat and walked to the marina grocery, where they bought Cokes, bananas, a box of jerk chicken, and several bags of chips.

Peyton helped her climb aboard and then loaded their supplies. He lifted the St. Christopher medal out of his shirt. "Ready?" he said.

Lisa did the same. "Ready."

After starting the boat, he checked to make sure they weren't anchored, then untied the Chris-Craft and carefully pulled out of the slip. This boat was bigger than the *Madame Queen* but a lot smaller than Finn's fishing boat. Peyton was mindful of traffic, particularly all the small watercraft at this end of the island. Only when he was some distance from the marina and made his way to Hawk Channel did he relax and bring the boat up to cruising speed. He glanced over at Lisa in the passenger seat. She had braided her hair to keep it from blowing wild in the wind, and she was wide-eyed, watching his every move.

"Everything okay?" he shouted over the noise of the motor.

"Everything's fine!" she shouted back. "I just can't believe you really know how to do this!"

"Would I *lie*?" he said, which made her laugh.

They cruised for an hour or so before Lisa broke out the Cokes and handed Peyton a chicken leg. He took a big bite. "Miss Wallace, you're a wonderful cook!"

"It's a family recipe," she said.

"Wally said there's a public marina in Islamorada. Shouldn't be more than an hour from here. I'll pull in so we can stretch our legs."

When Peyton found the marina, Lisa helped guide him into a slip. They secured the boat and walked to a waterfront café with a big screened porch, where a waitress led them to a table with a cross breeze and a great view of the water.

"I know I keep saying it over and over, but the ocean here is just incredible," Lisa said.

The waitress brought them water and menus, then came back to take their order and deliver Cokes.

"Think you want to be a boat captain when we graduate?" Lisa asked Peyton.

"Actually, I want to fly." Peyton told her about the plane rides with his dad and the pilot who gave him the aviators.

"So that's where you got those glasses. Think you'll join the Army Air Force?"

He nodded. "Gotta finish college first, but yeah — I think I want to join."

"What makes you want to fly?"

"I love goin' fast, but in a plane you get

height too. When you take off, you get to watch the ground disappear below, and the higher you climb, the more it feels like you could just reach out and touch the sky. I can't think of anything I'd rather do than fly. How 'bout you? What do you want to do?"

"Not many options for girls," Lisa said with a shrug. "We're supposed to either marry right out of high school or become teachers, nurses, or secretaries first — and *then* get married."

"Don't you want to get married?"

"Of course. I just don't like that it's expected, you know?"

"I get that," Peyton said as he poured a dollop of ketchup onto his fries. "I don't think you should do anything just because people expect you to. You oughta get to do what makes you happy."

The waitress delivered their food — a shrimp basket for Lisa and a cheeseburger for Peyton. Lisa dunked a butterflied shrimp into cocktail sauce and took a bite. "You want one?"

"Nope, I'm happy with my burger," he said as he sprinkled extra salt on his fries. "You know, Lisa, I've heard that pilots make really good husbands. I think I read that in the Army handbook."

She raised an eyebrow. "Oh, the Army handbook says that, does it?"

Peyton was devouring his cheeseburger. "Sure does."

"Well," Lisa said, dipping another shrimp in the sauce, "any pilot looking to marry me will have to let me fly with him now and again, because I'm sure not letting him have all the fun while I stay on the ground, hanging diapers on the line."

"I'll alert the Pentagon. No, wait — I don't want any competition. I reckon those other fellas are on their own."

Lisa stared at him with those eyes the color of the sea. "Are you just kidding around, Peyton?"

She looked afraid of his answer. Trouble was, he didn't know whether she was scared of a yes or a no. So he took a deep breath and told the truth. "Never been more serious about anything in my life."

Now Lisa was smiling. "Good. Me too."

When Eileen's suitcase arrived, Kate was home alone. She carried it to Peyton's bed on the sleeping porch and popped the latches, which opened with a *click-whap*. Kate had bought the suitcase with her own money, her first paycheck as a travel nurse. And now it held what was left of her life with Marshall, packed into pockets and compartments where makeup and hairbrushes used to go.

She slowly shuffled through the contents of the suitcase: cards and letters, playbills, framed pictures of happier times, many of them made on Tybee — Kate photographed at sunset, Marshall standing in the water, eyes closed, face turned to the sky. He was such a beautiful man. Kate could still see plain as day the line of his jaw, the high cheekbones and tan skin, the strong shoulders and graceful hands — everything.

She unwrapped the few pieces of jewelry he had given her — few but fine. He always told her she was too beautiful to cover up with baubles, but he'd bought her a strand of pearls, which she wore most often, a diamond dinner watch and a gold one for daytime, a delicate necklace here, a bracelet and earrings there — not a lot, but all of it special, chosen just for her.

In a corner of the suitcase was the small brown leather New Testament she had given him when he left for the Pacific. She picked it up and saw something tucked between the tissue-thin pages. It was a photograph of Marshall standing in front of a small stone church, surrounded by children holding candy bars and smiling. The picture was dated August 1945 — just a few months before Marshall came home. Kate turned the picture over again and again, staring at the image and hoping each time she flipped it over to find a clue written on the back. It remained blank. Maybe this snapshot captured the key to her husband's postwar struggles — a soldier's inability to help the helpless, to save the innocent? Kate had to accept that she would likely never know.

FORTY-FIVE

It was midafternoon when Peyton backed the Chris-Craft into a slip in Fort Lauderdale, relieved to have successfully completed his first ferrying job. Lisa went to the marina grocery to buy them a couple of Cokes while the dock manager inspected the boat and gave Peyton his money, then offered him another job.

"Boat's big enough to sleep on, so you won't have to pay for a room," Mack McGee said. "Pay's good. Fella needs it at a fish camp up around St. Lucie by the day after tomorrow."

"Cubano's?"

"Yeah, you know it?"

"I do. And I 'preciate the work."

"Happy to have the help." Mack showed him the boat, which was called *Skidaddle* and looked about the size of Finn's, then handed him half the ferrying fee.

Lisa came out of the grocery and gave him

a Coke as they walked back to the docks. "I can't believe we're doing this," she said.

"Doing what?"

"Riding a total stranger's boat out across the ocean, traveling the whole length of Florida by ourselves, never knowing where our next dollar is coming from . . ."

"Oh, that," he said with a smile.

"Yes, that."

"You mind doing it again tomorrow?"

"Seriously?"

"Yep. This one will take us to the little town where Gina's family lives. Maybe we can stop by and say hi."

"I'd love to meet them."

"They're gonna love you. Especially Gina. She quizzed me up and down about you. I guess now I know what it would be like to have a big sister."

"Did you ever wish for one — a brother or sister, I mean?"

"Not really. I guess I didn't have any idea what I was missing, if that makes sense. Hey, we should call Judy. She sure has been a big help to me."

"She likes you," Lisa said. "And that says a lot because Judy's picky. I'll give her a call and let her know what's up. I have no idea what my cousin has told Aunt Marilyn. Probably nothing. She'll want to stay in Key

West by herself as long as she can, and she couldn't care less what happens to me as long as I don't tell on her. I called her from the pay phone at the store and promised I'd keep my mouth shut if she would. But she can lie like a rug, so I have no idea if that did any good."

"Want to go to the beach for a little while?"

Lisa held her skirt out. "In this?"

"We can change on the boat. And I can spring for some beach towels. I am *that* loaded."

The beach in Fort Lauderdale was lined with dome-shaped cabanas, rented from little stands every quarter mile or so. Peyton rented one and spread two beach towels underneath it, then tucked a small cooler into the back before following Lisa into the water.

She was floating on her back, her long red hair drifting in the ocean.

"It's a beautiful thing to swim with a mermaid," Peyton said as he leaned back and floated beside her, reaching out to hold her hand. Gentle swells calmly undulated beneath them and kept them aloft.

"I don't have the fins for it," she said with a dreamy sigh.

The Florida sun was warming them from above, the water cooling from below. Peyton once again imagined an aerial image: he and Lisa lying on the ocean, her red hair fanned out behind her, his hand holding hers.

"Hey, Lisa?" he said. "What do you think we look like from the sky?"

A swell lifted them and gently laid them back down before she answered. "Are you going to ask me that every time we get near water?"

"Probably."

"Well, I think we look like there's no place else we'd rather be," she said, "and nobody else we'd rather be with."

Peyton and Lisa had finished an early supper and were walking back to the marina when a delivery truck caught her eye. "Well, now that's an appropriate name for an orange grove," she said. "Paradise Fruits."

They heard a loud voice and saw a burly man who looked like a prizefighter herding about thirty adults and children out of the marina store and onto the back of the truck. "You got your crackers and baloney, now get back in!"

The people climbing into the truck looked miserable, dirty, and ragged. More than that, they looked hopeless.

"What a horrible man," Lisa said. "We shouldn't stare at those poor people, Peyton."

Just as they were about to turn away, Peyton saw Bonnie and Jasper at the end of the line. "Oh, no," he groaned as he pointed at the children. "Lisa, that's them — the kids I told you about. That's Bonnie and Jasper at the end of that awful line!"

Lisa gasped at the sight of them. Jasper was clutching his sister's hand. Their legs were covered with scratches, and their clothes were filthy. Their parents were nowhere to be seen.

Peyton and Lisa stared at the children inching their way toward a truck filled with destitute, desperate-looking people who didn't seem to pay the other kids on board any attention at all. Peyton thought Lisa was about to cry. "We have to get them," she said. "We can't let them get on that truck."

The line was moving slowly, as one exhausted, defeated soul after another climbed aboard. Peyton and Lisa didn't have much time. No doubt convinced his charges had no energy to run and no place to go even if they did, the driver had taken his seat behind the wheel and cranked the truck, which was backed up to the front of the store. Jasper and Bonnie were standing on the porch that stretched across the front of the grocery, waiting their turn to climb on.

"Let's go around back." Peyton took Lisa by the hand, and they ran to the back of the store, through a small door, and up one of the side aisles to the front. The clerk, who was busy stocking his shelves with canned goods, paid them no mind. Peyton cracked the front door just enough to get Bonnie's attention. There were only three more workers ahead of her in line.

"Psssst! Bonnie! Bonnie, turn around!" he said in a loud whisper. Then a little louder. "Bonnie! Bonnie, come here!"

Slowly, she turned around. She wore the same dead expression as all the others — until she saw Peyton. Then her mouth flew open, and she suddenly came alive. He motioned for her to come back into the store.

Bonnie whispered something to Jasper, then pulled him backward into the store, never taking her eyes off the truck. Once inside, she wrapped her arms around Peyton's waist and burst into tears. "Please help us, Peyton. Please?"

"Climb onto my back. We need to get outta here before that driver figures out he's short a couple o' kids."

Lisa held her arms out to Jasper. "Will you let me carry you, sweetie?"

He timidly raised his arms and let her lift him. The busy clerk didn't even notice as two teenagers hurried out the back of the store with a couple of kids. Once on board the *Skidaddle,* they all went down below to a small captain's cabin, the children desperately clinging to Peyton and Lisa.

"It's okay, Bonnie," Peyton said as he held her on his lap and wiped her tears away with his hand. "Who was that man?"

Bonnie had collected herself enough to talk. "He bought us from Daddy."

"He *what*?" Peyton said.

"He bought us to work in his orange groves."

"Sweetheart, people can't buy other people," Lisa said as she held a whimpering Jasper, gently rocking him on her lap.

"If you're poor, they can do whatever they want to," Bonnie countered. "All I know is that after Mama died o' the pneumonia, Daddy carried us to the orange groves and a mean man named Hiram Elrod give him some money. Daddy said we had to go to work for Hiram and live at the grove. Said he couldn't find him another woman to cook and look after him with me and Jasper a-draggin' him down. I pick oranges an' Jas-

390

per puts 'em in boxes. Who's that purty girl holdin' Jasper?"

"That's Lisa," Peyton said.

"Is she a good person?"

"The best."

"Am I a good person?" Bonnie asked him.

"Absolutely."

"Then how come nothin' but bad things happens to me? If I'm a good person, that ain't fair."

"No, it's not. And I'm real sorry about that. But you found Lisa and me. That was a good thing, wasn't it?"

Bonnie smiled and nodded. "What you and Lisa gonna do with us?"

"Well, lemme see. Are you hungry?"

"Yes."

"We'll start by fixin' you something to eat. Then we're gonna put you to bed and figure it out from there. But I'll promise you this — you're never goin' back to that orange grove."

"Let's leave a light on so they won't be scared if they wake up and don't remember where they are," Lisa whispered.

Peyton switched on a small light in the cabin and led the way back up to the deck. Just as he and Lisa emerged, they spotted the burly truck driver and ducked down beside the captain's seat. He appeared to be questioning fishermen as they came off the dock because each one shook his head and walked on.

"What are we going to do?" Lisa whispered.

Peyton watched as the driver apparently gave up and disappeared inside the marina tavern. "We're gonna get out o' here. Will you help me?"

Lisa crept to the back of the boat with Peyton. He raised the anchor as she untied the ropes. Peyton knew the sound of a boat this size firing up and leaving the marina after sunset would likely attract attention, but he was willing to risk it to get everybody out of harm's way.

"Here he comes!" Lisa was watching the tavern as Peyton steered the fishing boat out of its slip and beyond the marina to open water. The driver ran toward the dock when he heard the boat, but he was too late to catch them. Peyton could only hope it was too dark to read the nameplate on the boat — and that Mack McGee wouldn't give them away to Bonnie and Jasper's tormentor.

The water was calm and smooth. Stars sprinkled the sky with light as the moon shone on the water. Peyton steered north toward Palm Beach and the public marina he remembered not too far from The Breakers. Without looking at Lisa as they skimmed across the water, Peyton said, "I'll bet you're braiding your hair."

"Roger that," she said.

"You sure you're okay with all this, Lisa?" Peyton knew he was getting both of them into a situation they had never bargained for.

"That horrible man scares the daylights out of me," she said with a shudder. "But it's an amazing thing that you're doing. You saved those kids' lives."

"No, *we* did."

"All I did was feed them. You're driving them across the ocean. No telling what would've happened to them if you hadn't found them." They traveled across the water in moonlight, riding in silence until Lisa said, "Nothing scares you, does it?"

He frowned as he thought about her question. "It's not that I don't get scared. I just try not to let being scared stop me from doing whatever I've made up my mind to do."

Lisa tilted her head back to let the wind cool her face. Bonnie and Jasper slept through it all as Peyton took them past Pompano, Highland, and Delray Beach, at last spotting lights from The Breakers off in the distance. He steered inland to the marina he remembered from his days there as a pool boy and backed into an empty slip, where Lisa helped him secure the boat.

"I'll be right back," he said as he disappeared into the cabin below. When he came back, he was carrying two Cokes, their beach towels, and a couple of small pillows. Peyton climbed onto the bow of the boat, where he spread the beach towels and propped the pillows against the windshield.

"What on earth are you doing up there?" Lisa said.

"Come on up and I'll show you." Peyton held the Cokes in one hand and helped Lisa up with the other. "I figure I'll sleep out here, and you can sleep down below with the kids. But I'm not sleepy. Are you?"

"No," she said, "I'm not sleepy."

"Well then, let's watch the show together."

"What show?"

"That one!" Peyton waved his arm at the open water, the occasional boat going by, the sound of music coming from somewhere on the beach. He helped Lisa settle in and handed her a Coke. "Here's to the future — when we can actually travel in a car like normal people."

Lisa laughed and clinked her Coke bottle to his. "I don't know about that. Car travel might be overrated. I'm starting to like the sound of water slapping against a boat."

"Me too. Also, I really like the sound o' your voice. I don't think I'd ever get tired o' hearing it."

"Even if it were reminding you to take out the trash?"

"Music to my ears." Just as Peyton leaned over and kissed Lisa, they heard a loud boom and looked up to see the sky showered with color.

"Now that's timing," he said.

They heard a scream from below deck right before Bonnie and Jasper came running up the steps, calling out to them. Peyton and Lisa jumped down from the bow and picked up the kids.

"It's okay," Peyton said to Bonnie. "It's just fireworks." He pointed up to the sky.

"What's fireworks?" Bonnie's eyes were as big as saucers, and her mouth flew open at the next burst in the sky.

"Just pretty lights for you to look at," Lisa said. "They're noisy, but they won't hurt you. Come on up here with us and we'll watch them together."

She and Peyton carried the children onto the bow and sat back down on the beach towels with the kids on their laps.

"Jasper, look!" Bonnie shouted as a big

red, white, and blue starburst exploded over the water.

Jasper's eyes were as wide as Bonnie's, but he didn't speak. He only gasped at the sound of the first few explosions, then buried his face in Lisa's shoulder.

Peyton put one arm around Lisa, still holding Bonnie with the other. Any passerby who saw the four of them silhouetted against the boat, looking up at sprays of color lighting the night sky, would have thought they were a family. And maybe that's what they were — a family trying to find the way home.

FORTY-SIX

At the marina bathhouses, Peyton and Lisa helped the children get a morning shower and wash their hair. Then they all went shopping. Lisa said kids should never have to wear dirty clothes that made them feel ashamed, so Peyton had asked around and found a huge souvenir shop that carried everything from seashell lampshades to toys and sundresses.

Peyton carried Jasper to the boys' section, while Lisa helped Bonnie find three sundresses, along with flamingo-covered underpants, a bathing suit, sandals, a comb, a hairbrush, and hair bows — all pink, her favorite color.

Lisa didn't want anything for herself, but Peyton loved giving her presents and found an abalone ring with a rose-gold band to match her hair. He tucked it into the front pocket of the coral shirt Millie had sold him. The right time would come, but it wasn't now.

Jasper kept picking up a small stuffed dolphin and squeezing it, so Peyton bought it for him, along with a soft mermaid doll for Bonnie. A store clerk helped them find child-size life jackets since there weren't any on the boat.

Carrying Jasper on his shoulders, Peyton looked on as Bonnie, sporting new clothes and holding what was likely the first doll she had ever owned, stared at herself in a tall mirror in the center of the store. Lisa had brushed her blonde hair — now clean and shiny — and pulled it into a ponytail held with a pink bow. Bonnie's sundress was pink with little white daisies all over it. "I can't get over it," she said, staring at her reflection.

"Get over what, honey?" Peyton asked.

"I look like a real person."

Lisa knelt beside her, gazing into the mirror.

"You gonna cry?" Bonnie asked Lisa's reflection in the mirror.

Lisa bit her lip and shook her head.

Bonnie reached up and held Lisa's face in her hands. "I didn't think I was gonna like you as much as Peyton, but I do."

Lisa kissed the top of Bonnie's head, then stood up and took her by the hand. "Jasper, you look mighty handsome in that sailor outfit," she said.

He grinned shyly at her from his perch.

"I ain't never seen you in clothes that was your size, Jasper," Bonnie added. "You look real nice."

The four of them had an early lunch at a café on the beach, then returned to the marina to buy their provisions and load in.

"We need to keep an eye on the weather today," Peyton said to Lisa. "The sky had a little red in it this morning, but I don't know if it was red enough for us to worry about it."

"Show me what to look for and I'll help you keep watch."

"That's the spirit, first mate," Peyton said with a little salute.

As he pulled the *Skidaddle* out of its slip and into open water, Bonnie sat on his lap, with Lisa holding Jasper.

"Can I put my hands on the steerin' wheel with yours so I can feel what it's like to drive a boat?" Bonnie asked.

"You bet. Don't you take us out to sea, now."

Bonnie laid her hands on top of his, which rested on the bottom of the steering wheel. Her eyes were fixed not on the expanse of turquoise sea but on the wheel. "Your hands are a lot bigger than mine," she said, looking down at them. "But I'm not scared of 'em. I won't ever be scared o' your hands, Peyton."

FORTY-SEVEN

Peyton dropped anchor and helped Lisa with the children. Everybody was ready for a snack and a break.

"I never seen one o' these before," Bonnie said as she examined the MoonPie that Lisa handed her.

"I'd bet a Coke you're gonna love it," Peyton said as he unwrapped it for her while Lisa helped Jasper with his. "It's kind of a cookie and kind of a cake with marshmallow in the middle and chocolate all around. Take a bite and see what you think."

Bonnie bit into the MoonPie and wiped some stray chocolate off her mouth. "That's good," she said as she chewed.

"How 'bout you, Jasper — what do you think?" Peyton said.

Jasper only nodded, his cheeks puffy with all the MoonPie he had stuffed into his mouth.

Peyton looked out at the water, which was

slightly choppy now. "Feels like the wind is picking up a little bit," he said to Lisa as a cloud passed over the sun.

"You're right," she said. "It's getting cooler too."

Peyton could see the sky growing darker as the children finished their snack. "Bonnie," he said, "I need you to take Jasper down below. Let Lisa put both of your life jackets on since it's a little stormy today. Can you do that?"

"Sure," Bonnie said, tugging at her brother's hand till he followed her.

Peyton hurried to the captain's seat, raised the anchor, and started the boat, traveling slowly through shallower water till he reached a suitable depth to open the throttle and let the *Skidaddle* fly.

Now clouds had completely blocked the sun, and the water was white-capping. As Lisa joined him at the helm, the storm moved in quickly, its winds growing stronger, with daunting waves beginning to form.

"I think you oughta go down below," he said to Lisa.

"No," she said. "I'm staying with you — unless I'm in your way."

"You could never be in my way," Peyton said. "How about grabbing a couple o' life jackets for us."

They had just fastened their jackets when Peyton saw a wave coming at them. He throttled back and aimed the bow of the *Skidaddle* into it, approaching on a diagonal as Finn had taught him. The boat rode up the wall of water and smoothly down the other side.

"Ha! How 'bout that!" he said to Lisa, who had covered her face with her hands.

When she looked up and realized they had cleared the wave, she jumped out of her seat, clapped her hands together, and threw her arms around Peyton. "We didn't die!" she exclaimed.

"Not yet anyway." Peyton pointed to another wave coming at them, smaller than the first but still formidable. He fought hard to remember every scrap of instruction Finn had given him and again rode a diagonal path to the crest of the wave, then glided down the other side.

Lisa braced herself as they pitched in the waves, climbing and descending one after another. Now and again, a big one would spray them both, leaving them soaked with salt water.

"Oh my gosh, Peyton, look!"

He immediately saw it, an enormous wall of water that was cresting just a few yards away. Peyton had a sudden vision of Will and the number 10 car barely missing a wave half this size. He knew he'd never be able to ride it to the crest. His only hope was to outrun it. He pulled the throttle back and, like a surfer inside the curl, ripped through the water with the wave rising overhead. He gave the *Skidaddle* all the power it had, shooting through a tube that seemed like miles and miles of blue water. Peyton could feel the spray from the wave crashing just behind them as the boat broke out of it.

More would be coming, but nothing like that one. Peyton could finally turn his attention away from the water long enough to see how Lisa was doing.

She looked stunned. Her eyes were wide, her face slightly pale, and she was gripping anything she could get her hands on to steady herself. "Did we just do that?"

"I think we did. You okay?"

"I'm not sure." She shook her head and her wet auburn hair as if to shake off the danger they had just come through. "I'm still thinking about all that water over our heads and what might've happened if —"

"C'mere." Peyton kept one hand on the steering wheel, reaching for Lisa with the other. She came to him, putting her arms around him and resting her face against his shoulder as he held her with his free arm.

"I think the worst is over," he said, pressing his cheek against hers.

She tightened her arms around him. "Even if it's not, we'll be okay. You'll make sure of it."

Peyton steered them through a series of smaller waves until finally the wind died down and they had nothing but pouring rain to contend with. He and Lisa were both soaked.

"Why don't you go below and check on Bonnie and Jasper — get some dry clothes on so you don't catch cold?" he said as he felt her shiver against him.

"What about you?"

"Oh, I'm an old salt," he said with a grin. "Throw anything at me — mosquitoes, crazy artists, crazy aunts — I can take it. I'm covered." He tapped the St. Christopher medal hanging around his neck.

Lisa kissed his cheek. "I'll be back."

Below deck, Lisa found the children on a cot together, with Bonnie's arms around her little brother. Jasper had fallen asleep, but she was wide awake.

Lisa sat down beside them and ran her hand across Bonnie's forehead. "It's alright, sweetheart," she said. "The storm's over."

"You're all wet," Bonnie said.

"I know, honey. There's an awful lot o' water out there."

"Is Peyton okay?"

"He's fine."

"Are you sure?"

"I'm sure. I'm going to carry a blanket up to keep some of the rain off of him. Will you and Jasper be alright till we can dock somewhere?"

"We'll be alright. But are you sure Peyton's okay? Are you really, *really* sure about him?"

Lisa kissed Bonnie's forehead. "Yes, sweetie. I am really, *really* sure about him."

FORTY-EIGHT

It was five o'clock in the afternoon when Peyton backed the *Skidaddle* into a slip at Cubano's. The dock manager inspected the boat and handed Peyton his pay. He and Lisa took turns drying off in the cabin before gathering their belongings and taking the kids to the fish camp café.

Once inside, Peyton immediately began looking for Gina. He saw her coming out of the kitchen with a tray of beer glasses for the bartender. She emptied the tray and was about to head back to the kitchen when she spotted him and stopped in her tracks.

"Hermanito!" she shouted, tossing the tray onto a table and throwing her arms wide. "You made it!" She ran to him and gave him a big hug, kissing him on both cheeks before stepping back to look at him. "You have changed, little brother. For one thing, you have children. Is this your beautiful Lisa?"

Peyton was beaming. "Yes. This is my beautiful Lisa. And I am her lucky Peyton."

Gina held out her arms and Lisa gave her a hug. "You can't imagine how much Peyton's told me about you and your family, Gina," she said.

"Likewise," Gina said. "And the *bebés* — who might they be?"

"This is Bonnie and Jasper," Peyton said. "Let's just say they were in a bad spot and needed some help, so we brought 'em with us."

"And your bike?"

"That's kind of a long story. It's gone, but I don't mind."

"Well, where is it? How did you get here? How are you getting to St. Augustine? Why —"

"Hang on, hang on. Let's feed the young'uns and I'll tell you all about it."

"You know what today is, don't you?" Gina said.

Peyton was confused. "You mean the date?"

"No, silly, the *day*. It's Saturday!"

"Oh, man, are we in luck!" he said to Lisa.

"You will all stay at my mama's — no arguments." Gina waved her hands in the air as if to swat away any objections they might raise. "This time, Peyton, you do not

408

have to work the bar. We are under new management." She motioned for them to follow her into the kitchen, where Peyton saw Mama Eva stirring a huge stockpot of what smelled like her ropa vieja and giving orders over her shoulder to three cooks.

"Hey, Mama Eva," he said.

She whirled around and threw out her arms. "Peyton, *mi bebé*!" she cried as he hugged her tight and kissed her.

He introduced her to Lisa and the children. "What's all this, Mama Eva?" he asked, waving his arm around the kitchen.

"My new kitchen!" she exclaimed, raising her hands and looking skyward. *"Gracias a Dios!"*

"Papa says Mama seemed sad with all the children grown and no crowds to cook for except on Saturdays," Gina explained. "So he bought her the café just a few days after your visit. Now it is spotless, the food is fresh and fantastic, and business is booming. In less than a month, my mama is famous for her cooking. All the fishermen from Jacksonville to Miami find an excuse to get here whenever they can. We screened in the back porch to seat more people."

"Can I get you all a bowl of my ropa vieja?" Mama Eva asked.

"No, ma'am," Peyton said, "not till the

whole family's here. Wouldn't seem right."

Mama Eva dabbed at her eyes with a dish towel. "You such a dear boy, Peyton," she said as she hugged him so tight he couldn't breathe. "Don't you worry. I fix you children some good food to hold you till the family comes after closing. We put the little ones to bed in a booth if they get tired."

He kissed her on the cheek. "I thought about your family every day that I was gone. Thank you for feeding us, Mama Eva."

Gina led them to a breezy table on the porch and called for another waitress to deliver Cokes. "No menus from now on. Mama decides what everybody eats."

"Hey, Gina, how's Rolando?" Peyton asked.

"I can't wait for him to see me in my wedding dress!" she said with a big smile. "And thank you for giving me your tips, Peyton. You did not have to do that."

"You didn't have to take me home with you, but you did. He's still in the Philippines, right?"

"That's right. He has rented a little house for us by the water. Can you believe that? My own house. I will not know what to do with so much room."

"I guess you'll have to fill it up," Peyton said with a grin, nodding to the children.

Gina threw her dish towel at him. "You are trouble. I have always known it. Keep an eye on him, Lisa, while I check on your food."

"What's that big smile all about?" Peyton asked Lisa after Gina had gone.

"These people love you," Lisa said. "You only stayed with them for a little while, and they treat you like family."

"I'm pretty sure they treat everybody like family."

"Maybe so, but I still think you're special to them."

"You will be too."

"What about me and Jasper?" Bonnie asked. "Will we be special too?"

"You two will be *super* special," Peyton said.

By the time Gina's family closed the restaurant, enjoyed their Saturday night gathering, and started home, it was nearly one o'clock in the morning. Bonnie and Jasper had long since fallen asleep, tucked into makeshift beds in one of the booths just like all the other children in the family. Gina's brother Ramone helped Peyton carry them to Mama Eva's house and put them to bed. Lisa slept with them so they wouldn't awake in a strange place and be afraid, while

Peyton took an empty bed in the brothers' room.

Before he fell asleep, Peyton said a silent prayer of thanks for this family's warmth and hospitality, for Gina's friendship, for Jasper and Bonnie's safety, and for Lisa's love — for that most of all.

"Promise me you will write," Gina said to Peyton. "You too," she said to Lisa.

"We promise," Lisa said with a smile, hugging her goodbye. "Oh, Gina, your family is amazing. I hope we have a family like that one day."

"Ah, so you are thinking about it!"

Lisa blushed, but Peyton couldn't have been prouder.

"Come here, little brother," Gina said, hugging Peyton and kissing him on both cheeks. "The little ones already on the boat?"

"Jasper's a little shy," Lisa said.

"Well, you give them both a kiss for me. Here is a sack filled with more of Mama's food than ten people could eat. You know where you are going?"

"We do," Peyton said. "And thank Ramone for putting in a good word with the dock manager. We'll get the boat to Daytona."

"You might have trouble getting ferry work from there."

"That's okay. Got a backup plan for Daytona."

"Alright then. Safe journey to you."

Gina waved goodbye from the dock as Peyton and Lisa untied the boat and pulled out of the slip. They waved to her one last time before they left the harbor.

Bonnie and Jasper, who had been playing below deck, came back up once the boat began moving. They took their usual spots — Bonnie on Peyton's lap and Jasper on Lisa's.

"I feel sad, but I don't know why," Bonnie said.

"It's always sad to leave a happy place behind," Peyton said. "And it's hard saying goodbye to people you love."

"You love all them people back there?"

"I sure do."

"You love me and Jasper?"

"Absolutely."

Bonnie thought for a minute. "Well, what about Lisa? Do you love her?"

"You better believe it."

"You sure got a bunch o' love in you, Peyton," Bonnie said with a sigh. "It's a wonder it don't spill out all over the place and make a big ol' mess."

FORTY-NINE

"Aunt Gert! Aunt Gert, come quick! There's a race car in your driveway." Kate had heard the sound of a big engine and looked out the living room window to see an older model Ford with the number 10 painted on the door.

"Katie, have you been breathin' ammonia in there, cleaning that bathroom?" Aunt Gert called from the kitchen.

"No! Hurry up!"

Aunt Gert made it into the living room and looked out the window just as Peyton climbed out of the car.

"He's back!" Both women screamed it together and nearly tripped over each other racing out the front door. "Peyton!" they yelled as they ran to him and smothered him with hugs and kisses.

"Hold on just a minute, ladies!" He laughed as he struggled to free himself. "I'll be right with you."

Peyton held the door open and helped three passengers out of the back seat while the driver climbed out from behind the wheel.

"Lisa?" Kate said. "I can't believe it's you, honey!" They hugged each other before Peyton introduced Lisa to his aunt.

"Miss Lisa, I have long waited to meet you, and you do not disappoint."

"I'm so happy to meet you, Aunt Gert. I'm sorry — I shouldn't call you that."

"Oh yes you should." Aunt Gert looked at Peyton. "I like her. She's grade A. Now who else is with us?"

"This is my friend Will Fournier, who gave us a ride from Daytona," Peyton said.

Will stepped around the car and made an awkward bow in the general direction of Kate and Aunt Gert.

"Well, we are in your debt, Will," Aunt Gert said as she and Kate shook his hand.

"And these two," Peyton said, "are Bonnie and Jasper."

Kate knelt down between the children and put her arms around them. "Hello there."

"Hello," said Bonnie, her voice breaking as tears rolled down her cheeks. Seeing his sister in tears made Jasper cry.

"Oh, sweethearts, what's the matter?" Kate said.

"It's a long, long story, Mama," Peyton said as he and Lisa picked up the children.

"I trust more information will be forthcoming, but for now, everybody into my house," Aunt Gert said. Will turned to get back in the car. "You too, Will. Get yourself in here. I've got questions and I want answers. I'm willin' to feed you for 'em."

Peyton hadn't realized how much he missed the sleeping porch at Aunt Gert's. St. Augustine had seen more rain than usual, she said, and the river was running high. Peyton could hear the swift flow outside and the calls of crickets and cicadas like voices harmonizing in a church choir. The palms and bananas surrounding the purple bungalow were whispering in the wind, which was blowing the rain outside, and thunder was rumbling off in the distance. There was no more peaceful place on earth than Aunt Gert's sleeping porch in an early morning thunderstorm.

Peyton wished Lisa were lying here beside him. Nothing would be more perfect than sharing a thunderstorm in the quiet darkness with her. Then again, sharing anything with Lisa made it perfect. Now that he had seen what it would be like to actually live with her, to have her beside him morning and night, he didn't know how he would get through the tedium of high school — of passing her notes in class and "no going out on a school night" and movie dates with everybody else in town. He felt married to Lisa and knew he always would.

Pirate climbed onto the bed and stretched out next to him. Peyton scratched the cat under its chin, which was the only affection it would tolerate, at least from him. "You're a poor substitute, ol' boy, but I guess you're all I've got right now."

Staring out at the darkness, listening as morning birds took over the night song of crickets and cicadas, Peyton wondered whether Lisa was fast asleep or lying awake, longing for him as he longed for her. Was it wrong to hope so? Nothing would ever convince him of that.

Aunt Gert fed Pirate his bacon before dishing out more of it, along with eggs, toast, and plantains, to a tableful of hungry guests. Peyton's mother poured the orange juice, Aunt Gert offered thanks for a safe return, and everybody dug in.

"Where's Lisa?" Bonnie asked.

"She's calling her sister back home," Peyton said. "Sure hope she gets good news."

"She did," Lisa said as she came into the kitchen and Peyton pulled out a chair for her.

Aunt Gert filled a plate for Lisa and set it on the table. "You don't look too happy about it."

"That's because I don't feel right about it," Lisa said. "Judy got hold of Bobbie Ann in Key West. She said she didn't tell anybody when I left. And she's happy to lie to her mother and say I got homesick and caught a bus to Savannah this morning. It's a two-day trip, so as long as I catch the bus in the morning, my folks will never know any different. I can go home and act like nothing ever happened."

"I take it that doesn't suit you?" Aunt Gert asked her.

"I don't like lying. But more than that, it's just so unfair to Peyton. He rescued me from my horrible cousin. He kept me safe. He risked so much for Bonnie and Jasper and found work so he could feed us all. It's not right for my parents to treat him like every other boy in high school." She reached over to hold Peyton's hand under the table. "He's not like them at all."

"Here we go again." Aunt Gert covered her face with her hands as if she just couldn't face young love in her house again.

"Peyton, I don't want to take the bus home," Lisa said. "I want you to get your license and drive me. And when we get there, I want to tell my parents everything you did to protect me and get me home. I'll figure out a way to keep Bobbie Ann out of it, but I want them to know what you did."

Peyton leaned over and gave Lisa a kiss without a thought to his mother or his aunt or anything else.

"Oh, dear heaven!" Aunt Gert said.

"Anybody home?" Finn was at the kitchen door. Peyton jumped up from his place and hurried to open the door for him. "I hear you did yourself a little boatin'!" Finn said as he shook Peyton's hand and clapped him on the back.

"You saved my life, Finn. You saved a bunch o' lives with what you taught me. I sure do thank you."

Finn shrugged it off. "Weren't nothin'. 'Course, if you was to spread it around at the VFW, why, I wouldn't object."

"Pull up a chair," Aunt Gert said. She fixed him a plate and a steaming cup of coffee as Peyton introduced him to Lisa and the children.

"I can't believe I'm sitting at the table with you!" Lisa said with a big smile. "I've heard so much about you."

419

"All true, if it was good," Finn said with a grin.

"Well then, it's all true."

"Oh!" Peyton's mother got up from the table. "I almost forgot something. I'll be right back." She hurried out of the kitchen and came back with a small square box wrapped in navy-blue paper and tied with a white satin bow. "Happy belated birthday," she said as she handed it to Peyton.

"Thanks, Mama." He untied the bow and unwrapped the box, which held a key nestled on a bed of cotton. Peyton turned it over and over in his hand, then looked up at his mother.

"What is it, Peyton?" Bonnie asked as she chewed on her third strip of bacon.

"It's a key," he said.

"To what?"

Again, Peyton looked at his mother, who said, "A 1947 Chevy Fleetwood convertible. The color's called Freedom Blue. Cream interior."

Peyton and Lisa both squealed and jumped up from the table. He lifted his mother and twirled her around the kitchen. "But — where is it?" he asked.

"Parked outside the courthouse so you can drive it right after we get your license. Aunt Gert says the clerk will let us use her

420

address."

"When did you have time to buy a car?"

"I didn't. Your daddy bought it right after Christmas. We had gone out to dinner and were on our way home when he spotted it at a dealership and decided then and there that you would be driving it. He bought it that night, and we took it to your Uncle Jimmy's for safekeeping. I asked Jimmy to have it delivered down here after you left for Key West."

Peyton turned the key over and over in his hand. "Daddy picked it out for me?"

"Yes," his mother said. "He was smitten with that car right from the start, and when they told him the color was called Freedom Blue, that sealed it for him. He said he couldn't think of anything better to give you on your sixteenth birthday than a little taste of freedom." She put her arms around Peyton and held him tight. "He loved you very much, son. Always remember that. Enjoy his gift. Make the most of it."

FIFTY

"But why can't we go to the courthouse with Peyton and Lisa?" Bonnie was not happy about being left behind, but Aunt Gert knew how to charm a child.

"Because I need your help," she said. "I can't make brownies *and* do all the tasting myself. Somebody's got to lick the spoon to make sure we get the chocolate right. Jasper, do you know anything about licking a spoon?"

He shook his head.

"Well, what about you, Bonnie?"

She shook her head too.

"Well, I'll teach you," Aunt Gert said. "It's a very important skill."

Bonnie and Jasper followed her into the kitchen and sat down at the table, watching her mix eggs, butter, sugar, and cocoa into a bowl. The more Aunt Gert stirred, the bigger their eyes grew.

"It's turnin' into chocolate!" Bonnie exclaimed.

"Yes, indeed, and now comes the critical part." Aunt Gert dipped two spoons into the batter and handed one to each of the children. "Go on," she said. "Lick your spoons and tell me how the chocolate tastes. This is our last opportunity to make adjustments."

Bonnie and Jasper licked their spoons clean and said they could find no fault with the chocolate.

Aunt Gert poured the batter into a buttered baking dish. "Well, that is such a relief, children. Thank you very much for your help." She slid the dish into her oven and set a timer. "Now, I'm afraid we'll have to hurry because we don't have much time. We need to get into our bathing suits and pack a picnic basket, because as soon as those brownies come out of the oven, we'll have to be on our way. There's a waterfall that needs our attention."

"What's a waterball?" Jasper asked.

"Water*fall*, Jasper. One of the prettiest in Florida. The water flows over rocks, down into a crystal-clear swimmin' hole. Do you children know how to swim?"

"No, ma'am," Bonnie said.

"Well then, we'll have to add that to your list of chores. From now on you'll have to

taste all the chocolate *and* go to the swimmin' hole every day till you learn how to
handle yourself in the water. I just hope
you're not too tired to ride in the *Madame
Queen* after all that."

Jasper smiled at Aunt Gert. "I'm very
strong," he said.

FIFTY-ONE

"Where's Bonnie?" Peyton and Lisa were saying their goodbyes at Aunt Gert's when he realized she was missing.

"She's on the sleeping porch," Peyton's mother said, "and I think you've got some unfinished business before you go."

He walked around back and stepped onto the porch, where he found Bonnie curled up on his bed, looking out at the river. She had been crying. Peyton sat down next to her and brushed her hair out of her eyes. "You know I'll be back, right?"

Bonnie nodded. "But not forever. You're gonna leave again at the end o' the summer. Aunt Gert said so."

"That's right. I've got to finish school — and you've got to start."

Bonnie climbed onto his lap and put her head against his shoulder. "I never been as happy in my whole life as I was with you an' Lisa."

Peyton stroked her hair and held her tight. "Remember in the hospital cafeteria when you told me I was grown? Well, I'm not. I'm more grown now than I was in Atlanta, but I've still got a ways to go. And you do too. You've done your level best to be a mama to Jasper. And you did a fine job. But now it's time for you to just be a kid without worrying about feeding anybody or protecting anybody. Let Aunt Gert and Finn look after you and Jasper, because they're real excited about it."

"Don't forget me — okay, Peyton?"

Peyton drove his new Chevy over the bridge to Anastasia Island and parked close to the water. He and Lisa were on their way out of town, back to Savannah, back to the real world, away from their island. But before they left, he wanted her to see the place where his parents met, his father's final resting place.

They took off their shoes and crossed the dunes hand in hand. In the morning light, they could see a sandbar just beginning to peek through the tide. Silently, they stood together, feeling the warmth of the sun on their faces and the Atlantic spray at their feet. Peyton reached into his pocket, took out the abalone ring, and slipped it on

Lisa's finger. He wrapped his arm around her waist, held her face with his hand, and gave her a kiss that held a promise — of love and protection for a beautiful girl who smelled like gardenias and tasted like a summer rain.

EPILOGUE

Summer 1967

Peyton stood on a short flight of long, white brick steps that led nowhere. Once they would have taken him to the lower porch of his grandparents' Greek Revival mansion — the same porch a dog named Jubal had leaped from to pursue a squirrel, the same dog that had spooked his father's horse during a fateful picnic long ago.

But the house wasn't there anymore. Once Peyton's embittered Uncle Julian seized control of the estate, he had the house torn down — his vengeance for a lifetime of perceived slights from the family patriarch. Knowing Uncle Julian, tearing down the house was the final assertion of his dominance over the family — of victory.

But like everything else about him, his victories were hollow. A carefully cultivated fortune left in his hands was doomed to blight. To finance his "visionary" real-estate deals, he had sold off the oil wells that fueled the family fortune. One failed development followed another, one bad investment heaping debt on those who came before, until finally, Uncle Julian was left with nothing but the family homeplace, which he transformed into the biggest trailer park in the state of Georgia. By the time his patrician neighbors found out, the trailer park was ready to open, but they swiftly put a stop to it, even engaging the governor for assistance. The park closed before it could open, and Uncle Julian, drowning yet another humiliation in whiskey at one of the seedier local taverns, mouthed off to the wrong mill worker and was found floating in the river three days later.

Now, here Peyton stood on the only remnant of an old family home, a stack of bricks and mortar that had escaped the wrecking ball. Granddaddy Cabot's long-pampered carpet of zoysia grass had fallen to neglect, as had the azaleas that used to flower in the spring. Rectangular concrete slabs with trailer hookups dotted the landscape like so many gravestones, with weeds and briars growing up between them. Peyton did indeed feel like he was standing in a burial ground. Even the Ghost Oak was gone — and good riddance. However unintentional its role, that tree had helped end his father's life. Peyton didn't think he could bear the sight of it, even after all these years.

"Promise me something." He turned to see his wife standing behind him. She had agreed to wait for him in the car — the '47 Fleetwood she had restored for his thirtieth birthday a few years ago.

He smiled down at her. "You think I have to promise you the moon just because you gave me back the car o' my dreams?"

"That's exactly what I think."

He descended the steps and kissed her. "Well then, I guess I'd better go to promising."

Lisa held both of his hands in hers. "Promise me you'll never come back here, Peyton. It's too much — it's just way too much."

He pulled her closer and held her against him. As always, Lisa was right. The memory of what had been, set against the stark reality of what remained, which was nothing, really — it was way too much.

At a sprawling Georgia Air Force base, Peyton parked the Fleetwood and helped Lisa out. Then he stepped back for a better look at the car and whistled. "Man, she's a beauty."

"You used to say that about me." Lisa

shook her head and laughed.

"And I still do, every single day. May I?" He offered her his arm as they made their way to the auditorium.

"Last time we were stationed here, you were a lieutenant. Back then, did you ever think you'd make colonel so fast?"

"Back then, I was just trying to get more flight time."

Lisa stopped and fussed with the medals on his jacket. "I'm mighty proud of you."

"Sure you don't want to go onstage with me?"

"No. You're the one she'll want. I'll sit with your mother."

Inside the auditorium, Peyton went to the stage and stood in the wings, peeking through the curtain to make sure Lisa found his mother. And then a long line of newly minted Air Force nurses filed in. There were the usual speeches and presentations before it was time for the pinning ceremony. One by one, the young women crossed the stage until finally, Bonnie's turn came.

She looked stunned to see Peyton standing there with her pin. "We're so proud of you," he whispered as he pinned her. They saluted each other before he escorted her offstage.

431

■ ■ ■ ■

Outside, Peyton and Bonnie stood in a shady spot with Lisa and Kate, waiting for the parking lot to thin out before heading back to Kate's house on Tybee to celebrate.

"I sure miss Aunt Gert and Finn on days like this," Bonnie said.

"Me too, honey," Kate said. "But I like to think they're looking down on us and smiling."

"Hey, Lisa," Bonnie said, "who's minding the munchkins?"

"Mama," Lisa said. "It's been a long time since she's had two kids in the house, let alone three, but she insisted. I hope they're not tearing the place apart."

"C'mon, everybody," Peyton said. "Let's see how many people can fit into the greatest automobile ever made."

Peyton's mother joined him on a wide deck overlooking the Atlantic. They stood by the bannister, looking out at the ocean, and watched as Bonnie stepped onto the sand down below and walked toward the water. She was carrying an old quilt Aunt Gert had given her. As she spread it on the sand, Peyton's mother sighed and said, "If ever

432

there were a young woman in need of a father right now, it's Bonnie. Why don't you go see about her, son?"

Peyton hugged his mother and headed for the beach, where he joined Bonnie on her quilt.

"Does the brass know you dress like the Beach Boys when you visit your mom?" she said with a smile.

"I don't see any need to trouble 'em with that information. Speaking of withholding information, you ever gonna tell me where Jasper is? You're gonna give yourself whiplash with all the ducking and dodging you've been doing."

Bonnie sighed and looked him square in the eyes. "He's in a commune in California. There. Now you know. He's a full-on hippie. And he's protesting the war."

"Is he happy?"

"Yes."

"Is he safe out there?"

"Yes."

"Well, if he's happy and safe, that's all that matters. Why didn't you tell me before?"

"You mean why didn't I tell an Air Force colonel that the boy he rescued is a hippie and a war protestor?"

"He served his hitch. Did his duty. He's got a right to feel how he feels about the war. Everybody's different, Bonnie. Serving in Korea made me want to be in the military for life. I guess Vietnam made Jasper never want to go near it again. That's his right."

They sat silently together, watching the waves break against the sand, before Bonnie said, "I've been thinking about some things — like Pine Mountain. And that hospital cafeteria in Atlanta. Mama lying sick and Daddy selling his own kids into hard labor."

"Shouldn'a happened, but it did. And you came through it strong. You've got a lot to be proud of."

Bonnie drew a boat in the sand with her finger. "When you and Lisa left Jasper and me with Aunt Gert, I thought I'd never see y'all again."

"We promised we'd be back."

"Promises never meant much where I came from."

"What's this all about, Bonnie?"

She looked at him and took a deep breath. "I just need to tell you before I lose my nerve — and before I ship out — that you changed my whole life, and Jasper's. And I know I don't have a right to say it, especially now that you've got kids of your own, but part of me will always think of you and Lisa as my parents. That made a lot more sense when I was seven instead of twenty-seven, but there it is. Do you mind? I mean, does it make you feel weird?"

"Makes me very happy. I learned a long time ago that there's all kinds of family, Bonnie. Some you're born with and some you're lucky enough to meet along the way. You and Jasper and Lisa and me — we'll always be family."

They stopped talking for a while and just listened to the waves rolling in.

"It's gonna be pretty rough over there, isn't it?" Bonnie said.

"Yes."

"How did you handle it — when you were in Korea, I mean?"

"I did my job the way I was trained to do it. That's what you have to hold on to, Bonnie. You've been trained by the best, and that training won't let you down when you need it the most. I know you won't be flying fighter planes, but you'll see the worst that happens up there when all the wounded start coming in. Just remember: Do your job exactly like you were taught, and don't let the rest of it get into your head. You've got what it takes and then some. You'll make it back just like I did. And when you do, I'll be there to meet your plane — might even fly it if they don't think I'm too old."

Peyton stood behind Lisa with his arms around her waist. They were looking through a doorway into his mother's living room. Lisa's parents had arrived with the kids, who were running back and forth between their three grandparents. Their youngest daughter was on Bonnie's lap, telling her a long-winded tale about the family vacation to Disneyland.

Lisa smiled up at Peyton and said, "We finally pulled it off — our own Cubano's Fish Camp."

The beach house was quiet. Everyone had gone to bed.

"You asleep?" Peyton whispered to Lisa in the darkness.

"No — you?"

They both stifled laughter as they struggled to be quiet.

"Want to go swimmin'?" Peyton asked.

"We haven't done that since the kids!"

"They all left their beds and climbed in with Mama, so I think we can pull it off."

They slipped out of bed and got ready for a swim, then tiptoed through the house and out the front door to the deck and down to the sand. Peyton held her hand as they ran into the moonlit surf, Lisa giggling like a teenager.

"What's so funny?" he asked her.

She looked up at the moon and shook her head. "I don't know. I guess I feel like we're getting away with something."

Peyton laughed with her as they swam out just a short distance from the shore and floated on their backs, looking up at the sky.

"Isn't that the Strawberry Moon?" Lisa said, reaching out for his hand.

"Sure is."

Out here in the Atlantic with Lisa, his children safe inside the Tybee Island house that had brought such comfort to his mother, Peyton felt bathed in good fortune as the silver light beamed down. A blissful moment from their first time on Key West floated by on a memory. And he couldn't resist a question for his wife.

"Hey, Lisa . . . what do you think we look like from the sky?"

ACKNOWLEDGMENTS

You never know where a story will come from. This one began in a conference room at *Southern Living* magazine, where my friend Holly Patterson Belk turned to me during a break from some meeting or other and said, "I've got a story to tell you."

Holly's original story about her father, Brigadier General Ben Lane Patterson Jr., contained all of these words: *bourbon, Thoroughbred, asylum, bicycle,* and *fighter pilot* — in that order. The part that sparked my imagination was something Holly knew only bits and pieces about: her father's solitary bike ride from Waycross, Georgia, to Key West, Florida, when he was just fifteen. He did it on a bet, having endured a family tragedy and a painful breakup with his girlfriend, Bette. (Not to worry. Bette Young was the love of his life. He won her back and married her. Holly knew her as "Mom.")

439

Peyton Cabot's family is entirely fictional, but the central event in his story is based on General Patterson's life. The bare facts are these: General Patterson really did ride his bike to Key West and back, sleeping in police and fire stations, thanks to a letter of introduction written by his hometown chief of police. He really did become locally famous as coastal newspapers covered his journey, and he did indeed take refuge at the Navy base on Key West after getting swarmed by mosquitoes. Like Peyton, General Patterson loved to fly, completing 101 missions as a US Air Force fighter pilot during the Korean War. (He was also the Georgia Bulldogs' biggest fan, but that's another story.) Everything else on Peyton's journey came from the imaginative world inspired by my own travels in the Florida Keys and by General Patterson and his wife as I came to know them through photographs and wartime letters that Holly shared with me.

I want to say a special thanks to Holly and her siblings, Daphne Patterson Asbury and Ben Lane Patterson III, for allowing me into their mom and dad's beautiful story so that it could inspire one of my own. This one will always be special to me.

I couldn't resist giving Peyton Cabot just

a little bit of my own dad, Junior Fraser, whose creative, adventurous, take-it-as-it-comes spirit always amazed me growing up. There's just a touch of Daddy in my protagonist. I don't think Holly will mind. There's room for both of our heroes in Peyton.

Many thanks to my husband, Dave; my parents; and my extended family, church family, and dear friends for their love and encouragement. Undying gratitude to my friend and agent, Leslie Stoker, without whom my stories might never have made it off my computer, and to the editorial team at Revell, especially two of the best editors I've ever had the privilege of working with. Kelsey Bowen has championed my stories and given me a chance to grow as a writer, thanks to her incredible insight, while Jessica English asks all the right questions and polishes my stories "like nobody's business," as we say in the South. Thank you to Gayle Raymer and her team for the original cover of my dreams. Many thanks to Michele Misiak, Karen Steele, and the marketing and publicity team at Revell for their constant support. Also, my sincere gratitude to Sid Evans, Krissy Tiglias, Nellah McGough, and the *Southern Living* staff for making it possible for me to pursue my stories, and to

Kristen Payne for helping new readers find me.

We won't talk about how long it has been since I've saddled a bike, so many thanks to Karin Fecteau, Grant Zondervan, Mari Root, and my unofficial Facebook cycling advisory board for cluing me in. (Author Erin Bartels even took time away from writing her wonderful novels to clue me in on the pains of biking.)

My boating skills came from Brette De-Vore's "How to Handle Boating in Rough Seas and Nasty Weather." Vintage video on KeysTV.com gave me valuable glimpses into yesteryear life on the islands.

Special thanks to the Sewell family for lending me the *Madame Queen.*

Special thanks to my beloved Aunt Joyce. She knows why.

Finally, thanks to all the readers who have welcomed me to signings and book clubs and shared my stories with your friends and family. You amaze me daily.

P.S. Thanks to Cheeto the cat, my constant companion, for standing on my keyboard to remind me when it's time to take a break. And feed him. Again.

ABOUT THE AUTHOR

Valerie Fraser Luesse is the bestselling author of *Missing Isaac,* which won a 2018 Christy Award, and *Almost Home.* She is an award-winning magazine writer best known for her feature stories and essays in *Southern Living,* where she is currently a senior travel editor. Specializing in stories about unique pockets of Southern culture, Luesse has published major pieces on the Gulf Coast, the Mississippi Delta, Louisiana's Acadian Prairie, and the Outer Banks of North Carolina. Her editorial section on Hurricane Katrina recovery in Mississippi and Louisiana won the 2009 Writer of the Year award from the Southeast Tourism Society. She lives in Birmingham, Alabama.